NAKED CAME THE SHARKS

JED DONELLIE and DEVORAH FOX

Mike Byrnes and Associates, Inc.
355 Keewaydin Lane
Port Aransas, Texas 78373

Also by Devorah Fox
The Bewildering Adventures of King Bewilliam series:
The Lost King, Book One
The King's Ransom, Book Two

http://devorahfox.com
ISBN: 0-9778245-4-3
ISBN-13: 978-0-9778245-4-0

DEDICATION

To Jerry Bateman, Don Lowe, and to our dear friend, Lynn Jones.

AUTHOR'S NOTE

This is a work of fiction. Therefore names, characters, places, and incidents are the product of my imagination or used fictitiously. Any resemblance to actual events, places, or persons living or dead is purely coincidental.

THANKS TO

Ian Ridout and Barbara Sanchez, who support my noveling efforts.

Mike Green, for sharp eyes and clever puns.

The members of the Rockport Writers Group, Port A Pens, and South Texas Scribes, for helpful comments and critiques.

Samantha Lafantasie and Diana Fabrie, who gave every jot and tittle their full attention.

The Office of Letters and Light for the carrot and the stick of Camp NaNoWriMo.

Alice Marks, John Rojas, Alan White, Kenneth Scott, Joyce Walters, DeeDee Shields, Andrea Dobson, John Howell, Phyllis Sayre, the Parrot Heads of Port Aransas, and Mike Daigle for their continued encouragement.

Lari and Iris Tonti, winners of the *Naked Came the Sharks* Great Character Auction. Your donation to the Parrot Heads of Port Aransas Wings 2013 "Latitude with an Attitude" lent the name Kurt Tonti to one of the book's characters, and helped to fund the work of the Animal Rehabilitation Keep and the Helping Hands Food Pantry. Thank you so much.

and thanks to Mike Byrnes, always.

CHAPTER 1—MORE THAN I BARGAINED FOR

"It's not right what they want to do here," Holly's father Clark Rivera had written. "Dredge The Gap, put up hotels on Isla del Tesoro. And a gambling barge. Can you believe it? It will change the entire character of The Island."

Would that be so terrible? Holly wondered. She sipped coffee from a cup that she had found in the kitchen of her parents' house. The glazed ironstone mug with a U.S. Navy insignia had been her father's. Feet propped on the back deck's railing, she looked out over the water of The Gap, a shallow inlet from the Texas Intracoastal Waterway cutting almost—but not quite—through Isla del Tesoro to the Gulf of Mexico. As a child she had always enjoyed sitting on the back deck, watching the sun rise over the water and following the flight of shore birds as they crossed the apricot sky.

She watched a flock of brown pelicans fly single file, evenly spaced, flapping muscular wings almost in unison. The leader caught an air current and one by one, each follower in turn stretched out his wings and took up gliding.

Holly sighed. If it weren't for her somber errand, her visit to the Gulf Coast could be a relaxing vacation from work...

1

...Holly flipped her long wavy auburn hair over her shoulder with a practiced toss of her head and stepped forward. "Holly Rivera Berry for the San Francisco Informer," she said. "Mr. Stochbaum, a group of people claim that the storage facility you plan to build will come at the price of Mission Dolores, a neighborhood treasure." With all the menace of a hunter racking a shotgun she clicked on her ballpoint pen and held it poised over her notepad, ready to take down Stochbaum's damning reply.

A short heavyset balding man, Stochbaum extended his thick neck to its full length, the better to raise his head high enough so he could look down at Holly. "That old decrepit building? That's no treasure."

Holly responded by stretching her slender frame as tall as she could get it and looked him in the eye. "It's an old church, a definitive example of Spanish Tudor architecture from the 1870s. A classic building—"

"Which didn't make the Register of Historic Places," Stochbaum countered. His gaze and tone of voice were steady but he crossed his arms over his chest.

Ah, a defensive gesture, Holly thought. She suspected she hit a nerve. "Only because the application arrived too late to make the deadline."

"That wasn't my fault," said Stochbaum. "The courier delivering the application had a traffic accident—"

"With someone who just happened to be on your payroll," Holly said. She jutted her chin and Stochbaum took a stumbling step backward.

Score, Holly thought. Defiant, she crossed her own arms...

...and spilled coffee into her lap, bursting the bubble of her fantasy.

"Shit!" Holly clapped her hand over her mouth and looked around, anticipating her father's chiding at the unladylike utterance, but she was alone.

She set the cup on the arm of the Adirondack chair and blotted her dampened bathrobe with a napkin. Holly gazed out over the water and sighed. Blighted by a billboard directly across The Gap the view was less spectacular than she remembered. In his letters, her father Clark had complained about it enough. The huge sign promised that the Tejas Bonanza Casino Resort was "coming Spring 2002," just a couple of years away. The sign blocked what once was an unrestricted view from the back deck of her childhood home across The Gap to the Intracoastal Waterway shoreline of Isla del Tesoro. The two-mile-wide barrier island buffered the city of Bonafides from the Gulf of Mexico.

At least the seaweed-scented breeze was pleasant, though as the sun rose higher the day would change to another June scorcher in South Texas. The daytime high was forecast to be in the nineties, the humidity stifling.

Just yesterday Holly had left her San Francisco home and flown into Bonafides's Sky Marina International. Unfortunately she was in Bonafides not to lounge on the area's many beaches but to deal with her father's death. Wasn't forty-nine too young for a fatal heart attack? she asked herself. Worse, it appeared that Clark Rivera's life had been cut short just as he was getting somewhere with his latest obsession.

His most recent, and last, letter had arrived three months ago in San Francisco neatly addressed to the attention of Señora Holly Rivera Berry. Holly kept using her maiden name after her marriage to her San Francisco boyfriend, thinking "Holly Berry" alone was a little too cute for a hard-boiled journalist. She retained the "Berry" after the divorce when she discovered that while "Holly Berry" tended to provoke giggles, it was at least memorable.

Her father's letter began *"Mi hija bonita y testaruda."*

Holly snickered. She was not Clark Rivera's "sweet and stubborn daughter," but his black sheep daughter. As far back as she could remember her relationship with her father had been contentious, part of the reason for her relocation to San Francisco after graduating from college.

Holly returned to the letter, twisting a strand of hair around her finger. As a teenager she started the hair-twisting deliberately in a futile attempt to put any kind of wave into her bone-straight thick black hair. It hadn't worked, nor had hanging upside down by her knees from her bed's footboard resulted in her growing taller and slimmer. She was still petite and round and her hair wasn't anything like the soft, wavy, auburn mane of her fantasies. Not only that, now she was stuck with a nervous hair-twining habit.

3

Her father had written the rest in English for which Holly was grateful. They didn't speak much Spanish in the home when she grew up. In retrospect she was surprised that her dad remembered any, not to mention used it. As a youth, he had had no great love for his Mexican heritage, called himself Clark instead of Carlos Gabriel, and dropped his traditional second surname. Holly wondered if her father's Hispanic rebirth was part of his preoccupation with this whole Rivera family legacy thing or if he had been having mental as well as physical problems.

Perhaps that explained his objection to the proposed development. The Gap could use a little improvement. The acreage earmarked for the new projects was on poorly drained land unfit for anything other than fishing shacks and remote beach cottages. Like this home of Peanut Volkman's, their neighbor two houses down. It was far less grand than the Rivera's four bedroom villa, but like most of the houses on this block, Peanut's had its own fishing pier. Holly waved to Volkman, headed out now with a rod over his shoulder for some early morning casting.

Apparently, Bonafides had grown since she'd been gone. Someone—the nameless, faceless "they" of her father's letters?—had found some use for this area on the Isla del Tesoro's Intracoastal shore. Dredging The Gap, a shallow natural channel, would cut a boat-worthy route through The Island. There were times in The Gap's history when it had been deeper and open to the sea, the forces of wind and water making it an actual channel between the Gulf and the Intracoastal Waterway. For all of Holly's life, though, it had been barely two feet deep in places and blocked as it approached the Gulf. Hardly deep enough to drown in much less navigate, she thought. Boaters had to moor their vessels fifteen miles away in the deep water marinas of Turtle Point or trailer their boats and launch from those marinas to get to the Gulf.

"They claim that dredging The Gap, making the Gulf more accessible will increase the area's attractiveness," Holly's father had written.

What would be so bad about that? Holly wondered. That would raise property values and wasn't that a good thing?

Even now, a wave-runner screamed up The Gap, a plume of water spouting from the SeaDoo's stern like a rooster's tail. The pilot made a wide turn and sent a small tidal wave surging against Peanut Volkman's pier. Volkman flipped him off.

OK, maybe not a good thing for everyone, Holly acknowledged, picturing flotillas of large boats crowding the narrow passage.

Volkman turned, caught her eye, and flipped her off too.

Now what was that all about?

"Anyway, the land's not theirs to develop," her father insisted in his letter. "It's ours."

Holly chuckled. Oh, sure, Dad. That old Rivera land grant story. Holly's grandmother, *Abuela* Carlotta, would regale the family with tales of how the Mexican government had granted her husband, Don Carlos Gabriel Rivera Valdez, much of the north end of Isla del Tesoro. It included the bank of The Gap on which stood the Rivera house not to mention Peanut Volkman's and everyone else's on the block. No one ever took Abuela Carlotta seriously. The old woman was daft, had been even before her husband had died.

"Isla del Tesoro—Treasure Island—is our treasure," Holly's father finished. "Yours and your brother's. Your legacy."

A sudden gust whipped Holly's hair across her face. She tucked it behind her ear and twisted a strand. Speaking of her brother, where was Tres? Why hadn't he met her incoming flight? At the very least he could have met her here last night to greet her and let her in the house. Holly was as surprised as she was relieved to discover that she still had a key to the house on her key ring but why hadn't Tres answered her calls?

This was just like Tres. He was born twelve days past his delivery date making everyone wait on him and they'd been waiting on him ever since. Lazy, spoiled, useful as a hen with teeth. Why her parents doted on him was beyond Holly. Could it be that her Dad was more traditional than even he liked to think and simply valued his son more than his daughter? Maybe Clark

Rivera had a hidden machismo streak. That would certainly explain why Holly had always found pleasing him to be a struggle. It could even be the reason why she got the ground floor bedroom while Tres's had been upstairs along with the master suite.

She sighed again. Tres was still her brother—all the immediate family that she had left now. Last year their stepmother, Taffy, divorced Clark and ran off to England with a count or earl or something. Apparently Taffy decided the earl's legacy had more materiality than the one alleged by her mother-in-law. Taffy hadn't lived to find out. On her honeymoon, she was beaned fatally by a polo ball. It was odd but Taffy's death softened Holly's feeling toward her stepmother. She had not much cared for the woman any more than she did the man whom her brother became, unkind as that sounded.

Just look at what brother Tres had gone and done now. Holly twisted her hair tighter. He had without so much as a "may I?" planted their father virtually overnight in some remote little corner of Riprap Ridge, itself practically at the city limits. Only afterward did Tres call Holly to tell her that their father had died and been buried. Holly wondered if she would have gotten even that news had Tres not found his sister named as executrix of the estate.

Riprap Ridge! Was that any way to treat their father? Holly and Clark hadn't been close but he was her father. He deserved better and Holly was going to see that he got it.

She fingered the empty coffee cup. It was about time she got moving. The sooner she started, the sooner she'd finish and could get back to her life in San Francisco. Get back to her newspaper job, too. Weekly deadlines did not permit long absences.

Too bad, though. She enjoyed sitting here, soaking up the sea breezes and bird song. This had been her longest stretch of doing nothing in how long? There was indeed something enchanting about this location. Not that San Francisco didn't have its share of captivating waterfronts and water views. Just not from her Mission District apartment.

She gazed across the water and visualized the shrubby island shoreline bristling with marinas, hotels, shops, parking lots. It'd be different alright. Here she had been wondering if like Abuela Carlotta, Clark Rivera had developed a few snags in his fishing line. A reaction to his early retirement? Maybe all the Riveras went nuts as they got older. Holly grimaced and realized that she saw her father's obsession with the property in a new light and it wasn't just the dawn breaking.

Holly left the deck, reentered the house through the sliding doors to the great room, and picked her way across it toward the kitchen with growing annoyance. Pillows and cushions that belonged on the couch and chairs lay on the floor. Books and magazines made an unsightly pile to one side of the teak cocktail table. She paused at the entry to her father's study and frowned. Cabinet doors were slightly ajar and drawers hung open with their contents pulled partway out. An avalanche of papers and folders cascaded across the top of her father's huge desk. Where was Artemisia, the housekeeper? If Holly didn't know better, she would figure this to be Tres's mess. He probably used the house for some mega party and hadn't bothered to clean up afterward. Holly couldn't imagine what the luxury condo Tres now called home looked like without someone to pick up after him.

Holly twisted her hair. Speaking of Tres, where was Narcissus now?

CHAPTER 2—THE MORNING AFTER THE NIGHT BEFORE

White-hot light blasted in front of his closed eyelids. He covered his eyes with his palms and clutched at the excruciating pain in his forehead. Lowering his hands, Gabriel Carlos III "Tres" Rivera observed that the blinding light was not a nuclear blast, only the sun glaring through his condo's balcony door.

He lit a cigarette. Fuck! Was he so wasted last night that he didn't even close the blinds or the drapes? He hoped that the eternal snoops across the way enjoyed the performance, assuming there was one.

Tres's only clear memory was of working on a pickup in the Dragon Lady bar. Been a while since he had been that stoned. The tangled condition of his fine Peacock Alley bed sheets and his sore body suggested one of two things: either the World Wrestling Federation had staged a primo match in his bed or it had been a night of passion. The condom snagged on the woven sea grass headboard confirmed it: last night's affair had not been an officially sanctioned WWF match. Shame he didn't remember but thank God the pickup, if there was one, had already cleared out. Nothing worse than facing a strange body the morning after.

Unsure that his tormented head was still attached, Tres eased his body upright and cautiously lowered his feet to the Berber-carpeted floor. A glimpse of the time displayed by the coral-colored Moonbeam bedside clock finally registered serving as an immediate sobering agent.

Holy *mierda*, two p.m.! He should have met his sister Holly hours ago. Well, rightly, last night. She was going to be mighty pissed. His cell phone bulged with missed calls from last night. He'd been vaguely aware of the buzzing vibrating phone dancing around on the bedside table but was too busy to take calls. Now she was going to be ape-shit furious. Her favorite taunts of years past echoed in his mind. "I know you can't help being born stupid but do you have to keep having relapses?" And, "Assuming you ever grow up, do you plan to be anything other than Daddy's little pet?" She could land some low blows when she got going. He sighed. The sooner he got over to Dad's house the less time she'd have to work up even more creative tongue-lashings.

What was it with that girl anyway? he wondered. Always striving to please their parents, especially their father. Nothing she did ever seemed to impress them much whereas no one ever seemed to expect much of him, Tres realized early on. As a youngster he'd decided his role was to get his big sister to lighten up.

Ricocheting off furniture and walls like a demented ping pong ball he staggered to the bathroom. Tres raced through his usual morning—or as was more often the case, his afternoon—showering and shaving routine, using extreme caution to avoid cutting anything vital. His light olive complexion looked a bit wan today. Tres poured some Acqua de Gio cologne into his palms and smacked his cheeks to bring up some color. He Visine-d the red from his eyes, round and dark as his sister's, and tied his long dark hair in a ponytail. He'd have to do something about those bags under his eyes. A dab of Preparation H? Sunglasses today for sure, he decided.

The sight of his body made him grin in appreciation. True, at five-foot-six he was somewhat height-challenged but his small stature only emphasized his generous genital endowment which over the years he found to be a desired trophy in many a bedroom. Other men might have to suit up for a night of clubbing by slipping the cardboard core from a toilet paper roll down the front of their pants but not Tres Rivera, no sirree.

He tucked his fitted Nik Nik shirt into his bell-bottomed Angel Flight pants, all the better to show off his slim torso. Vintage Wearhouse had charged him a small fortune for the authentic garments but Tres felt it was worth it to have the genuine articles and not some cheesy knock-offs. The ensemble really called for platform shoes but his Converse low tops worn without socks looked just as nice and added the right note of casual elegance.

Hmm, something else was needed. Yes, his bone-colored straw Fedora. He spied it perched precariously atop a bottle of Gran Patrón Burdeo tequila, unfortunately empty. He plucked the hat from the ornately carved crystal stopper, snugged it onto his head, and fingered the brim.

Another smoke, several cups of life-sustaining coffee, and a handful of aspirin later, Tres felt it might just be possible to deal with his sister. He'd make a stop on the way to the house; pick up some flowers or something.

In the kitchen, Tres made a final inspection of his appearance in the gleaming chrome surface of the Dualit toaster, about the only thing for which he used the appliance. Looking good, he decided.

He strode out to his car. Amazing. Despite the lost night, the green Jaguar sat shaded in its assigned parking space. Tres paused and studied his reflection in the car's shiny glass window. His grin was rueful. If he didn't get money, soon and in serious quantity, it was only a matter of time before both the Jag and the condo would be repossessed.

CHAPTER 3—MORE HERE THAN MEETS THE EYE

She *had to make it on time, she just had to. If she could get to the newspaper office before tomorrow's—really, today's—edition went to press, she could splatter the front page with evidence of Moneywell, Inc.'s, shenanigans the same day their stock was to go public. Ace reporter Holly Berry drove at reckless speeds on San Francisco's winding, hilly, night-dark streets, dictating her story into a recorder clutched in her right hand. Her left hand on the wheel, she gripped a cup of caffeine-rich coffee (her sixteenth) between her knees. When a car pulled out from nowhere and cut across her path, she hit the brakes, jostled the coffee, and spilled the hot liquid...*

...on her feet. Holly stood in the doorway to her father's study and studied the fresh coffee stain on the carpet. Great—something else to clean up besides this office, which she barely recognized. That her father had made some changes to it since Holly last saw it was an understatement. Gone was the sleek "New Traditional" office suite that Taffy selected. Instead, the room was filled with massive pieces, darkly stained and deeply carved in the style characteristic of Mexican provincial furniture. A brightly colored serape draped an oxblood-red tufted-leather divan whose cushions lay askew. The serape's stripes clashed with the red-and-green plaid wallpaper and velvet drapes remaining from the original bourbon-and-branch-water cattleman's-club look that Taffy chose. Holly shuddered.

She wondered where was the pewter cross that apparently had once hung on the wall between the divan and the armchair. All that remained of the cross was the faint outline it left on the wall.

Holly weaved around the piles of paper stacked on the floor, sifting through them for checking account registers, insurance policies, and title certificates. She collected an armload but there was no room for them on the desk which was cluttered with dog-eared books, papers, and yellowed photocopies and faxes. Holly picked up the divan cushions, put them back into place, and piling the papers to one side took a seat on the other. Her heel bumped up against something under the divan. She got to her knees and found more books and papers shoved under the furniture, as well as the missing cross. What was it doing under the divan? she wondered. Maybe it had fallen off the wall and slid underneath. A heavy, ornately engraved piece, it bore splotches of crusty brown tarnish. Resolving to clean the piece and rehang it later when she had time, Holly left it under the divan and retook her seat.

She picked up a sheet with a strange drawing on it. The illustration looked like a map. On closer examination she could see it was indeed a map but not of any area she recognized. Nothing on it revealed what area had been charted. Holly twisted a strand of hair. The legends and labels were in a spidery script that gave the document an air of age. Running along the top, print in a small modern font indicated that the sheet was Page 2 of a fax. Holly searched through the papers and found what appeared to be Page 1. The boilerplate cover sheet gave the address and phone number of the Ridge Pack 'N' Mail that sent the transmission. Halfway down the page, a short message read, "Clark, I do believe you have a legal leg to stand on. I'll call you. Rusty."

A legal leg to stand on regarding what? Holly wondered, and who was this Rusty?

Before Holly could ponder any more questions, her cell phone emitted her chosen ring tone, the opening bars of Gloria Gaynor's "I Will Survive."

The caller was Holly's boss, the publisher of the *Mission Crier*. "How's it going there, Berry?" he asked in a tone that clearly demanded "Why are you still there and not here?"

"Not well, I'm afraid, sir," Holly answered. "My dad's affairs were in a bigger mess than my brother led me to believe. It appears it's going to take me a day or two longer than I had anticipated."

"I understand. These things are never simple. Take as long as you need," he replied, though he unmistakably communicated, "If you value your position with this paper, you'll wrap it up fast and get your butt back here on the double."

"Yes, sir. Thank you, sir," Holly said, but he had already hung up.

When yet another bell rang, Holly needed a second hearing before she could determine it was the door and not the phone in her father's study. Nimbly as an Olympic track star, she jumped the paperwork hurdles in her father's study, cleared the living room obstacle course, and got to the door on the third ring. The door's beveled glass panes revealed a long-limbed curvaceous woman. Her sugar-loaf blond hair was so bleached as to be nearly transparent. A large silk monarch butterfly pin perched on the haystack of hair. A short, sleeveless, pink-pastel sundress that was unmistakably Lily Pulitzer revealed a medium dark toast tan that gleamed in testimony to many well-oiled hours in the sun or possibly a tanning salon.

Holly opened the door and the woman held out a perfectly manicured hand. Large fancy gold rings with chunky gemstones adorned several fingers and an armload of wide David Yurman bangle bracelets encircled her right wrist.

"Holly, hi. Cilla Esquivel from down the street. Remember me?" the woman asked.

"Of course," Holly said, although the Priscilla Esquivel Holly remembered had been dark-haired, heavier, and not quite so stylin', or at least what passed for stylin' in Bonafides, whose

13

sartorial standards were somewhat casual. This wasn't San Francisco after all, or Dallas, or Houston. Or Austin, or San Antonio, or Victoria, or even Corpus Christi. Shorts, flip flops, and tees or Columbia fishing shirts were pretty much the uniform of the day.

Priscilla Esquivel stepped through the door without waiting to be invited.

"Please, come in," Holly said to the woman's back. "May I offer you a cold drink?

"Why, I wouldn't mind that at all, it's fixing to be a hot one," Priscilla replied. "Please accept my condolences on the loss of your father," she said and headed for the living room before Holly could stop her.

"Excuse the mess—" Holly began.

"Oh, no need to 'pologize to me, Sugar, I understand. Housekeeping's the last thing on your mind right now. It surely was the last thing on mine when my Jaime died." Cilla strode through the living room, looking to the right and left and occasionally nodding her head. "Yes, a terrible loss."

"Jaime?" Holly asked, trying to recall when Mr. Esquivel passed away, or even if she had been aware that he had.

"No, your father. A terrible loss. Even if all we were to each other were people who lived on the same block for about forever, it would be a shame. But lately we had grown so much closer."

"Oh?" Holly had been on her way to the kitchen to get her visitor a beverage. At Priscilla Esquivel's remark, she turned and hustled to keep up with the woman who aimed straight for Clark Rivera's study. Close to her father? How close? Holly wanted to know, and since when? Before or after her father's divorce? Holly wondered anew about her stepmother's desertion.

"Yes, regarding the sale of the house."

"Sale of the house?" Holly realized that she sounded like an idiot echoing everything Priscilla Esquivel said but she had no idea what the woman meant.

"Why of course, Sugar. Oh, I guess you didn't know. I'm in real estate now."

Holly wasn't surprised. It was a popular occupation, especially among the wives of the men stationed at the nearby Naval Air Station. The Navy wives found that their membership in an itinerant community made selling houses an easy way to supplement their husbands' government incomes.

"Have been ever since he died," Cilla continued.

"My father?"

"No, Jaime," Cilla said. "Had to do something with myself." She stopped at the entrance to the study. Her brow furrowed, she scratched her head through her poufy hair with a long, painted fingernail. The butterfly pinned to her hair fluttered. After a moment, she took a step towards the serape-draped divan.

"Please, let's find somewhere else to sit and chat," Holly said. "This room's an even worse mess." She took the woman's elbow and tugged her out of the study.

"And I haven't done too badly, if I may say so, Sugar." Cilla allowed herself to be led away with some resistance. "Must be doing something right to get elected president of Oink."

"Oink?" Holly repeated, sounding more like a pig now than a trained parrot. Gently, she guided Priscilla Esquivel toward the front door.

"O-I-N-C," Cilla spelled out. "On the Intracoastal Neighborhood Committee. You know, Sugar, I happen to have the inside edge on a development deal that could greatly benefit everyone on this street." She turned on a pink strap-sandaled heel. "Tell me, Sugar, what do y'all plan to do with this ole house?"

"Do?"

"Surely you're going to sell it, aren't you?"

"Probably," Holly replied. Her life was in San Francisco now. A villa in Bonafides would just be an anchor keeping her unnecessarily tied to this city. She doubted Tres wanted it. More likely he'd be happy to have a share of the proceeds of a sale. "I haven't given it much thought."

"Of course you haven't. But you're going to have to, and soon. Why not let me help ya, Sugar? Here's my card." Cilla pressed a business card into Holly's hand. A color photo of a broadly-smiling Cilla took up most of the card. On the scant space that remained, in a microscopic point size that Holly found barely legible, Cilla had crammed the numbers for every type of telecommunications device available to New-Millennium Man: telephone, fax, car phone, cell phone, pager, and e-mail address, as if Cilla didn't live right down the street where Holly could find her whenever she had a mind to. "Call me, Sugar."

"I'll do that," Holly practically pushed the Esquivel woman out the door, closed it, and leaned against the solid wood for support. Some condolence call.

OK, back to her father's study and the matter of legal legs on which he could stand. Maybe the sender of the perplexing fax could shed light on the matter.

CHAPTER 4—NO TIME LIKE THE PRESENT

The creak of the door hinges warned Holly that someone was coming. Oh, no, caught red-handed rifling through the confidential files of precinct committeeman Harvey Bloughtorch! Holly knew that she absolutely mustn't be discovered, not before she'd gotten the goods on Bloughtorch. She stashed the file back in its drawer, shoved the file drawer shut, and looked for a place to hide. There, in the closet...

"Lucy, I'm home."

At the sound of her brother Tres doing his Ricky Ricardo impersonation, Holly snapped out of her fantasy and to her embarrassment found herself hiding not in the office closet of a precinct committeeman but in the shower stall of the bathroom adjoining her parents' master bedroom suite. She had planned to reclaim her old bedroom downstairs for her brief stay in Bonafides but found that Taffy had repurposed it into a personal home gym and filled it with exercise equipment.

Holly stepped from the shower stall into the bathroom, got an elastic from the vanity drawer, and gathered her hair into a ponytail, all the better to keep herself from twisting it. She met Tres halfway on the stairs.

"Hi, Sis," he said. "Or do I call you Holly or Holly Berry?"

"Apparently you don't call me at all," Holly said with a glare.

Tres gave her his little boy smile, the one that worked like a charm on everyone else. This afternoon the wattage didn't quite match the brilliance of his shirt, painted with what looked like a mural from some small Italian family bistro, nor was his grin as wide as his vintage flared pants. Ridged seams ran like railroad tracks from waist to cuff. It was beyond her why Tres went to such great lengths to make a decades-old fashion statement. Perhaps the '70's lounge lizard look appealed to some women but to Holly he looked like an overage pool boy who watched too many reruns of *The Lifestyles of the Rich and Famous.* Why in this heat he didn't wear shorts and a T-shirt like everyone else she did not know. Leave it to Tres, though. He never broke a sweat, literally or figuratively.

"Sis is fine," she said. "Why didn't you come to the airport to greet me? Or meet me here or even answer my calls? Where the hell have you been?"

"Oh, in and out," he said with a devilish grin. "And in and out and in and out. You get the picture."

"Unfortunately, I do." Positioned one stair step above him Holly stood practically head-to-head with her brother. She took advantage of the added height and looked him straight in the eye. "I can't believe you buried Dad before his body was even cold."

Tres made his eyes big and round and pouted, all the better to look wounded. "I did the best I could, under the circumstances. That old doctor was doddering around, you weren't here..."

"What old doctor? What are you talking about? Doctor Franklin isn't that old."

Tres drew on his cigarette. "I didn't call Doctor Franklin. I called Doctor Roberts."

Holly frowned. "Doctor Roberts, Doctor Roberts. You don't mean Doc Billy Bob? Is he still practicing? Is he even still alive? That guy's older than dirt."

"He doesn't practice much but he's still licensed." Tres held up an index finger. "And he's a JP. I thought he could pronounce Dad and get him out of the house. I was just trying to be efficient. Like you would have been." Tres leaned over and, catching his reflection in the brass banister, smoothed an eyebrow with his thumb.

Since when did Tres know the particulars of Texas law that required a justice of the peace's signature on a death certificate? Holly wondered. Maybe he had done some growing up in her absence but she'd ponder that some other time. "Why on Earth did you bury Dad out in Riprap Ridge? What were you thinking?"

"Hell, I wanted to put him in Oceanview but they wanted big bucks." Tres turned on his heel and stomped down the stairs. Dodging the obstacles littering the floor he crossed the oversized Persian rug to the wet bar at the opposite end of the living room where he poured himself a drink. He held up the blown glass decanter in invitation.

"No thank you. Tres, that's Dad's special Old...Old...Whatever."

"I don't think he'll miss it." Tres paused to check his reflection in the decanter's shiny surface before setting it down. He cast a glance around the room, then ducked down and pulled an ashtray out from under an upholstered wingback chair.

"Nice. Don't tell me Dad didn't leave plenty of money, not to mention enough for a decent funeral."

"Dad left plenty of money, sure, but the only one who can get near it is you. You're the execu-trickster." He tapped his cigarette ash into the ashtray.

"That's 'executrix.' So spend a little of your own, for God's sake. You'd get it back. And please don't smoke in the house, at least not while I'm here."

Tres pouted and put out his cigarette. "I did what I could with what I had."

"Which probably wasn't much, considering you're perennially broke. What do you do for money, anyway? Do you even have a job or would that be too much like work?"

Tres merely grinned.

"You could have waited to bury Father until I got here."

"And you would have gotten here in plenty of time if you'd taken some time off that oh-so-important job of yours." Tres crossed his arms over his chest. "I thought you'd be pleased. You were always hammering on me to be a man, take charge—"

"Instead of being Mommy and Daddy's pampered pet?"

"So what are you going to do about it? Re-bury him?" Tres chased his laughter with a swig of Old Whatsit.

Holly paced a little circle on the Persian carpet then wheeled to face her brother. "You know, I just might."

Tres whipped around to face her.

"Don't look so shocked," Holly said. "Now that I think of it, it sounds like a great idea. We'll have a reception in his honor at the house afterward. You can help."

"Help?"

"Oh, don't worry. Nothing hard. Just help me think of the people who should be notified."

Tres smiled. "Now that I can do."

CHAPTER 5—TWO'S COMPANY, THREE'S A CROWD

The sun blazed through the west-facing picture windows and baked the living room but Cilla Esquivel was damned if she was going to spoil the view of her carefully tended palm trees by drawing curtains. Cilla started toward the thermostat to summon more coolness and noticed a familiar black BMW pulling into her driveway. She detoured to the front door as attorney Sidney Qownsill stepped from his car. Cilla opened the door just in time to catch the man scratching under the sweat-darkened ribbed band of his knit watch cap. It was way too hot really for any hat except perhaps a sun visor but Sidney Qownsill could hardly be seen without his trademark Green Bay Packers hat.

"Why Sidney Qownsill, what brings you down here in the middle of a perfectly-good billable hour?"

"Hi, Baby Doll, how's by you?" Sidney Qownsill asked. "Don't you look purty as a petunia in that summer dress?" He leaned against the door jamb and grinned at her. "TGIF, honey," he said. "Saving th' city from economic disaster at the hands of those stubborn 'aginners' is tirsty work, eh? How 'bout goin' for a drink with me by The Tropics? It's been such a scorcher today, believe you me. Figured you'd enjoy a cool one to wind down."

"Why that's the best offer I've had all day," she said, although the Tropics wouldn't have been her first choice. "I don't have any good news to share with you if that's what you're hoping for. We can sure chat about the progress of all the sell-outs though. You drive, I'll buy?"

"Don't be silly, I'll buy. I gots th' firm's credit card." Sidney Qownsill patted her arm. "We will be talking business, won't we?"

"Oh, to be sure," she said with a wink.

"Lock up then and we'll be on our way."

A few minutes later they drove onto the crushed shell of the local lounge's parking lot. Right on the beach, The Tropics' circular *palapa* bar was surrounded by tables, chairs, and Tiki torches. The Tropics boasted "the best margaritas in town"—what Bonafides bar didn't?—and 60 different kinds of imported beer. Apparently, "imported" meant "from anywhere but here" since Blue Moon and Fat Tire were on the Imports list.

They took seats at a battered wood table. Cilla signaled for the waitress who was already on her way to their table.

The waitress, clad in shorts and a skimpy bare-midriff top, asked Sidney, "The usual?"

"You betcha," he replied.

"And for you, Ma'am? We've got a special on margaritas today. Two for one."

"Sounds good to me," said Cilla. She wondered what Sidney would be getting.

The waitress winked at Sidney and sauntered off.

"Whoa," Cilla said. "Is she a friend of yours or what?"

"Well, I do come here a lot, but she's dating a friend of mine," Sidney Qownsill replied, still grinning. "No need to be jealous. I'm all yours."

"Gee, Sidney, I wonder what your wife would have to say about that."

Sidney chuckled. "You know what I mean."

Cilla wasn't entirely sure that she did.

He tapped out a cigarette. "Not to change the subject, but how's it going with th' sell-outs? The Riveras throw in the towel, eh?"

"Not quite," Cilla answered. "But I'm not anticipating a problem."

"No problem?" Sidney frowned. "Towards th' end there, Clark Rivera was adamant against dredging The Gap. He was bound and determined to stop Tejas Bonanza from buying th' Intracoastal property."

Cilla shrugged. "But his daughter Holly doesn't seem to have an issue with it and apparently she's the executrix of the will. To hear Tres tell it, she left her heart in San Francisco, so I think it's just a matter of time."

"Well, time's a wastin'," Sidney said.

"You don't need to remind me," Cilla replied. "I've already spent the money I'm going to make on the transaction."

"Ah, here's Adella w' our drinks." Sidney Qownsill let out a sigh of relief.

The waitress set two margaritas in front of Cilla and a huge bottle of beer before Sidney.

"Not a margarita, Sidney? They're so refreshing on a hot day."

"Couple-two-t'ree beers is what I was tirsty for," Sidney said. "I'm Wisconsin-American, Cilla, it's my heritage, don't you know?"

Wisconsin-American. That was rich, Cilla thought. Sure he came to south Texas from what was originally a family of Cheeseheads but that was generations ago. Sidney himself was a native of Bonafides. His law firm trumpeted that fact in all their advertising.

"Ain't every place in town where you can get a Schaeffers neither," Sidney said.

Another of those "imported" beers, no doubt. No wonder he wanted to come here. Cilla shifted on the wobbly weather-beaten resin chair which didn't feel all that sturdy. She suspected that when she stood she would have white chalky stuff all over the seat of her sundress. She cupped her margarita and said, "This is

23

the way to end a busy week. Cheers and here's to a quick end to this housing sell-out."

Sidney Qownsill took a deep swig. "Uff-dah!"

From his expression, Cilla could tell that he recognized someone approaching them and twisted in her chair to see who it was.

"Well, Sidney Qownsill," said Tres Rivera. He pulled out a chair and sat between them. "I thought that was your Beamer out there in the parking lot, guy."

Would have been hard to miss with the black-and-white cowhide upholstery and the CHEDR vanity license plates, Cilla thought. And Tres? He looked like he had just time-travelled from some all-night disco. Given the day's heat, a Hawaiian shirt and shorts would have been far more appropriate than Tres's *Saturday Night Fever* ensemble.

"Looks like you have too many margaritas, Cilla. How 'bout sharing the blitz?"

Cilla scowled but slid one over.

Sidney Qownsill winked at Tres. "How's by you, Tres? Haven't seen you in a day or two. We were just talking about you and wondering how soon you were going to hand over th' estate."

"If it were up to me I would have dumped it last week." Tres said.

Cilla doubted that his sour face had anything to do with the tartness of his margarita.

"There going to be a problem with that, hey?" Sidney Qownsill asked.

"Surely your sister is eager to divest herself of it and get her buns back to San Francisco," said Cilla.

"You'd think. I dunno. Toward the end, there, Dad was making some serious noises about family legacies and all that crap. Holly may think she needs to keep it for its sentimental value."

"Then you've got to convince her udder-wise," said Sidney Qownsill. "Take her someplace. Wine her, dine her. Take her to the best place in town. Shouldn't be too hard to figure out where, it's not like we're up to our asses in five-star restaurants."

"Yeah, she might like that. Holly doesn't get waited on much. Too bad, though. Dad's funeral? Wiped me out. Much as it pains me to admit it, I find myself financially embarrassed."

"That is too bad, Sugar," said Cilla.

"'N so," said Sidney Qownsill.

Under the table, Cilla slipped a bill from her purse, folded it, and tapped Tres on the knee. He had no sooner taken the money from her with his left hand when she saw his right, and Sidney's left, slide under the table.

With a noisy slurp, Tres finished his drink. "Well, I'd better be going. See if I can't give Sis some help with divesting Dad's assets."

"Go 'head," Sidney Qownsill said. "And be quick about it."

CHAPTER 6—ALL IN A DAY'S WORK

Rusty Burger walked into the Marina Bar, Grill, and Bait Shop and trudged across the scuffed and stained pine floor to the small bar nestled in the back. Not an authentic bar, it was just a chipped Formica countertop perched atop the half wall behind which Joe Eddie manned the cash register and kept the big-ticket merchandise. Which was okay because the Marina Bar, Grill, and Bait Shop wasn't really a bar. Joe Eddie didn't have a liquor license so he didn't actually sell beer. He gave the beer away. What he did sell was the container. Patrons could choose a six-pack from Joe Eddie's cooler and pay for the bottles or cans that just happened to be filled with beer.

Some patrons took their beverages to go along with bait and other supplies for a day of fishing. Those who didn't have any fishing planned were welcomed to stay and shoot the shit with Joe Eddie. From garage sales and sidewalk dumps he had scavenged enough rickety stools, threadbare webbed lawn chairs, and a couple of three-legged tables to provide something of a sitting area. Or one could take a seat on a bench on the dock, watch the boats on the somewhat sluggish section of the Intracoastal Waterway known as the Lagoon, and chat with Joe Eddie through the pass-through window.

For that matter, Rusty thought, not only wasn't the Marina Bar, Grill, and Bait Shop much of a bar, it wasn't much of a grill either unless you counted the hot dogs in the countertop roller cooker, some of them roasted to the point of petrification. If they weren't tough enough, you could always stave off hunger with a Slim Jim.

The Marina Bar, Grill, and Bait Shop wasn't much of a marina, either, although boats could tie up to the small private dock at the back.

The afternoon breeze blowing in from the mucky Lagoon through an open door didn't smell too bad. It wasn't anything like cool but at least the air moved.

Rusty plucked a six pack from the cooler. Settling down on a spindly bar stool, he removed a faded Cabela's ball cap from his head, set it on the bar, and ran his hands through his curly red hair. He pushed aside a damp smudged copy of Bonafides's newspaper, *The Daily Breeze*, that was turned to the Sports page. He'd already read the fishing report that morning and noted with chagrin a story about a former client. Jimmy "Full Throttle" Ipswitch's fondness for amphetamines had put the brakes on the street stock racer's promising career.

Rusty held up one long neck. "Hey, Joe Eddie, run me a tab, it's been a rough afternoon." The day had been hot and the "brown tide" algae bloom had challenged him to provide his angler customers a satisfactory haul.

Joe Eddie grinned a mostly toothless smile and said, "I'll run yer tab but I need an installment. Ya didn't pay last week's tab."

"I'll pay up tonight," Rusty replied. "Made a little from today's outing. Got another tour scheduled tomorrow. These tourists are sure itchin' to catch drum and redfish out there. But it wears me out. I'm bushed."

Joe Eddie laughed and added, "Don't slam too many brews down too fast. The Ridge Pack 'N' Mail sent a message over for you. Sounds like some gal is lookin' for you. Let's see." He rummaged around the ancient cash register. "Yeah, here's the message. Holly Berry Rivera is her name."

"Rivera?" Rusty frowned. Only Rivera he knew was Clark Rivera and he was dead. Had a heart attack just a couple of weeks ago and was buried in Riprap Ridge, a gritty section of Bonafides' Lagoon shoreline west of the Marina. Rusty took a long thoughtful swig and pitched the empty bottle into the trashcan alongside the bar. "I'd better have another. I have a bad feelin' about this."

Joe Eddie let out a long slow whistle. "Check this out, my man. Never seen a gal in a skirt and heels stroll into these parts."

Rusty looked over his shoulder. A petit, curvaceous woman with long black hair approached them. Her slim navy skirt, white blouse, and high heels did seem out of place in the Marina Bar. Typically gals wore jeans and halter tops in cool weather, shorts and tube tops on warm days, and footwear ran toward cowboy boots or flip flops. The overdressed woman's leather heels kept catching in the floor's many knots.

Rusty chuckled. "Must be lost. This sure isn't a fancy dancy club for Happy Hour. Look sharp, Joe Eddie, maybe she's from the Liquor Board, come to see if your license is up to snuff."

"If she's got a problem with my operation I'll just tell her I got my mouthpiece right here."

Rusty held up his hands in self-defense and shook his head. "Me? Your lawyer? Like you could afford my services."

"With the kind of tab you run here, not only should I get free legal advice, so should my heirs."

"'Heirs' implies you have something to bequeath."

The woman strode up to the counter, propped her forearms on it, then reeled back and checked the elbows of her silky white blouse to see what might have soiled them. "Excuse me," she said to Joe Eddie. "I'm looking for Rusty Burger."

"And who might you be, pretty lady?" Joe Eddie asked.

"My name is Holly Berry—"

"Holly Berry?" Joe Eddie chuckled. "Jingle bells."

"Holly *Rivera* Berry," she said firmly. She rummaged in a blue leather purse that exactly matched her shoes and produced a business card. Joe Eddie looked it over. He lifted an eyebrow and he handed the card to Rusty.

Sure enough, it proclaimed her to be Holly Rivera Berry, with a San Francisco address. The card bore the logo of some publication called the *Mission Crier* and her title, "Staff." A writer? Maybe a reporter? Hoo boy, Rusty thought, here comes trouble.

Joe Eddie looked a question at Rusty, who shrugged and said, "I'm the man. What can I do for you?"

Holly Rivera Berry twisted some strands of hair around her index finger and said, "Clark Rivera was my father. You sent him a fax. The origination point was Ridge Pack 'N' Mail. Carla suggested that I might find you here."

Rusty smirked at Joe Eddie. "So much for handling all my correspondence needs with discretion."

Holly Berry continued, "The fax said something about my father having a leg to stand on. You sent him a map. What was that all about?"

Rusty replied, "Since your dad is gone, I don't see that it matters anymore."

"It matters a great deal. I just came in from San Francisco and I'm trying to settle my dad's estate. If there's an asset in dispute—"

"Forget it. It's nothing for you to worry your pretty little head about. Take it from me. Get your business settled and get back to the bigger City by the Bay. Leave the legal heavy lifting to someone who knows what he's doing."

"Excuse me?" The woman took a seat on a stool and looked him in the eye. "I'm the estate's executrix and if there is heavy lifting that needs to doing, I'm certainly capable of it. And anyway, I thought you were a lawyer. At least that's what Carla told me. Although if you are a lawyer, why is your office address the same as the Ridge Pack 'N' Mail?"

Rusty shifted on his seat, nearly upsetting its precarious balance, and looked away. He stared at the familiar pictures on the wall of various big game fish catches and marine memorabilia. He looked back at Holly. "All the better to get here in time for happy hour. Not that it's any of your business."

"It is if it concerns my dad's estate," Holly replied. "I need to know what is going on. What does that map have to do with anything?"

"Look, little lady," Rusty replied, "Clark is dead. Just go back home and don't worry about it. It's too late now anyway."

Holly Berry looked at him and sighed. "I hoped that you might be able to shed some light on this. I guess I was wrong. I don't imagine any light could penetrate the fog in your head." She slid off of the bar stool and added, "By the way, Mr. Burger, I'm afraid you'll be receiving an invitation to a real memorial for my father. He'll be reburied, with all the respect due him, at Oceanview tomorrow. I've invited everyone who might want to honor him. Apparently I mistook you for someone who cared about Clark. Do us all a favor and stay home." She turned on a blue leather heel and stalked out.

Rusty polished off his beer. "She's exhuming him?"

Joe Eddie scratched his stubbled cheek. "Who ever heard of do-overs on a funeral?"

Rusty shook his head. "This I gotta see."

CHAPTER 7—MONEY TALKS

Holly stood under the cottonwood tree's meager cover and focused her lens. *She centered the viewfinder on the bedraggled woman crouched over a distant row of strawberry plants. Holly snapped the picture hoping that the shutter's noisy click wouldn't betray her position. If she could get these photos back to the paper, she could show that the migrant worker crisis was far from over...*

"*Señorita?*"

Holly blinked.

"*Hay más?*" asked the dark-haired woman before her.

What is she asking me? Holly wondered. Oh, right: Is there more? "The baseboards, too, Artemisia," Holly replied.

"Bes—borts?" the housekeeper asked, her brown eyes rounded the way they got when she pretended not to understand.

"Baseboards." Holly reached down and tapped the dust-covered molding along the wall's bottom edge. As if the woman didn't know what she meant. Rivera family hired-help for many years, Artemisia understood English perfectly well, had to in order to communicate with her employers Clark and Taffy. Holly didn't speak Spanish fluently by any means but in a pinch she could understand it and make herself understood, just from listening to Grandfather Don Carlos and Abuela Carlotta. Holly had picked up a little more in the largely Hispanic San Francisco neighborhood in which she now lived. Her stepmother, Taffy, being Anglo, had no such advantage. It was possible that after Taffy's death-by-polo Clark had declared the Rivera home a Spanish-only zone. However, Holly suspected that Artemisia's sudden monolingualism was selective, enabling her to hear only what she wanted to hear.

The telephone rang. Holly waited for Artemisia to answer it but the woman intently caressed the "bes-bort" with a dust rag.

"Never mind, I'll get it," Holly said. She lifted the receiver of the reproduction candlestick phone on the nearby end table. "It's probably the caterer."

It wasn't. It was Holly's boss, the *Mission Crier's* publisher.

"Tell me something good, Berry," he said. "Tell me there's a good reason why you're still there and not boarding a plane bound for 'Frisco."

"Sir, how did you get this number?"

"I'm a journalist, remember?"

Holly was for the moment speechless. Somehow she had never quite thought of her boss as an actual journalist.

"You're not answering your cell phone," he said.

Cell phone. Where was her cell phone? Maybe it needed recharging.

Holly twisted a strand of hair around her finger while she tried to think of a response. "My apologies, sir. I have it recharging." Had she even remembered to bring a charger? "I, uh, hope to be getting on that plane Monday."

"Make it tomorrow. We have a deadline, you know. Remember deadlines? Deadlines as in: we live and die by them?"

"Yes, sir, I remember deadlines. Sunday we're having a funeral for my father."

"I see. Then I'll expect you Monday morning. Have a good flight."

"Thank you, sir." Holly replaced the receiver. "Not the caterer," she said to Artemisia, as if the woman cared. "Mmm, what's say we move on to my father's study? That might actually be more critical at this juncture than the baseboards." If she and Artemisia could plow a path through to the desk, Holly might be able to access the papers she needed to settle the estate and be on a plane tomorrow night. Once home in San Francisco she wouldn't care if reception guests complained that the Rivera baseboards had been dusty.

Holly started for the study, Artemisia in tow, when the phone rang again. Holly looked at Artemisia, who stared back blankly. Holly dashed toward the study and jumped over the hurdles that blocked the path to the desk phone. "This has got to be the caterer," Holly said.

It was, and they were happy to inform her that they could be at the Rivera residence tomorrow afternoon with the menu she had requested. They could set up and clean up. However, due to the short notice they would not be able to provide servers. Did Ms. Berry want to go ahead with her plans anyway?

She was going to have to. She had already notified so many people. She turned to Artemisia.

"Umm, please—uh, *por favor*—*mañana*—tomorrow?—after the funeral? The, uh, reception?"

With raised eyebrows and upturned palms, Artemisia said, "*No comprendo.*"

"Reception—*fiesta?*" A *fiesta* was more party than a post-funeral reception was likely to be but Holly couldn't think of any other word to describe it. "I need your help. *Necesito su ayuda.*"

"*Quizá.*"

Now what did that mean? Holly wondered. "I'll pay you, of course."

"*Anticipo. Cientos dolares,*" Artemisia replied.

Anticipo? What could that be? Holly twisted her hair while she tried to remember. *Anticipo* meant anticipated, maybe? Payment—in advance? That must be it. "Oh, yes, in advance. Naturally."

Holly picked her way out of the office, ran upstairs to the guest bedroom, and returned with her wallet. She held out a fifty. Artemisia took it and looked at her expectantly.

"A hundred?" Holly squeaked.

Artemisia smiled and plucked another bill from Holly's wallet. She lifted the hem of her Dallas Cowboys tee-shirt and tucked the bills into the pocket of her denim shorts. "*Gracias. Hasta mañana,*" she said, and marched out the door.

CHAPTER 8—OVER MY DEAD BODY

Holly hung back a few car lengths hoping not to be detected. Tailing turned out to be more difficult than she had expected, especially in a tomato-red PT Cruiser, especially when she didn't quite know where her quarry was going. She thought she was familiar with this part of town but there was so much here she didn't recognize. Suddenly, the heavily-chromed white Cadillac that she followed made an unexpected turn. Holly had to speed up so as not to lose the target. She cut someone off and the other driver communicated his displeasure with a loud blast of his horn. The noise...

...burst her fantasy bubble and she was back in Bonafides, following the hearse bearing her father to his new burial site.

Two days ago when her brother failed to meet her arrival at the Sky Marina International, rather than pay a rather hefty fare for a cab ride out to her father's house Holly rented a car. The PT Cruiser seemed like an economical choice and she picked the jaunty red color thinking that the cheerful hue would help keep her spirits up.

Now, turning off the city's scenic Shore Drive and easing through the tall wrought iron gates of Oceanview Memorial Park, she felt almost embarrassed. The car's bright finish seemed lurid, almost rude, in this subdued setting. When she lived in Bonafides, Holly always thought "Oceanview" something of a misnomer since the view was not of the ocean but of Bonafides's bay. Well, the cemetery's permanent residents were beyond quibbling about the inaccuracy and they could hardly appreciate the view, she decided. No doubt the beautiful grounds were for the survivors. Indeed, Holly found that the neatly trimmed oleander hedges and live oaks silhouetted against a cloudless blue sky conveyed peace and serenity.

The PT Cruiser's tires crunched loudly as she wound slowly along the broad asphalt path past acres of emerald green lawns dotted with white headstones and vivid flower bouquets.

One particular plot overflowed with an abundant mound of flowers, wreaths, small statues, candles, and slips of paper. No sooner had Holly noted the extravagance than she realized this must mark the interment of country-western singer/songwriter Xavier "Hobby" Melendez. For decades, Hobby worked the Rib Circuit: honkytonks, dives, and small town fairs like the Sticker Burr Jubilee and the Fire Ant Festival. Then "The Only Love I Know," a song that he licensed for a toilet-paper commercial, went Number One and put Hobby's hometown of Bonafides on the national map for fifteen minutes of fame. Hobby turned out to be a one-hit wonder except in Bonafides. There he continued to delight his legion of loyal fans on his own variety show which aired weekly on public access cable TV. After his fatal ejection off a barroom mechanical bucking bull while taking a break during one of his gigs, Bonafides observed the anniversary of his death like some kind of municipal holiday.

In the distance, sprinklers launched plumes of water over Oceanview's luxuriant grass. Holly could imagine the water bill. In his letters, her father had complained about the lack of rain. Oceanview probably had to run sprinklers all day, every day, in order to keep the grass so green.

Keeping cemetery grass green had turned out not to be a problem for the proprietor of Watkins Funeral Home and Auto Detailing, the Riprap Ridge cemetery that Tres had chosen for Clark's final resting place.

"Astroturf," proprietor Hambone Watkins told Holly. He looped his thumbs through his suspenders and snapped them proudly. "I ain't no fool to pump tens of thousands of gallons of water into a lawn during drought season. Hell no. This here Astroturf is a honey of a cost-saver over real grass, savings I can pass on to my customers, and it looks just as good."

Hambone also offered the option of digging one's own pit, an economy measure Tres apparently declined. Speaking of digging, Ham didn't have much of an objection to the exhumation as long as Holly was willing to bear the costs. He had a waiting list for plots in his small cemetery. "People are dying to get in here," he'd said with a cackle, and planned to offer the newly available burial site at a special rate, since it was "already broke in."

Holly had to admit there wasn't anything special about the exuberantly green grass here at Oceanview, at least not from where she sat behind the wheel of the PT Cruiser following the hearse as it lumbered through the cemetery. The ornate white hearse had been her choice, though Hambone Watkins had offered to transport Clark to Oceanview free of charge, as long as Holly paid for the gas. Lavishly tricked out with high rise wheels, chrome roll bars, and flame graphics enlivening its bright blue sides, the Ford F150 dually Ham proposed to use didn't seem appropriately funereal.

"Yeah, it's a little unusual," Hambone said, scratching his head under a Shiner Bock ball cap. "But it's another of my cost saving devices. See, it's four by four and I use it to go fishing when I'm not hauling around dearly departeds. Since I consider it my personal vehicle, I don't charge it up against the final expenses."

Nevertheless, Holly said, she'd go the extra expense for a genuine hearse. Unfortunately, one garish red PT following a white hearse didn't make for much of a cortege. Tres should certainly be in the procession. Where was Tres?

Holly hit the brakes as the hearse slowed, turned, backed, and stopped, a blindingly white blaze in the summer sun alongside the dark pit of a freshly dug plot. Holly parked the red PT Cruiser at a discreet distance behind the more sedate Cadillacs, Mercedeses, and BMWs and walked to join the people who already stood beside the grave. She approached a young man in the dark suit and Roman collar and held out her hand.

"Hi, I'm Holly Rivera Berry," she said.

He took her hand in his own sweaty one and pumped it vigorously. "Ms. Berry, I'm Father Lorimar. It's a pleasure to meet you, albeit under these sad circumstances. And let me say on behalf of the diocese that we're sorry we couldn't accommodate your request. I know you asked for Father Margolis but I'm afraid he's—"

"Passed on. So I was told." It had been a long time since Holly—or any of the Riveras—had been to church, but she remembered the Father Margolis of her childhood to be a kindly old gentleman. She asked if he could officiate at her father's burial and realized too late that if he was been old then he was likely to be dead now, as proved to be the case. Instead, the diocese had offered her the services of this one Father Lorimar, so young he seemed not only just out of the seminary, but just out of high school.

"I hope you don't find this reburial too strange," she said.

"Well, it is unorthodox, I'll say that," Lorimar replied, his brow furrowed. "Moving the poor man from his final resting place."

"There wasn't anything final about it. It was temporary."

Father Lorimar pressed his lips together, then nodded. "I do understand your wanting to honor your father properly. Clearly he was much loved by many. Look at all the people who are already here to pay their respects."

Indeed, quite a crowd had already formed. Men and women stood under the meager cover of a portable *ramada* that shaded them from the sun but did little to cut the heat. Their strained smiles and sweaty brows belied their attempts not to appear uncomfortable or impatient.

She should greet them all and thank them for coming. Where to begin? Maybe with that guy, that good-looker. Though not terribly tall, every inch of him was a winner. He even looked cool in his finely tailored dark blue suit which really set off his blond hair. Who was he? He held himself with an air of confidence as if he were well known and respected and knew it. Maybe it would be too obvious to start with the handsomest guy in the bunch. Besides, he seemed preoccupied. He was standing in close conversation with Senator Candida Schultklopfen, a big hero in these parts.

The senator much preferred her nickname Candy, and Holly couldn't blame her. Holly had learned the story from her father. At Candy's birth, her parents sought to honor their baby daughter by naming her after the ingenuous protagonist of Voltaire's famous short novel, Candide. In an attempt to feminize the hero's name, they inadvertently tagged their poor child as an infectious yeasty fungus. Holly sympathized. When she married her San Francisco boyfriend and became Holly Berry, she learned firsthand what it was like to go through life saddled with an awkward moniker.

Perhaps the handsome guy with Candy was a member of her campaign. The senator recently put a virtual lock on her reelection by securing federal funding for the headline-making Rattlesnake Rotunda, an urban development project. The huge domed shopping and office complex now sat securely in a square of inner city Dallas, replacing several blocks of decaying antebellum homes that were mowed down to make way for it. Rattlesnake Rotunda made Candy even more popular, especially with Realtors, developers, lenders, and contractors. The folks whose homes were leveled weren't too crazy about the senator, it was true. However, they were too busy finding affordable replacement housing for themselves to help get someone else elected.

Holly's gaze picked out a familiar face. She started toward the silver-haired older gentleman who resembled a clean-shaven Kentucky Colonel. Head of Barnes Bank, Noble Barnes stood by the Riveras in the early years when Clark first left the military and went into the grocery store business. Widowed many years ago he was a popular "plus one" at society events.

Barnes met Holly halfway and pulled her into an avuncular hug. "Holly, how good to see you," he said. "It's been decades, little girl. Too long."

"You're looking well, Noble," Holly replied. "Success suits you."

"Yes, yes, that it does, but I can't say I don't miss the old days when banking wasn't such big business. It's hard competing with these megalithic financial corporations that keep coming into town gobbling up all the locally owned banks."

"I'm sure it is," Holly said, her voice drifting off along with her attention. Tres had arrived, showing no restraint at all but bringing his green Jaguar to a skidding stop beside the hearse. If the dramatic arrival hadn't drawn sufficient attention, his clothing certainly would. His bright rayon Hawaiian shirt pictured saronged wahines whose toplessness was mitigated by strategically placed lei necklaces. Tres checked his appearance in the Jag's side view mirror and ground out a cigarette before searching the crowd. Instead of coming to stand at Holly's side, he headed straight for Senator Candy and her handsome companion. Holly twined a strand of hair around her finger.

Father Lorimar whispered in Holly's ear. "Is everyone here? Shall we begin?"

"Yes, I believe so. No, wait, here's some last arrivals."

A rusty old pistachio-green Jeep, its radiator grill hidden behind a bank of white PVC pipes for holding fishing poles, joined the lines of cars at the curb and discharged two men. Holly smiled as she recognized the plaid-shirted, blue-jeaned, and Stetsoned Sam Hill, an old friend of her father's. Historian, folklorist, balladeer, Sam Hill had been a professor at the college when Holly was young, where he was as renowned for his support of the local drinking establishments as he was for his epic poems. Sam claimed he wasn't drinking, he was gathering material for his poems but as the college grew so apparently did Sam's alcohol problem. Grants went to other, younger people in the department until Sam came to be regarded as just an old drunk willing to tell stories to whoever would listen.

It was a shame, really. Holly remembered Sam from his glory days, when he knew everyone and everything. He made a presentation to her grade school class and inspired her interest in becoming a writer. With the memory of Sam's decline, Holly pressed her lips together then frowned at the sight of his companion. Despite her discouraging parting remarks, Rusty Burger had decided to attend. In honor of the occasion, he dressed in his formal best: clean blue jeans, roper boots, and leather-trimmed suspenders. He trotted a step or two behind Sam Hill, hair coppery in the sun. The rumpled redhead's stumbling gait seemed to indicate that he was drunk, following figuratively as well as literally in Sam Hill's uneven footsteps.

"Ms. Berry, I think we had better get started," Father Lorimar said. "It is a little warm out here and folks are getting restless."

"Yes, yes, by all means," Holly replied, twisting her hair and keeping a watchful eye on Sam Hill. Rusty Burger caught the attention of Senator Candy's companion and even at this distance Holly could discern that the two men were not best buddies.

The pallbearers took their places. Holly smiled and nodded gratefully at the men that her brother Tres suggested as attendants and who agreed despite the short notice. She recognized Edison "Parvo" Pulitiz, media magnate, and Sam Hill. The other man was Ted Creaser, a Bonafides police detective. Though Holly was meeting him for the first time his reputation preceded him. Creaser had a bit part in the *Busted!* TV reality show. The real stars of that episode, a team of San Antonio detectives, pursued a fugitive all the way to Bonafides. They apprehended the bad guy during a karaoke performance in The Laughing Gull bar. Detective Ted Creaser happened to be in the audience and leaped into action to help corral the felon. Creaser got his five minutes of fame when he snagged the prize for the night's singing contest by default after the winner was hauled off in handcuffs.

As the coffin bearing Clark was slid from the hearse, Tres and the other three men took their positions and grasped the handles. By the way they struggled it was clear the coffin's weight was formidable. Holly wished that Tres had found two additional men to share the burden.

Parvo Pulitiz, Ted Creaser, Sam Hill, and Tres began their slow procession from the hearse to the graveside. They just about reached their goal when Tres stumbled. The other three men lost control of the coffin. It tipped and Gabriel Carlos "Clark" Rivera rolled out face down onto the grass.

The collective gasp sounded like a sudden gust of wind. For a moment everyone stood in stunned silence. Shaking off her shock Holly rushed toward her father's body only to be blocked by Detective Ted Creaser's considerable bulk.

"Stand back, Missy," Creaser said as he rolled the body face up. Senator Candy's handsome companion scrambled across the lawn to help Creaser return Clark Rivera to his coffin.

"He's my father," Holly replied.

"It was our fault. We'll take care of it," Ted Creaser replied in an authoritative tone that said he brooked no argument and which had undoubtedly served him well in his law enforcement career.

Almost instinctively, Holly stepped away but not before she noticed something that clouded her mind throughout the service.

She heard hardly a word of the prayers and psalms that were meant to soothe her soul, of the eulogies that had been carefully crafted to honor her father, or of the belabored benediction that Father Lorimar offered to conclude the ceremony. Throughout it all, a single question dominated Holly's brain: why did a man who supposedly died of a sudden heart attack have a big crevasse in the back of his head?

In a daze, Holly allowed Father Lorimar to escort her toward her car. What he surely meant to be words of comfort were an unintelligible buzz in Holly's ear. Half her attention was still on what she saw before Candy's companion retrieved and replaced the divot of skull that had flown across the lawn: the disturbing image of father's head cracked like a melon. The other half of her attention was on the noisy altercation behind her. Rusty Burger and Senator Candy's handsome acquaintance no longer merely exchanged angry glances. Now they exchanged angry words. Handsome Guy gave Rusty Burger a shove. Rusty Burger shoved back. Handsome Guy pushed at the redhead hard with both hands. Reeling from the shove, Rusty Burger stumbled, lost his footing, and fell into Clark Rivera's open grave.

CHAPTER 9—THE MORE THE MERRIER

In this crowd of San Francisco luminaries, Holly would be sure to get the story. The opening reception for the new San Francisco Museum of Sourdough Science and History had brought out any and everyone who was rich and famous, or rich, or famous, or wanted to be either or both. However, they were so busy trying to impress each other they all ignored a shy young woman with prematurely gray hair. She should have been the center of attention since it was her family's endowment that made the museum possible. Holly recognized her as Cattus Wrinkley, granddaughter of Elijah Wrinkley. Elijah Wrinkley claimed to have isolated the lactobacillus sanfranciscensis bacteria that gave San Francisco sourdough its unduplicated flavor. Allegedly, Cattus had the coveted original San Francisco sourdough starter from the mid 1800's which she kept alive in an undisclosed location. Maybe Holly could make her acquaintance, get the young woman's confidence, and a hint as to where Cattus kept the dough. Holly crossed the room, approached Cattus, extended her hand in greeting...

...and splashed her drink on her own forearm.

She blotted it with a cocktail napkin and twisting a strand of hair, scanned the Rivera living room. Where was Artemisia, the housekeeper and server-for-today? She should be circulating among the guests making sure everyone had something to eat. Getting something to drink didn't appear to be a problem. The liquor flowed faster than the Aguacate River after a gully washer. Ted Creaser would have a field day with all these potential DWIs leaving the reception. At the rate people were getting drunk Holly worried that she'd be liable under the dram laws. She really needed her guests to get some solid food in their stomachs but her server was nowhere to be seen.

Instead, Holly spotted another damn potted spruce. Apparently, when Artemisia had called for floral arrangements the florist had misunderstood. Instead of hearing that the customer was Holly Berry, he misinterpreted the instructions to mean that the customer *wanted* holly berry. He sent over, at no small expense considering the season, a number of the small, spiny-leafed bushes potted in red and green containers. To complete the display he included several small spruces laden with tinsel and red-and-green beribboned evergreen wreaths. The place looked and smelled like Christmas instead of a funeral reception. The only one who didn't seem out of sync with the holiday theme was an attorney Tres had introduced as Sidney Qownsill. That Qownsill wore a Green Bay Packers knit cap to a funeral reception in June had Holly wondering if the man wore that hat everywhere all year long.

Holly resumed her search for Artemisia and spied her holding a full tray of mini-*taquitos* and making goo-goo eyes at Handsome Guy from the funeral, who returned the favor. Holly seethed. Partly it was anger over Artemisia's dereliction of duty and partly it was jealousy over the attention Artemisia received, attention Holly wished she got. Holly chided herself. She shouldn't be harboring such lustful thoughts at a time like this. She should be thinking about her father. Well, just how could she be expected to wax sentimental and play hostess-with-the-mostest at the same time? If only Tres would help. Where was Tres, anyway?

Oh, there, next to the garlanded fireplace, chatting with that attorney Sidney Qownsill and Priscilla Esquivel from the neighborhood association. Whatever the topic of discussion was the three seemed to be in agreement as they nodded their heads vigorously. Good. Maybe Tres would charm the woman out of her obsession. Priscilla Esquivel called or visited at least once a day. Although she would always ask how Holly was holding up and was there anything she could do to help, the conversation always seemed to turn to what Holly planned to do with the house. Surely Cilla wouldn't bring that up now. Holly figured she was about to find out. The trio headed her way.

"Lovely service, Sugar," Cilla said. "And Oceanview is a much better choice for your father's final resting place than— what was the name of that cemetery?"

"Watkins Funeral Home," Tres answered.

"Watkins Funeral Home *and Auto Detailing*," Holly said and scowled at Tres.

Tres shrugged and lit a cigarette.

"A nice turnout," Cilla said.

"Beauty," Sidney Qownsill said, looking around the room.

Indeed it was. The attendees included everyone who had been at the burial and then some. Who were these people?

"Now that you've got your dad squared away, I expect you'll be anxious to leave us," Cilla said. "Any idea what you plan to do with the house?"

"I really hadn't thought about it. I've been a little busy." Holly tried to keep the irritation she felt out of her voice.

"Of course you have, Sugar," Cilla said. "You know I did offer to help." She batted her long, mascaraed lashes and Holly found it hard not to blink back. Hadn't powder blue eye shadow gone out decades ago? The woman had spiraled a black ribbon around her piled-high blond coiffure giving new meaning to the term "beehive hairdo."

"Really ought to sell the place, Sis," Tres said. "I don't need it. I have my condo. And I don't think you want this big ole millstone anchoring you to Bonafides."

"What's anchoring me to Bonafides is the matter of Father's death." Holly shuddered at the memory of what she saw at the cemetery.

"I can't help you there, Sugar, but I could help you unload this house," Cilla said. "I happen to know a real motivated buyer. If you like, we could step into your Dad's study and talk it over."

"C'mon, Sis. What do you say?"

45

Before Holly could reply, the sound of a spoon tapping a goblet made a bid for their attention. Across the room, Sam Hill vaulted onto the cocktail coffee table. Holly winced as Sam's boot heels carved a long scratch in the teak.

Sam harrumphed. "Can I have y'all's attention?" he asked. Not waiting for a reply he continued. "At the funeral, the Reverend Lorimar delivered a right fine eulogy."

Father Lorimar's fair skin, already reddened by his morning in the fierce sun, got even redder.

"But he don't know Clark the way I knowed him. I could tell you some stories—"

Holly could recall a time when that announcement would be greeted by enthusiastic cheers and whistles. This crowd looked at Sam Hill with expressions of pity, irritation, and disgust. Holly wondered if Sam's mangled grammar was a deliberate attempt at country humor or if he was drunk.

"Why I recall when we was in the Navy together, a couple of teenagers flying sorties over Okinawa. I was scared to death, I can tell you. I didn't know if the noise in my ears was the wind rushin' past, or bullets flying by, or just my nerve takin' flight. I was the coldest I've ever been in that plane and it didn't have nothin' to do with the altitude or that it was a glass canopy. I was that scared. Then one of our engines failed and I'm yelling, 'Clark, get us out of here!'

"But Clark, he wouldn't give. 'Hell, Sam,' he said, 'I went to a lot of trouble to get us in this position and we ain't givin' it up til we're done with it. Now keep shooting.'

"So I keep shooting and all the time I'm prayin', 'Hail Mary full of grace, get me out of this fuckin place'—beggin' your pardon, Father, ladies—"

No one seemed to mind the profanity. They were too busy chuckling at Sam who, crouched atop the coffee table, mimed a gunner frantically firing, removing his hands only to clasp them in prayer, then just as frantically grabbing for a wildly free-swinging weapon.

Artemisia passed by with a tray of drinks.

"Ah, the Red Cross," Sam said. He grabbed two drinks, downed one and said, "Bless you, darling.

"Yes, I got a lot of credit for that mission but I'm here to tell you the credit should have gone to Clark. He was the one to stick it out when the going got tough. I was just along for the ride." Still holding on to his imaginary machine gun, Sam swayed as if astride a bucking bronco.

"As if one successful career wasn't enough, after Clark retired, with honors, he went into business with hardly a cent to his name. But just like he did in the skies over Okinawa, he hung in there and made a success of it.

"I see you nodding over there, Noble Barnes, like you had something to do it with. Well, maybe you did at that." Sam held his arm out and pointed at Barnes. "That man there took a flier on a flier—an ex-Navy flier. Paid off, though, didn't it, Barnes?"

Holly saw Barnes smile sheepishly.

"'Course that wasn't the first or the last time you received a payoff, was it, Barnes?"

Noble Barnes' smile, and those of several others, faded as he pondered the meaning of Sam's remark.

"You know," Sam said, "There was a time when you couldn't hardly open the paper without reading somethin' good about Clark. Like all the community organizations he supported with company profits, and the free Thanksgiving turkey giveaways, and like that."

A murmur of appreciation for Clark's philanthropy rumbled in the audience.

"Yup, that was the heyday for the paper, wasn't it, Edison?"

"Hear, hear," said Edison Pulitiz. He owned several media outlets and published the Bonafides newspaper, formerly the *Bonafides Intelligencer,* now the *Daily Breeze.* He grinned and his chest seemed to expand.

"You were quite the go-getter yourself back then, weren't you, Edison?" Sam said. "Never say die, you were one hell of an investigative reporter."

"That I was," Pulitiz said, his distant expression revealing his enjoyment of the reminiscence.

"You didn't care who the subject was, or how powerful or high and mighty. You hung onto a story like a dog with a bone. Parvo, they called ya. Dogged determination."

"Dogged determination." Parvo Pulitiz parroted and punched the air with his fist. "That's what it takes to get the story."

"'Course, now you're just a dog," Sam Hill said. "A low-down yellow bellied mutt."

"Yellow bellied—" Pulitiz stopped in mid-sentence, his mouth agape.

"And," Sam continued, "that rag you call a newspaper ain't fit to paper-train a puppy."

Pulitiz's face turned stormy.

Uh oh, Holly thought. Sam's gone too far. She needed to get him out of here. How, without embarrassing him? Why didn't Tres help? And where in the hell was Tres? Oh, there, with the handsome mystery man. Apparently Tres knew who he was but now was not the time to try for an introduction. Holly had to do something about Sam.

She started across the room. Sam Hill reached into his jacket, fished out a flask, and took a long swig. "Parvo, you publish company press releases and call it 'news.' You wouldn't know a real story if it jumped up and bit your butt. Like how a bunch of grab-ass developers greased the city council's palms and got it to steal the Rivera land right out from under Clark's nose. 'Eminent domain,' my ass." Sam scratched his bewhiskered chin. "Or is it manifest destiny? I get 'em confused. Well, either way, the Riveras wuz robbed. You wouldn't know anything about that, would you, Sidney Qownsill?"

"Hey!" Sidney said, his face pinched tightly.

Sam went on. "But so what if the Riveras were robbed? We're pretty flexible when it comes to the law around here, aren't we, Creaser?"

"Why you sonofabitch!" Creaser made as if to charge at Sam.

"Now hold on just a minute," came a voice near the door. Holly turned and spotted Rusty Burger. When had he come in and how had Holly missed him? Dust dulled his red hair, dirt streaked his cheek, his jeans were wrinkled, and loam clotted his boots. He grabbed Creaser's shoulders and spun him around. "You leave him be."

"Now you hold on," Creaser said. "I was just gonna shut him up before he pissed off someone important."

"Like who? Pompous Ass?"

The handsome man who had been standing with Tres approached Rusty from behind. "Who you calling an ass?"

Rusty Burger wheeled around, saw the new adversary, and delivered a right uppercut to the man's jaw. "And that's for trying to bury me prematurely back there at the cemetery."

"Ohmigod," Holly squeaked. "Somebody do something!"

Tres started toward the embattled pair but before he got to them, Sam Hill took Rusty by the arm and led him toward the door. "Come on, young fella. I could use a drink but I'm too drunk to drive and don't want to ruin old Creaser's day here by making him actually do some work."

Rubbing his knuckles, Rusty let himself be led from the house. Holly breathed a sigh of relief along with her guests who returned to eating, drinking, and talking. She crossed the room to where her brother stood with the handsome guy who was palpating his jaw.

"I am so, so sorry," she said. "Can I call a doctor for you? Get you some ice?"

The man grasped his chin and ratcheted it from side to side and back and forth as if working his jaw back into place. "I'm fine," he said. "Fortunately for me, his aim is about as good as his judgment. Speaking of judgments, I'll get mine as soon the courts open tomorrow, you can bet on that."

"Still, please accept my apologies." Holly held out her hand. "I see you're a friend of Tres, but we haven't been introduced. I'm—"

"Holly," he said. "Tres's sister. Got to be. Look at you, the two of you could be twins. Tres, why didn't you tell me your sister was a knockout? She's got those same simmering dark Latin features only they look better on her."

Tres pouted. "Hey!" He checked his reflection in one of the shiny ornaments on a nearby tree.

"'Scuse me, Tres. You'd think I was born in a barn. I've been woefully negligent in showing my hostess my deep appreciation for her hospitality." He took Holly's elbow, which she didn't mind at all, and led her over to the fireplace. "I'm Larry Pomposas. I'm the county district attorney."

"Why yes, of course. I knew you looked familiar. I think I've read about you."

"In San Francisco?" Larry's grin widened.

"Yes. I understand you're slated to be the next governor of the Lone Star state."

Larry Pomposas all but ground his toe into the carpet and said "shucks." "Well, I don't know about that. I'm happy to stay right here, doing what I can for the citizens of Bonafides. That includes former citizens who are here to settle their father's estate. Maybe I can be of some help there. Gratis, of course. Wouldn't want anyone to think I was working a private case on taxpayer time."

Holly didn't think she needed any help in the legal arena but Larry didn't have to know that. Truth be told, she wouldn't mind getting a look at his briefs—legal briefs, of course. "You know, I could use some help. Goodness knows Tres hasn't been much use. Oh, he's a dear. I love my brother, but..."

Larry smiled. "You don't have to make excuses to me. I wasn't born yesterday. Just because Tres and I are friends doesn't mean I'm not aware of his limitations. So maybe we could get together for lunch. You could let me know just how I may service you. Tomorrow too soon?"

"Tomorrow would be great," Holly said. She wondered if he was aware that his offer could have a double meaning and thought perhaps he just might.

"Then tomorrow it is." Larry leaned forward and kissed her.

Holly felt the blood rush to her face, partly in shock and partly in reaction to what had been a great kiss.

Larry gave her a devilish smile. "I hope you didn't think me too forward, but what could I do?" He pointed up above their heads. "Mistletoe."

CHAPTER 10—MONEY OFTEN COSTS TOO MUCH

Smiling, *Holly laid down the* Bonafides Daily Breeze. *The report about her engagement to District Attorney Larry Pomposas hadn't been relegated to what passed for a Society page these days but ran as hard news. The portrayal of Larry as a serious possibility for Governor gave her a thrill. Even more rewarding was the description of the future Holly Rivera Berry Pomposas as formidable in her own right. "The beautiful, talented, and award-winning Ms. Berry will be an asset to the Governor's mansion," the story read...*

Gloria Gaynor proclaiming that she would survive woke Holly out of a pleasant dream. She glanced at the digital clock on the night stand. Had she really slept in till nine-thirty? She reached for her singing cell phone.

"Hello," she mumbled.

"Berry," replied a familiar voice. "Why aren't you here?"

"Sir, I just buried my father yesterday," Holly stammered to her boss at the *Mission Crier.*

"Great. Then you have no further reason for being there and not here."

"Actually, sir, my father's death seems to have, well, raised some new questions."

"Yeah? Well, can't you find someone to help answer them? You're needed here. I have a paper to put out. Or have you forgotten?"

"No, sir." Holly twisted her hair. "It's ever on my mind. In fact, I took some steps yesterday to do just as you suggested: get some help. I'm meeting an attorney later today."

"Good. Then I'll expect you here tomorrow. Come straight to the office. Don't even think about going home first."

"No sir, I won't."

"Tomorrow, Berry." With that, he hung up.

Holly no sooner put her head back on the pillow when another phone rang and sent her pulse zooming. She picked up the house phone extension on the nightstand.

"Holly, Larry here. Sure hope I didn't get you up with the birds."

"No," she said. Larry, thank goodness. "I was just fixing myself a cup of coffee. I did sleep in a little late this morning, though."

"You deserve it," Larry answered. "Say, I was wondering if we could have dinner tonight instead of lunch. I'm thinking The Pilothouse on top of the Baygarden Hotel. The view of the city is too good to be true but it's best seen at night."

"Sure," Holly replied, twisting her hair. "I think I'd like that. What time would you like to meet?"

"Meet? I had planned to come pick you up."

"Don't be silly. You're already downtown, aren't you? No need for you to drive all the way out here just to turn right around and go back. Twice."

"Not that I'd mind in the least but that's very thoughtful of you. Well, then, why don't you meet me in the bar at seven-thirty? We can have a drink before dinner and watch the lights come on over the city."

"Sounds like a plan to me," Holly said.

"Oh, Holly," Larry added, "just pull up to the entrance drive. Valet Service will park your car free as a breeze. We'll get your stub validated in the restaurant."

"Okay. See you in the bar."

Valet Service, my ass, she thought. Sounds like he's done this a few times. A smooth operator, no doubt about that.

Holly jumped out of bed and threw on a shorts set. She stood before the full-length mirror twisting her hair around the fingers of her right hand. She'd have to do a little shopping. Holly hadn't packed anything that would be suitable for her date tonight. Date. Tonight. With the handsome, powerful future governor Larry Pomposas. She smiled at her reflection, turned, and skipped down the stairs to the kitchen grinning.

Holly brewed some coffee, poured it into a travel mug, and headed for the front door, primed for a quick dash to Marshalls or Steinmart. She opened the door to find Priscilla Esquivel on the other side.

"Sugar! Just the gal I wanted to see," said Cilla.

Well, yeah, Holly thought. Who else were you expecting to find here? "Good morning, Cilla. I'm sorry but I don't have time to visit. I've got an errand—"

"Honey, you're in luck. Running errands is my stock in trade. I do know my way around town and where all the best bargains can be found. What are you in the market for?"

"Something's come up that I didn't anticipate when I packed and I need a dress."

"A dress. I know just the place. Finders Keepers. I shop there a lot." Cilla opened the passenger door to her white Mercedes sedan. "Hop in, Sugar. I'll drive and you can tell me all about San Francisco. I'm sure you're dying to get back there."

Cilla sped along Bonafides's Livingston Freeway as if hers was the only car on the road, leaving Holly sending up silent apologies to the other motorists that Cilla cut off and prayers for their safe arrival. Finally Cilla turned into a small shopping plaza of red brick shops with arched windows and doors, white columns and trim. A sign in flowery script declared the corner store to be Finders Keepers.

Clearly Priscilla Esquivel was a frequent visitor as she and the clerks who met them at the door were on a first name basis.

"Can I offer you a glass of wine?" asked one woman whose nametag proclaimed her to be Sally Finders.

At nine a.m.? "No, thank you," Holly said, thinking longingly of the travel mug of coffee sitting in the Mercedes's cup holder, untouched because Cilla said she didn't allow the consumption of food or drink in her car.

"A nice sweet tea, then? It's already awfully hot out there," said Sally. "Evian water?"

Cilla appeared at Holly's side and handed her a dress on a hanger. "I think this one has your name on it, Sugar. It was crying to me from the rack. Go try it on."

Grateful to escape Cilla's grasp, Holly excused herself and ducked into a try-on room. She shed her shorts and top and wriggled into the dress.

Clad in red, white, and blue star-spangled Spandex and wielding her Power Pen, Super-Holly had just struck another blow for Truth, Justice, and the American Way when...

"How're ya doin' in there, Sugar?"

Priscilla Esquivel's voice brought Holly back to the present.

"I wanna see, darlin'. I'm sure you look fantastic. Come out and show me," Cilla called through the dressing room door.

Holly studied her reflection in the full length mirror and blinked. Solid sequins paved the dress from scooped neck to thigh-high hem. Even in the dressing room's wimpy fluorescent light, the cocktail dress was blindingly stunning and Holly wasn't sure that was a good thing. The sheath that Cilla picked out for her relentlessly hugged Holly's roundness and she thought that she looked like a walking disco mirror ball.

A little black dress a previous shopper had left on the hook looked more like Holly's speed. She peeped at the size and price tags. Both were within her range so she slipped it on. Yeah, that was more like it. The slimming effect of the dark color and the vertical seams made her feel at least an inch taller and the back vent at the hemline was darn frisky.

"Sugar? You gonna show me how cute you look?"

Holly quickly squirmed back into the dress of many mirrors and stepped outside the room.

"Oh, don't you look precious?" Cilla said. She waggled her finger and Holly did a reluctant pirouette. "Perfect. Oh, I wish I had your figure. Those curves must drive the boys wild. Sold."

Holly returned to the dressing room to put her shorts back on, slung both dresses over her arm, and strode to the check out. Maybe she could get the LBD slid into her bag without Cilla noticing.

"You're taking it?" Cilla clapped her hands. "Wonderful. Because I found the perfect shoes to go with it." She held up a pair of slingbacks that looked like something Tres would wear if he were a woman: iridescent silver lame with platform soles and four-inch heels. "They're Stuart Weitzmans."

Holly winced. No way that she could afford a Stuart Weitzman coin purse much less an entire pair of his shoes.

Cilla handed her charge card to the cashier. "I'll get this, Sugar," she said.

"Cilla, I couldn't possibly—"

"Nonsense, Sugar. I shop here a lot. I have Frequent Finder points. Believe me, they're going to end up owing me money."

"I did find this one other dress..."

"The little black number? It's rather conservatively tailored. Well, I'm sure you'll find lots of practical uses for it for business functions back in San Francisco and you'll be there soon enough, won't you? The least I can do is get that for you too after what you're doing for me."

Holly raised her eyebrows in question.

"Letting me handle the sale of your house, of course. I do appreciate the confidence that you have in me," Cilla smiled and handed Holly the shopping bag.

Home again, her nerves sufficiently jangled, Holly made herself a fresh cup of coffee and started for the back deck. As she slid open the glass door, the front doorbell chimed.

Now who could that be? It was too early for Tres and besides he had a key.

Holly looked out the front door's beveled glass on her way to the entrance hallway and noticed for the first time how gritty the glass was. All the windows needed washing badly. What were the chances she could get Artemisia to...nah.

She saw an old Jeep in the driveway and recognized the color and the PVC pipes that hid the radiator grill. Now what is he doing here? Holly forced a smile on her face and opened the door. "Good morning, Sam. Please come in. What brings you out so early?"

"Holly, I've come by to apologize. About my behavior at your dad's funeral and the reception."

"I see. Look, I was just having a cup of coffee. Go on out to the deck and I'll bring you a cup too. It's nice and breezy out there and it's still in the shade." Holly watched him walk slowly and struggle onto a tall stool. She shook her head as she went back into the kitchen and thought that Old Sam didn't seem to be doing so well. She wondered if he had already had a little Irish in his morning coffee. Holly placed two ironstone mugs on the tall deck table and sat opposite Sam. "Thanks for the apology."

"Well, maybe not so much an apology as an explanation. Bet you thought I was drunk."

"Not just me. So did everyone else."

"That's the idea. Everyone thinks I'm swacked and I get to say what I couldn't if they thought I was sober."

"Well, maybe. But does anyone pay attention?"

"Enough. At least it puts the sleazebags and con artists on notice that they're not getting away with anything. I've got their number. Which I get 'cause people tend to be a little unguarded in their speech when they think there's only an old drunk around to hear."

Holly sipped her coffee. "I don't know, Sam. Could backfire on you, you know?"

Sam waved away her concern. "Hey, it's about all the fun left to an old geezer like me. Don't worry yourself about it."

"I won't. Frankly, I've got too many other things on my mind to let that little bit worry me. There's something strange going on about Father's death." Holly reached for her mug and took a sip. "I thought he had died of a heart attack. No one said anything to me about him also having a huge dent in the back of his head. Don't you think someone would have noticed?"

"Good question. Wish I knew the answer." Sam sighed and also took a sip of coffee. He rested the mug on his jeans-covered knee. "It was a might bit strange, I'll give you that."

"Well, I'm going to look into it."

"How?"

"I'm not sure yet. Review the death certificate? Talk to Hambone Watkins? I don't know, actually. Maybe I can get some advice from someone in an official capacity."

"Like who, for instance."

"Oh, well, like Larry Pomposas. I'll be seeing him tonight as a matter of fact."

Sam made a face like he'd smelled something nasty.

"Sam? I could see there was no love lost between Larry and that friend of yours."

"Ah, Rusty Burger."

Rusty. What a character, Holly thought. Why in the world had her father gotten involved with that clown?

"Holly, I need to share some information with you about Rusty," Sam said. "I don't think he made too good an impression on you and he really is a nice chap."

"Are you kidding? That drunken ignoramus." Holly started to twist her hair around her fingers. "He picked a fight. Two fights."

"He's no drunk but even if he were, maybe he's got a right to be," Sam said. "Rusty is a lawyer, or was. He has been suspended by the bar association, framed by the D.A. on false charges."

Holly paused in mid-sip and frowned. "False charges? Why ever?"

Sam looked across the water toward the billboard for a few minutes before answering. "Rusty was working with Clark to figure out this land grant business. Meanwhile, this bunch of developers is aimin' to build this monstrosity around The Gap like there was no question they had a right to."

"Developers? Like who?"

"Parvo Pulitiz has kept the names out of the paper. Some corporation which I'm sure is a shell. Still, someone could probably find out who the members are if he knew where to dig and had a mind to."

"Let me guess: That someone is Rusty."

Sam nodded. "On your father's behalf. Him nosing around pissed someone off. Next thing ya know there's some drugs in his car. Needless to say, old Rusty is lucky to be suspended and not disbarred. Or in prison. Or dead."

Holly released her hair and scooted forward on her stool. "Like my father? Who supposedly died of a heart attack but had a big crack in his head. You don't think...?"

"No, Missy, I don't think. I try very hard not to think. It could be fatal."

"Sam!"

"I do hear, though. I listen and I hear."

"That's all very well and good but I think I need to do something more than simply eavesdrop and hope to learn the truth."

Sam drained the rest of his coffee and all but slammed the mug on the table. "You're hardheaded, Holly. I'm strongly suggestin' that you should just go back to Frisco and quit worrying your pretty head about all this. If you ask too many questions around the wrong people you might get hurt." Sam got to his feet. "Still, if you insist, I say go see Rusty. He may be fool enough to stir up a hornet's nest but he is a man you can trust. I trust him. Hell, I gave him power of attorney to act for me if I can't."

"What do you mean, 'if I can't'?"

He gave her a wry smile. "I'm not getting any younger, dontcha know."

Really? From what she'd seen, Rusty Burger couldn't be trusted to put the right shoe on the right foot but she had a lot of respect for Sam. Maybe she needed to be more open-minded about Rusty Burger.

"OK, this 'drunken old fool' is off to see what kind of trouble he can get into." Sam winked. "You take care, little lady."

Holly watched him walk slowly through the house to the front door. He waved before he went out the door.

"Well I'll be," Holly muttered. What, she wondered, was Rusty Burger doing for lunch today?

CHAPTER 11— MORE SINNED AGAINST THAN SINNING

Holly *pushed open the heavy wooden door. The docks were a dangerous place for a meet especially this time of night. Nevertheless, if she wanted to break the story about the corruption in the longshoremen's union, she needed the information this whistleblower had promised to tell her, but only if they met in secret...*

The heel of Holly's sling-back sandal caught on the decking and the jolt brought her back to the present time and place. The heavy board-and-batten door wasn't the ingress to some den of thieves but merely the entrance to the Marina Bar, Grill, and Bait Shop, and it was bright daylight, not the middle of the night. Nevertheless, her heart still raced. Sam Hill suggested that she take Rusty Burger a little more seriously, something she found hard to do considering his law office effectively was a decrepit Lagoon dive practically in Riprap Ridge. While she was eager to talk to the man she definitely dreaded this confrontation. She didn't quite believe that he wasn't simply a drunken ass and now suspected that he might be a drug addict to boot, if not a drug dealer.

Twisting her hair, she squinted to get used to the dim lighting. Sunlight cast a bright path on the floor at far end of the room next to the bar where the rear door out to the dock stood ajar. She wrinkled her nose. The Lagoon smelled ripe today. At times in its history there had been a free exchange of water between the Intracoastal Waterway and the Gulf. When straits like The Gap silted in, sections of the Intracoastal became sluggish. The Marina Bar, Grill, and Bait Shop stank of stagnant salt water, decaying algae, and stale beer. How could Burger stand this dump?

Holly approached the bar with mincing steps. Damn, her sandaled feet were getting dirty just crossing the floor.

She could see Burger sitting at the bar. His cutoff khaki pants revealed tanned legs. His plaid western shirt at one time might have been red but had faded to rose. It also may once have had sleeves but all that remained of those were ragged armholes. Burger sat with his elbows propped on the bar and his fists planted against his jaw. Holly slid onto the stool next to him. Burger dropped his hands. The smile that broadened his face didn't hide his bloodshot eyes.

"Well hi there, little lady," he said. "What brings you out to my neck of the woods?"

"Could we sit outside?" she asked. "I've got a few questions that I need answers to and Sam Hill tells me that you've got them."

"Well, hon, we can slide over there," he answered getting off of the stool.

Holly slipped down from her chair and clutched Rusty's arm. "Let's get one thing straight, Mr. Burger. I'm not your 'hon' so please don't call me that. My name is Holly."

He shook her hand off and laughed. "Well 'Holly' is fine with me or would you rather I called you Ms. Rivera?"

"'Holly' will do," she answered.

"Fine. Then none of this 'Mr. Burger' stuff. Call me 'Rusty.' Would you like a beer and some nachos while we chat?" he asked. "Joe Eddie, how about some of your signature Seafood Nachos?"

"Not for me, thank you," Holly answered. She was hungry but debated the wisdom of eating seafood nachos in a bait shop. She'd hold out for later when she could dine in high style at the Pilothouse with Larry Pomposas. She went out the back door to the deck and gingerly took a seat on the bench which didn't look much more solid than the splintered, cracked, and weather-beaten wooden deck railing opposite. Through the pass-through window at her head she heard Rusty give the order for snacks. He stepped out on to the deck and strode nonchalantly over to her with none of the stumbling gait from yesterday. She wondered if like Sam Hill Rusty Burger played at being the drunk for his own purposes. On the other hand those bloodshot eyes seemed real enough. It was too bad, too. He had rather nice eyes, a clear green the color of the Gulf on a sunny day. Sure, he was a little thick around the middle but his broad shoulders and chest did a good job of holding up his shirt. His khaki cutoffs showed off sturdy thighs.

Whoa, girl, hold on here. What are you thinking?

"So, Mr. Burger—Rusty," she said, "Sam Hill told me that you were a lawyer and that you're temporarily suspended."

Rusty straightened. "Say, is that what you came here for? To rub my face in that? Okay, I guess you're mad about me throwing punches at your reception and you're probably right. I was out of line. But the bastard Pomposas deserved it. He planted those drugs on me and then had the balls to get me suspended." His anger seemed to drain the blood from the whites of his eyes and the green of his pupils intensified.

"I'm sorry for your problems with Lar—I mean, District Attorney Pomposas—but that's no concern of mine. What I really want to know is what do you know about my father's death? I don't believe he died of a heart attack. Not with his head bashed in."

Rusty paced along the dock. "You should care about my problems with Larry Pomposas. He ruined me and he could make life difficult for you if you cross him. Holly, you don't know what you're getting into. You should just let it be. Get your butt back to the big city and do whatever it is you do. What do you do, anyway?"

"I, uh, I work for a newspaper."

"Oh, a journalist, huh?"

"Actually, I'm the, uh, I put the paper together."

"Ooo, excuse me, you're the editor, of... what was the name of that paper again? The *Examiner?*"

"No, the *Mission Crier.*"

"What's that, one of those muckracking, rabble-rousing free papers?"

"It's a free paper, yes."

"Some kind of business journal, then, right?"

"Not exactly."

"Well, what then?" Rusty frowned, then grinned, his eyes twinkling. "Oh, don't tell me. It's a shopper, like the *Pennysaver.*" He laughed. "You paste up an advertising rag."

Now it was Holly's turn to frown. "It's not a rag, it's a very highly regarded paper. We win awards. We have huge circulation," she said but she would have had to shout for Rusty to hear her over his guffaws.

Rusty wiped the tears from his eyes and took a swig of beer. "Well, Lois Lane, there's a story here all right, not that you should go poking into it even if you were a real journalist. I believe that your father was murdered because he wouldn't sell out to the cartel."

"Murdered? Cartel? What are you talking about?"

Joe Eddie arrived and set two beers and a basket of what passed for nachos in the Marina Bar, Grill, and Bait Shop on the bench next to Holly. To her the nachos looked like Doritos topped with squeeze cheese.

"Thanks, Joe Eddie," Rusty said. "Bring us another round just like that in about ten minutes." Rusty set down his empty and helped himself to a fresh bottle. "It's all about the proposed Tejas Bonanza development. You know, if The Gap were deeper, boats could use it to get out to the Gulf faster. That'll make the area around The Gap more attractive, worth developing. Tejas Bonanza Corp. plans to put up hotels, marinas—"

"I know that. So? What's the problem? Why don't they just go ahead and dredge The Gap?"

"Because it's not theirs to dredge. It's government property. So Tejas Bonanza needed the city's cooperation. Not to mention state, county, and federal since some of the land is theirs. That's where the cartel comes in." Rusty took another swallow of beer. "Tejas Bonanza needed a bunch of people at all levels of government pulling for this."

Holly twisted her hair. "OK, but what's my father got to do with it?"

Rusty helped himself to some nachos. "Nothing unless you believe, as he did, that the land doesn't even belong to any government. It belongs to him. Lotta money and reputation at stake if that's true. You can see why the cartel would want your father out of the way. I have no idea who did it exactly but I wouldn't be surprised if Mr. Pomposas and his crew had their fingers in this mess."

"Cartel?" Holly replied. "Oh, that's rich. So it's not just one man you're up against it's an entire cartel? Let's be honest here. You're just ticked because the DA had you suspended. He doesn't seem to me like he's capable of murder. And why would he? What motive could he possibly have?"

Rusty looked more worried than angry. His green eyes had turned murky the way seawater did when the wind blew hard. "You don't know anything about him. He's an ambitious man."

"And what's wrong with a little ambition?" Holly asked. "Maybe it's enough for some people to sit in smelly bars all day drinking beer and eating—yuck—squeeze cheese." Cheese that did indeed smell fishy, she thought with a shudder.

His cheeks bulging with nachos, Rusty pouted. He took a swallow of beer to wash it down and said, "Hey, this is nutritious stuff. Ya got all four o' your food groups here: fat, starch, salt, and alcohol."

Holly rolled her eyes. "I'll pass. I have a dinner engagement this evening and I don't want to ruin my appetite much less show up blitzed."

Rusty took another swallow and grinned. "A dinner engagement? Anyone I know?"

"Oh, no," Holly stammered. "Just an old friend from high school days. I'm sure you don't know him. So what do you mean by Lar—I mean Mr. Pomposas's ambitious plans? What could he possibly have to do with Clark's death?"

"Nothing that I can prove at this point."

"See? Cartel, indeed. Even if my father found that the Rivera land grant was legitimate and even if that stood in some developer's way, nobody murders over something like that. It's too easy to get what you want legally," Holly said.

"I'll say," Rusty grumbled, and picked up another cheese-laden chip. "I will tell you this. My little guide business is an eye opener. There's something suspicious going on in The Gap and the Gulf."

"Is that so? Maybe that's what Clark found out. Maybe that's what got him killed."

Got him killed. With a start Holly realized that she seriously entertained the notion that her father had been murdered. She absentmindedly picked a cheese-and-hot-pepper laden chip from the basket and munched it, then clutched at her throat. "Ohmigod," she gasped.

"What? Are you okay?"

"I forgot how hot jalapeños are." She grabbed the second long neck and drank it down.

"Oh." Rusty ducked his head but not quite low enough to hide his grin.

"Maybe I had better go out on your boat with you some time," Holly said.

"To nose around? Forget it. I'm not giving Pomposas another chance to ruin my life."

Holly tipped her head and flashed a coy smile. "No, no, no. Just to play tourist. I've always loved going out in the Gulf."

Rusty choked on his beer. "Is this supposed to be a date with the Captain?" He leaned back and braced himself against the dock railing which creaked ominously. He scooted over a couple of inches to lean on sturdier section and Holly again found herself noting the huggable contours of his torso.

"A date? Sure, uh—"

Rusty made a wry face. "Now who's zooming who? Okay, I can see you're not giving up."

"I'm certainly not leaving town until I know the truth about my father's death."

"Then I guess I'd better keep an eye on you." His tone was bantering but his face wore a worried expression.

Holly laughed. "You're going to keep an eye on me?"

"Hey, you wanna come on the boat or not?"

"I want to come on the boat.

"Let me see. I do have a trip planned on Friday. Fishing trip, mostly, but they can pretty much handle themselves so you'd have my undivided attention. Wanna come along for the ride? I can't promise any espionage. In fact, I'll be doing my best to avoid it. But you'll enjoy the outing."

Holly wasn't so sure about the "undivided attention" part but didn't want to pass up this chance to find out more about what might have happened to her father. "Okay, Cap'. Count me in." She drained her beer and stood. What was she getting herself into? she wondered. She must be crazy to be getting involved with this nutcase. "You've got my card. Give me a call and let me know what time we sail." Maybe by Friday she'd have her father's affairs straightened out, the mystery of his death resolved, and she'd be well on her way back home.

"Will do," Rusty replied. He stretched forward to grab another beer from the bench. "I'll talk to you soon. And keep a sharp eye out," he called just as she stepped back into the shop.

He should have taken his own advice. As Holly turned to wave, Rusty leaned nonchalantly against a too-weak section of railing. It gave way and he toppled into the water.

CHAPTER 12—ALL'S FAIR IN LOVE AND WAR

The elevator stopped with a musical chime and the doors sighed open. Holly stepped out into the dimly lit foyer of the high-rise's top floor. She was grateful that the thick carpet muffled her footsteps. It was late and no one was about but the building was hardly abandoned. She would have to be careful if she was going to slip in, get the information she needed, and slip out without tipping her hand.

Suddenly, a slim, blond-headed woman in a middy blouse and long navy skirt appeared. "May I help you?"

Holly shook her head to clear it and refocused. No, she was not high atop San Francisco's Transamerica Title building about to snoop around some corporate executive's suite. She was at the Pilothouse restaurant on the twentieth floor of the Baygarden Hotel, one of Bonafides's two bay-front skyscrapers, the other being the Shorefront Suites office building. She looked around. While it wasn't the sky lounge at the Top of the Mark, she had to admit the restaurant did offer an impressive view of the Bonafides shoreline and bay.

"Are you dining now, or would you like a drink in the bar?" the hostess inquired.

Holly caught her reflection in the mirror across from the elevator and liked what she saw. The short black sheath dress accentuated her figure. The wicked Stuart Weitzman heels that Cilla Esquivel had chosen provided a pop of color—well, more like an explosion but they did draw attention to Holly's shapely legs. The ensemble ought to wow Larry Pomposas for sure.

"I'm meeting someone in the bar," Holly answered.

"Would that be Larry Pomposas?" the blond asked.

"Yes."

"He just called and said to tell you that he would be a few minutes late," said the hostess. "He already placed an order for you at the bar. Mr. Pomposas said you were fond of Cutty and soda. He also wanted me to seat you in the couch section on the far side of the bar so that you won't miss the city lights coming on."

Cutty and soda? Not hardly, and Holly questioned what gave Larry the impression that she liked it. Holly didn't know whether to be miffed or not at the man's presumptuousness but she followed the hostess through the nautically themed setting. A mounted tarpon, swordfish, and shark hung on the wall across from the hostess station. Holly wondered what the fish did to deserve ending up like that. Oh well, this was Bonafides where catching fish was as much about sport as it was about eating. At the entrance to the bar, she passed a marble table decorated with a brass diving bell filled with orange and yellow artificial flowers.

The restaurant and bar took up the top two floors of Baygarden, the rest of which served as a hotel, with the bar elevated above the dining room. Windows stretched from floor to ceiling all the way around providing a spectacular view. As Holly crossed in front of the bar she grinned. A sailor figurine stood in the middle of the liquor bottles. He clutched a bottle in his upraised hand and his nose lit up in red neon.

Following the hostess, Holly went down three steps to a classy couch and coffee table arrangement. The couch had an Egyptian look with curved legs and broad gold and navy stripes. Not very nautical, Holly thought. Then again, the ancient Egyptians had been accomplished sailors so maybe it was apropos at that.

The bartender had already deposited her Cutty on the glass-topped table. Holly sat on the corner of the couch and looked out the window. As dusk fell, Holly thought it strange that the lights of the high-arching Treasure Island Bridge in the distance failed to come on. The bridge connecting Bonafides to Isla del Tesoro was practically a city trademark. The lights of buildings along the shoreline twinkled pleasantly enough, though.

The bartender walked down the steps toward her. "Larry just called and he's on his way up. He requested a Jack Daniels. Can I get you another Cutty?" he asked.

"No, thank you," Holly answered. "I'm fine."

The bartender chuckled. "Are you? Doesn't look like you've even tasted your drink. Is anything wrong?"

"Not at all." She took an obligatory sip of her drink and smiled. On a first-name basis with the bartender, huh? Larry must be a regular around here.

"Hi, Sweetness. You're a sight for sore eyes," Larry said as he approached the couch. He sat down next to her and kissed her on the cheek. "Sorry I was delayed. I had to take a conference call unexpectedly. Better late than never, huh?"

Holly looked up into his deep blue eyes and trembled. Looking into those eyes was like diving into a sparkling, clear blue swimming pool with no bottom. Could be dangerous. She'd better watch herself, she thought, twisting her hair.

"Are you cold?" Larry asked. "You shivered."

"No, it's just the Cutty," Holly answered. "But I think I'm ready to tackle some food, if you are."

"Sure," Larry said, waving his hand at the hostess. "Would you take our drinks down to the table? I reserved one on the south side."

"No problem," the hostess said. "Hipolito will be your waiter, as you requested. Just follow me."

"You're a dear," Larry said. He took Holly's hand and pulled her up.

Holly held Larry's arm and they followed the hostess down a short staircase to the dining room. Their square table was covered with a white linen tablecloth. A candle in a hurricane glass with a metal stand adorned the center. Soft blues-y music filled the air. Holly could hear chatter from other tables but it wasn't distracting. Five huge majestic columns stood spaced along the window side. Bleached canvas sails tied back with gold rope draped either side of the columns. The plush navy carpeting had an ornate gold rope-and-anchors pattern.

Larry pulled out a chair and Holly took her seat.

A short, dark-haired waiter approached. His white middy blouse made his toast-colored skin appear even darker. In keeping with the nautical theme he also wore bell-bottomed navy pants and Topsiders. "Hi," he said. "I'm Hip. I'll be your waiter this evening." He set glasses of lime-garnished ice water on the table and handed them each a large cork-covered menu. "May I suggest our house wine? We are featuring a smooth merlot to go with our steak dinners, and I would particularly recommend the Texas Chateaubriand tonight. We also have a light Chardonnay, if you prefer one of our fish or chicken entrees."

Larry looked up at the waiter. "Thanks, Hip, but I'm sure Holly would prefer to choose for herself. She's a woman who definitely knows her own mind."

Holly wished he had thought of that before ordering her a cocktail she didn't want.

The waiter departed to give them some time to consider. Holly studied the menu. The many seafood selections gave it a coastal flair but an abundance of beef and game dishes reminded patrons that this particular coast was in Texas.

"Take it from me," Larry said, "You should get the Texas Chateaubriand. It's an eight-ounce cut of tenderloin and it's definitely worth the trip. In fact, that's what I'm going to have."

Funny, that had been the waiter's recommendation. Still, Holly hadn't quite finished perusing the menu. She reached for her water while she considered her options. She looked out the window. The lights all over town twinkled. "The view is truly breathtaking, Larry. San Francisco is scenic but this view of Bonafides is also pretty awesome."

Larry pointed to the building next door. "That's Shorefront Suites," he said.

"Offices, I know," Holly said.

"Well, it's the el primo address not just for businessmen but for some peregrine falcons that nest on top. Bet you didn't know that."

Holly admitted she didn't.

"It's too dark to see them now, but I'll get Hip to tell you about them."

The floor of the Shorefront Suites building across from them was dark except for a Coke machine burning brightly in what Holly assumed was some kind of employee's lounge. "Oh, look. Two people just walked into that lounge. Kind of late for anyone still to be working. I wonder why they're in the dark. Some kind of secret meeting, you think?"

He chuckled. "What an imagination you have. It's probably just security guards," he replied. "Oh, here's Hip. We'll have the Texas chateau and you can bring us the merlot."

Holly frowned. And here she'd been just about ready to order the pecan-crusted snapper. Well, steak would be fine too.

"After you place our order, Hip, come back and tell Holly about the falcons."

"Of course," he replied as he left.

"Larry, security guards don't shove each other around," Holly said, twisting her hair. "Besides one of them has awfully long hair to be a guard." In the unlit room, silhouetted by the dim light of the Coke machine, the two figures were featureless dark shapes. Still, one guard seemed to have long thick ponytail.

"Could be a female guard," Larry said. "Doesn't look to me like there's any shoving going on. They're probably just on break, goofing on each other."

He should know, Holly thought. She'd seen Larry do some pretty effective shoving of his own lately.

"Here's Hip with our wine," Larry said.

The waiter poured a small amount into a crystal wine glass and handed it to Larry. "Is this to your liking, sir?" he asked.

Larry sipped. "Very good, Hip."

Hipolito filled their glasses. "I'll be back shortly with bread and salads," he said.

"The falcons, Hip!" Larry said.

The waiter looked anxiously towards the kitchen. "Sir, let me just get—"

"The falcons?" Larry prompted.

The waiter sighed. "Every year the same pair of falcons come back and nest on the top of Shorefront Suites," he said, his delivery somewhat rushed. "This year one of their babies, a female, also came back. The females are larger than the males. Yesterday two males came and fought for her. They fight with their talons and dance around. It's really something to see. The female just waits and whoever wins is her mate. She and her suitor have flown off to find their own nesting place. They can't stay on the Suites because it is already claimed by her parents. Peregrine falcons mate for life."

"What a neat story," Holly said. "I wish we could see them."

Larry raised his wine glass. "We'll just have to come back again when it's light enough. How long will they be here, Hip?"

"They stay for a little more than a month before they fly down to South America," he answered. "Excuse me. I really must go. I'll be back with your steaks."

Holly looked over to the Shorefront Suites building. The people in the lounge area were gone. She wondered what the confrontation had been about.

"How long will you be staying in Bonafides? No doubt you're eager to get home to Frisco. If there is anything I can do to help you settle your father's estate, I'm at your service."

"I would like some answers concerning Clark's death," Holly said.

"What do you mean? Tres tells me it was certified that he had a heart attack." Larry shifted around in his chair.

"Didn't you see at the funeral? His head was bashed in," Holly said. "That doesn't usually happen from a heart attack."

"Now, Holly, you're letting your imagination get the best of you." Larry drained his wine. "I'll bet Clark hit his head on something when he fell."

Hipolito brought their steaks and Holly kept the conversation casual, restricting her comments to interesting plot turns on *Law and Order* and machinations on *Survivor*. Her thoughts were jumbled. Why did Larry change the subject every time she said anything serious? So much for getting any information from him. Could there be any truth in what Rusty had said? Why was Larry so interested in helping her settle the estate?

The waiter interrupted her thoughts. "Can I get you any dessert?

"None for me," Holly answered.

"Oh, don't be silly," Larry said. "Sweets for the sweet, sugar for my honey. Hip, bring Holly a slice of cheesecake."

The waiter was off to fetch the unwanted dish before Holly could protest. Afraid it would offend her host to waste it, she forced it down.

Hip returned to clear the dessert plates and Larry said, "Call down to valet service and have them bring our cars up from the garage."

Holly noticed that Larry signed rather than paid the bill. I guess he really is a regular here, she thought.

At the driveway, Larry opened the door of Holly's PT. He pulled her close to him and kissed her. "I hope we can do this again soon," he said.

"I had a great time," Holly answered, trying not to burp. The cheesecake sat heavily on her stomach. "Just give me a call."

As she drove off, her thoughts wandered back to the scene in the lounge of the Shorefront Suites. Like the cheesecake, something about it just didn't sit right.

CHAPTER 13—AND SO TO BED

"We need to talk. Tomorrow, one-thirty p.m., usual place. Be there."

That sonofabitch, Larry Pomposas thought. He punched another cell phone number and voiced the same message to a second listener.

Calmer now having taken action he allowed his mind to drift. It had turned out to be some evening. He hoped Holly hadn't seen too much of what had transpired in the lounge across the way in the Shorefront Suites skyscraper. She shouldn't have seen anything but she had. Seems like we are taking one step forward and then two backward. He wondered who the skirmishers were. Looked like Sidney Qownsill and Tres. That Tres could get into more trouble than a politician at election time. Larry would have to keep the boy on a shorter leash.

A few minutes later Larry's cell phone rang. He looked at his caller ID and decided not to answer. It could wait until tomorrow. Tomorrow he'd also call Holly and tell her what a nice evening it had been. He needed to keep that going in the direction in which it was headed. She was one sweet little thing. Tres was no slouch in the looks department and his sister wasn't either. She and Tres could be twins.

Larry tilted down the rear-view mirror to get one more look at himself before pulling away from the Shorefront building. He grinned. His detractors—yes, he had a few, some people just had no sense—accused him of considering himself God's gift to the world but the fact of the matter was that it was true. District Attorney at thirty-five. Might be governor someday. Sooner than later if he could put this Gap channel thing over.

He loosened his tie and opened his shirt's top button to admire the seahorse medallion hanging from a simple gold chain. He always scored when he had the seahorse with him. He patted his shirt pocket. If the medallion didn't do the trick, this little treat would. Ted Creaser had gotten it for him from the evidence locker. Just as Larry's date with Holly Rivera Berry had been as much about business as pleasure, his next meeting would be too although in this case the pleasure might be just as important as the business.

Earlier in the evening, Larry had put the top down on the new Audi convertible. Its cerulean blue color complemented his blond hair and blue eyes. Owning an Audi was a bit impractical since Bonafides didn't have an Audi dealership. However, Larry was in Austin often enough on business that getting the car serviced wasn't that much of a problem.

He picked up his car phone and dialed a number he knew well enough. He changed the phone to the other ear and muttered, "Come on, answer the phone." So near yet so far. He had just about given up when the call connected. Music played in the background.

"And just who might this be?" a familiar voice asked.

"You know who this might be. What took you so long to answer? Or should I ask, 'are you alone'?" Larry smiled and relaxed, knowing this wasn't going to be a dry run.

"And why wouldn't I be alone? You're not here. How soon are you going to get here? I've missed you."

"I'm only two blocks away, and you aren't going to miss me much longer," Larry replied. "Get ready, because I've got ants in my pants."

"Please drive carefully. That's some kind of weird fog that's rolling in. Fog in June. You'd think it was January."

"Never fear, Larry's here. I could get there with my eyes closed."

"I like it better when you keep them open," came the husky reply.

"Stop it," Larry said. "You'll be the death of me."

Moments later, Larry reached his destination. He was glad this condominium had its own garage with an entrance off the public road. Larry's divorce was long over but he still had to be careful for appearance's sake. Couldn't be caught with his pants down, not at this address.

He didn't have to ring the penthouse's bell. The door opened wide and he was greeted by open arms, pulled into the room, and given a kiss that was avid and genuine. When he surfaced from the deep tongue tangling, Larry said, "Great appetizer. Let's get to the main course."

"You're right, it's been too long. Once a week isn't enough. Come on, get comfortable. I've fixed you a drink."

"Never mind the drink," Larry said. "I need another kiss from my special angel."

Their embrace became more fervent, their breathing heavier. Clothes seemed to shed themselves of their own accord. Drinks forgotten, they stumbled toward the bedroom, their bodies entwined.

"Larry, oh Larry, don't ever stop," Tres said.

Larry paused only long enough to close the bedroom's vertical blinds. Tres forgot to do that enough times that Larry was pretty certain it was deliberate. As much as Tres might want everyone in the condo to know who his lover was Larry needed to keep that a secret.

"Whoever said 'business before pleasure' wasn't the brightest bulb on the Christmas tree," Larry panted as they fell on the bed. With calculated diligence that rivaled the best military campaign, he administered the kisses, touches, and strokes that he knew pressed Tres's buttons and before long the young man was transported to another dimension.

Larry breathed deeply with satisfaction. Good to know that Tres was still enthralled. He probably had him right where he wanted him but just to make sure, he said, "I have a little something for you."

"Oh, you shouldn't have," Tres replied, but he had the lean and hungry look of a dog awaiting an expected treat.

Larry produced the cocaine Ted Creaser had gotten for him. "Just one line's worth but it's all yours."

"I would share," Tres said although his expression begged Larry not to ask.

"That's okay, sweetness. Have at it." Larry congratulated himself. He'd managed to orchestrate their previous snorting sessions so that Tres thought that they both indulged which Larry would never do. He couldn't afford to be that much out of control.

Tres eagerly sucked the powder up his nose. Larry leaned back against the pillows and watched Tres react as the drug took hold. Just as when they were having sex, Larry found it to be a definite thrill watching Tres surrender while Larry kept his wits about him.

Control. Yes, that was what it was all about he decided as he watched Tres lose it. Self-control. Sure I'm handsome, intelligent, Larry thought. So are a lot of other guys, so is Tres. The difference was that Larry never got carried away. He always kept his eye on the ball and his hands on the wheel. That was his edge.

"Oh, yeah," Tres cried, stretching to his full length on the bed and drumming his heels on the quilted comforter. "Top o' the world, man. Standing on top o' the world."

Chuckling, Larry slipped from the bed and picked his trousers up from the floor. Any minute now Tres was likely to launch into a really bad Van Halen rendition.

Tres propped himself up on his elbows. "Hey, you're getting dressed."

"Better go while the gettin's good," Larry said. While you're still high, he thought. When Tres came down he tended to get pouty and maudlin. "The way this fog is moving in, if I wait much longer I'll have to drive through pea soup." Larry buttoned his shirt. "Fog in Bonafides in June, who woulda thunk? Must be some kind of weird front blowing in."

"Blowin' in, blowin' in the wind," Tres sang a few lines from the Peter, Paul, and Mary classic. He laughed. "Hey, you can't go yet. You haven't even told me how the meet went with Holly."

"It went just fine." Holly looked so much like her brother it had been like being on a date with Tres. Larry was going to have to be especially vigilant. It simply wouldn't do to call out Tres's name at some inopportune moment. "I'm playing her like a violin. I've got her convinced she could use my help with your father's estate. Before long, she'll be dancing to my tune and begging me to play."

"Great," Tres said, giggling.

Great for me, Larry thought, patting his medallion. Not so great for you, little buddy. It's the beginning of the end for you. Once I've got Holly marching to my tune I won't need you to intervene. You become expendable and given that you know way too much about me, the sooner the better.

CHAPTER 14—CLEAR AS MUD

Sam Hill grimaced as he walked across Bay Club parking lot to his Jeep.

Damn, when had all this fog rolled in? This was an odd time of year for fog in Bonafides. True, it had been hazy a few hours ago when he arrived aboard the Naval Air Station-Bonafides. Maybe a cold front had blown in. In any case, now he could barely see his rig. Clearly he had stayed longer than he thought and that was the only thing clear in the thick swampy air.

He glanced at his watch and sighed. Midnight already? Those old geezers on the base could listen to his stories all night long then linger another few hours to tell their own. Not that Sam minded. He needed any paying gig he could get since Bonafides University had cut back his classroom hours.

Sam chuckled. Now part of the state university system, Sam would always remember that the institution got its start as a small private liberal arts college founded by two men, Montgomery Hardley and Alvin Knott. Shortly after acquiring the college the university system had gone to great lengths to rename it, changing the logo, the letterhead, the signage, and even the name of the football team. They could try to brand it "Bonafides University" all they wanted, Sam thought. It wouldn't do any good. Even new students referred to it by its old name. It was just too much fun when asked, "Do you go to college?" to smile and reply, "Knott Hardley."

Sam sighed. The short courses they assigned him to teach these days gave him so little time to cover so much. He wished he could go back to full sessions but those plum jobs went to the young bucks. They had no objection to teaching the gut courses, the ones with sexy names like History Rocks or 20th Century America According to the Sunday Comics. Those candy-coated courses got all the enrollments.

When I was younger I would have fought for academic integrity, he thought, but no more. Now he was too old for the stress or the bureaucracy. The world of academia, of art, had changed. These days it was all about marketing. He didn't like what higher education or the arts had become and no longer had the energy for or the interest in clawing his way to the top.

Sam lurched as he reached for the handle to his Jeep then chuckled. Most folks thought he stumbled because he was drunk. As he had told Clark's girl Holly, it was a great disguise. In fact, he was mostly just getting old and struggled with an aging body wracked with arthritis. Even now, tired and stiff as he was, bending down to pick up his dropped keys was a painful exercise. He would be ready for a nightcap when he got home. Just for medicinal purposes, of course.

The drive home along the length of Shore Drive traversed the city from east to west. Not a short drive but given the absence of traffic at this hour it wouldn't take long. He'd get there sooner if he could travel at a respectable speed. Instead, the fog had him creeping along at well under the posted limit.

Still, maybe he could make good enough time to pop into the Redfish Club, catch last call, and see if any of his buddies were hangin' out.

Sam snatched a rag from the floor to wipe some of the grunge off the windows. It would be hard enough to see with all this fog. He didn't need all this sea salt that had blown in from the Intracoastal and settled on the glass.

Car windows weren't the only thing that took punishment from the base's waterfront location. Situated on the point between the bay and the Intracoastal, NAS-B continually struggled with the elements. When not waging more heroic wars the sailors battled the destructive effects of wind, salt, and rust. The sanding, priming, refinishing, and repainting were never-ending chores.

It was true, "rust never sleeps." Now who did that one, Sam wondered. Ted Nugent? Neil Young? No doubt one of the students in B.U.'s so-called Music Appreciation course could tell him. Young, he decided, not Nugent, and congratulated himself for remembering that bit of trivia. Not such an old man after all if he could still call up that kind of data.

After a few swipes across each window panel, Sam climbed into the Jeep and drove out of the lot. He picked up a little speed once he passed the base security booth and got on the road leading away from the base and toward the city. Though he knew that homes lined the road on his left, he couldn't see them through the fog. Heck, he couldn't see the water of the bay just a few yards to his right. His headlights hit the wall of fog and splayed out into uselessness. On a good night he could see the lights of Shore Drive rimming the bay front ahead like salt on margarita glass. In this impenetrable dark murkiness it was as if he'd been transported to another planet.

God, help me get home safely, Sam prayed.

Though the road here was posted for 50 miles per hour, Sam slowed to 30. It wouldn't be hard to oversteer and go off the pavement. No guardrail separated the water from the roadway, just an earthen shoulder and a line of jagged concrete riprap.

Sam heard the vehicle come up behind him before he saw it. He couldn't believe his eyes. Some fool was driving in this fog with no headlights. And fast, considering how quickly he'd appeared in Sam's rear view mirror. Sam shook his head. Some sailor had stayed too long at the Base Beach Club bar, no doubt. Sam tooted his horn. "Put your lights on, idiot," he yelled, as if the other driver could hear him.

Sam accelerated, hoping the other driver would see him and move to the left lane before he connected with Sam's bumper. "Goddamn, he's not switchin'."

Sam yanked the wheel and swung his Jeep into the left lane. The other vehicle followed him and hit Sam's bumper. The Jeep jolted forward into the oncoming lane. Sam pulled the wheel to the right to get back into his own lane. He knew he had overcorrected when his tires jounced on the shoulder's rough surface. He struggled to return to the pavement.

The asshole had his lights on now, at high beam. What the hell was his problem?

A streetlight briefly illuminated the vehicle. Sam went suddenly cold. He knew whose vehicle that was. There was no mistaking that paint job.

OK, so maybe I went too far at Clark's funeral, Sam thought. Does that give anyone call to scare an old man half to death on a foggy road?

Sam felt the Jeep climb and figured he ascended the short overpass that took the road over the water. On the downhill side a ritzy subdivision would be to his left. Sam planned to aim for that. He'd pull up to the first house he came to, knock on the door, and get help. He didn't care whom he might disturb at this hour. He'd apologize later.

Wait, was that subdivision gated? Damn! He drove past it so many times, why couldn't he remember? He could remember Neil Young but not a gate. Didn't matter. If there was a gate he'd just crash through it. That would raise an alarm for sure.

The pursuer kept right on Sam's tail. Sam felt another jolt as they made contact. This time his Jeep hit the pavement's edge and he felt his rig lean over on two wheels. Sam yanked the wheel to the left and his Jeep righted itself. I'll never be able to outrace him but I can sure try, he thought. "Your ass is in a sling if I can just get away," Sam yelled and mashed the accelerator to the floorboard.

As Sam crested the overpass, the pursuing vehicle slammed into him. The Jeep flew into the air. Sam gripped the wheel for dear life. The Jeep plunged into the night-black Gulf. Water as choking as the fog flooded in.

CHAPTER 15—GETTING DOWN TO BRASS TACKS

The rain pounded Holly's head and ran down her back. She was soaked to the skin but her position outside the window provided the only place where she could stand and eavesdrop on the conversation inside. She hoped the call that was the subject of her investigation would come through before she died of exposure. At last, the phone rang...

The ringing doorbell snapped Holly out of her reverie and summoned her out of the shower. Hair dripping, she scrambled into clothes which then clung to her still-damp body. Her navy skirt, white blouse, and heels were getting more of a workout on this trip than she had anticipated. Her clothes had the limp been-through-the-wash-one-too-many-times look. At this rate, she'd have to make another visit to Finders Keepers to buy something less bedraggled to wear.

She raced down the stairs to see who disturbed her at this ungodly early hour. Through the door's glass she could see a Federal Express delivery man, his white shirt already wilted and sweat-stained with the humidity and heat. A large box leaned against tanned legs showcased by blue walking shorts.

Right behind him stood Priscilla Esquivel. Here to grind me about the house, no doubt, Holly thought. The woman had become a major pest. Cilla's palm-tree-print sundress, necklace of chunky bright-colored wood beads, and ankle-wrap wedge espadrilles made Holly think of Carmen Miranda.

"Holly Berry?" the Fed Ex man asked.

"Yes," Holly said, although she realized that her hesitant tone made her sound not entirely sure. It wasn't her name that gave her pause, it was the package. Of the people who knew she was here, who would be sending her something FedEx, and what could it be? She signed the tablet the delivery man held out. He handed her the large box. "Have a nice day."

"You too," Holly mumbled, glad she wouldn't be the one running around town delivering packages on an already hot and sticky day. With gratitude she retreated into the house's air-conditioned comfort, Cilla Esquivel hot on her heels.

"Your paper, Sugar," Cilla said, and held out the *Daily Breeze*, rolled and sheathed in a thin plastic bag. "Thought I'd save you the trouble of coming out to fetch it. It's already hotter than Hades out here."

At first Holly had thought to cancel Clark's subscription. Once she realized she would be here a while she decided to keep the paper coming. She had remembered the *Daily Breeze's* previous incarnation, the *Intelligencer*, as a reliable source of information ranging from world events to surf reports. She found it surprising that short of a few wire service stories, the refashioned *Breeze* contained no world news in it at all, hardly any national or state news, and the coverage of local events was light and fluffy. That was how Holly liked her biscuits, not her news reporting. Nevertheless the ads, of which there were many, proved to be a good source of information about goods and services in a city that, like the paper, had changed greatly since she had been here last.

The newspaper once was very different, with informative in-depth articles and investigative reporting. It may have even inspired her to get into journalism, although it was only by the most creative stretch of the imagination that one could call her job of laying out a shopper "journalism." She felt her face grow warm with embarrassment remembering Rusty Burger's derisive laughter.

Yes, the local paper's heyday was many years ago. Sam Hill hadn't been talking out of his hat at the reception when he accused Pulitiz of turning a fine newspaper into birdcage liner.

Speaking of Sam Hill, there was a picture of him on the front page. The accompanying headline and story were below the fold. What was Sam up to now, Holly wondered. The answer would have to wait until later because Cilla patted her arm.

"Well, Sugar, that was quite a lovely thing you did for your father Sunday," she said. "Unusual, but lovely. Thank you for inviting me. I appreciated the opportunity to pay my respects. Again."

"No problem," Holly said. She wished the woman would leave so that she could (a) get dressed and (b) see what was in the Fed Ex package. Holly saw from the return address that the sender was her boss. Not a good sign.

Although Holly didn't move to let Cilla further into the house, the woman didn't get the hint. She held her ground in the foyer.

"I'd invite you in, but as you can see," Holly held her arms out at her sides, "I'm still dressing."

"That's quite all right, Sugar. No need to stand on ceremony with me. We're neighbors, after all. At least until you sell this place. You just go about your business. I'll make myself at home." She started off to the left, toward Clark's study.

Holly headed her off at the pass. "Excuse me. If you're looking for the kitchen, it's that way." Holly pointed to the right.

Cilla smiled. "I know that, Sugar. Well, I do believe I will get myself a cool drink after all. It's already blazing out there."

Holly hadn't been out of Texas so long that she had totally forgotten about southern hospitality. "Let me get that for you," she said, and followed the woman toward the kitchen.

"Don't trouble yourself, Sugar," Cilla said. "I know where everything is."

Indeed she did, as she went directly to the cupboard that held the iced tea tumblers.

Holly had her hand on the refrigerator door handle when the phone rang. She picked up the kitchen extension.

"Berry," came a gruff voice she knew all too well: that of her boss. "Don't think that by turning off your cell phone that you can avoid me. I know where you live."

"I can see that, sir," Holly said, twisting her hair.

"So you got the package."

"Just now. I haven't even had a chance to open it. Hold on a minute, sir." She put the call on "hold." "Excuse me," she said to Cilla. "I think I'd better take this in the study."

Her elbows propped on the kitchen island, a smiling Cilla Esquivel smiled even wider.

Holly dashed to her father's office and picked up the desk extension. "I'm back, sir."

"That box? It's the paper, Berry," her boss said. "I figured if you wouldn't come to work, I'd send your work to you. Get out your art boards, your Xacto knives, and your hot wax. Unless you can find a better way, you're going to paste up that paper the old-fashioned way."

Unless she could find a computer that happened to be loaded with the obscure software she was accustomed to using, Holly was going to have to do just that. She wondered if Edison Pulitiz would let her borrow a terminal at the newspaper office. After the drubbing he took from Sam Hill at her father's house, Pulitiz probably wouldn't be inclined to do Holly any favors.

Her stomach did flip-flops. She had been using DesktopPress to lay out the paper digitally for so long, she wasn't sure she remembered how to do it by hand, with agate rulers, blue pencils, and Rapidograph pens. Her boss hung up and Holly waited a beat to see if there were any other noises on the line, like the kitchen extension phone receiver being replaced on the switch hook.

If Cilla Esquivel had been listening in, she had made it from the kitchen to the study in record time. She stood in the doorway and pursed sticky stoplight-red lips in a big Marilyn Monroe pout. "I can see by the look on your face, Sugar, that that wasn't good news."

"Oh, nothing I can't handle," Holly said, twisting her hair.

Carrying two glasses of iced tea, Cilla strode into the room, moved some file folders aside, and made herself comfortable on the divan. She handed Holly one of the cold drinks. Cilla snagged the pewter cross, still half under the couch, with her heel. "What's this?" She bent down and reached under the divan to extract it.

"Something of my father's," Holly said. How had Artemisia missed it while straightening up? "Just leave it there."

"Why Sugar, I do believe I've seen it hanging on the wall, right there." Cilla pointed to the bare spot above her. "I could help you—"

"I said leave it," Holly replied. For some reason, the thought of Priscilla Esquivel fondling Clark's things didn't sit well. "I'll get to it."

"All right, Sugar. No reason to get testy. I'm here to give you some good news. Now that you have no further need for this house, you'll be happy to know that I have a buyer ready, willing, and more than able."

"Who said I didn't need the house? Tres?"

"Not at all. I just assumed, now that you have Clark buried, you'd be heading home. Especially since you have to get back to work."

"So you were listening in."

"Listening in?" Cilla bolted up, hands on hips. "Why I never... I just assumed, since you have a job—"

"I'll go back when I'm good and ready."

"And when might that be? Because you see, Sugar, this buyer wants the whole Playa Rico block. He's already made offers, generous offers, to all the other homeowners but the buy is contingent on him getting the entire block. No hold outs. Which, I'm afraid, right now is what you are. Sugar, you are holding up the deal of the century." Cilla bit her lower lip and twitched her hips in excitement.

Ah hah, Holly thought, no wonder Peanut Volkman gave me the finger that morning out on the deck. Clearly her neighbor wanted to sell and the Riveras held up the works. "Well, I'm sorry, but I have higher priorities right now."

"Such as?"

"Such as getting the facts about how my father died."

Cilla's smile faded. "Facts? But Sugar, Clark died of a heart attack. Everyone knows that."

"Everyone but me. There's something else going on here and I mean to find out what." With a hand on Cilla's back Holly all but pushed the woman from the study and toward the front door. "Until I do I'm staying and I'm staying in this house."

At the sound of a ringing phone Holly said, "Gotta go." She ejected Cilla, closed the door, and sprinted for the kitchen extension. Now who could this be? Holly grabbed the phone and growled into the receiver, "Yeah?"

"Hey, Sis. Are you okay? You sound terrible," replied Tres.

"Oh, it's you. Sorry. That Cilla woman was just here nagging me about selling the house. She's really getting on my nerves," Holly said.

Tres laughed. "Don't let her get to you. She means well, really. Why not sell the house? It's not as if you're going to keep it once you're done here."

"But meanwhile I need a place to live," Holly replied.

"You could always get a nice hotel room or a suite. Even a condo."

"Hey, I'm comfortable in the house. I guess I like being surrounded by familiar things. Maybe it makes Father feel less, well, gone."

"All right. We'll talk about this some other time when you're not so pissed off."

"Dammit, I'm not pissed off."

"Sure. Whatever. Look, I'm just a few blocks away. Did you forget we have an appointment with Noble Barnes?"

"No. I'm just about ready. His office still in that same old little bank building?" Holly asked more calmly.

"Oh, no. He's come up in the world. The main branch is in Shorefront Suites. He's on the lobby floor." Tres said, "Hey, I'm in the driveway now so pop on out."

Holly hung up, grabbed her purse, and headed out the door. She double-checked to make sure the door was locked just in case Ms. Esquivel tried breaking and entering to sell the house in Holly's absence. Holly hurried across the lawn and climbed into Tres' Jaguar where he sat admiring himself in the mirror. She was grateful to be the passenger. It gave her a chance to mark all the changes in town as they traveled from the Treasure Island Bridge and drove the length of Shore Drive west to downtown. New housing subdivisions, new apartment complexes, new shopping plazas. She wondered who was doing all this buying. How did people pay their rent? Bonafides wasn't the site of huge industry. Fishing and beer drinking were pretty much the city's gross national product.

Tres turned off the street and slotted the Jag into the Shorefront Suites parking garage. They entered the street-level lobby. In contrast with the outdoor temperature, the high-ceilinged space was positively frigid. Holly thought the air conditioning bill must be astronomical. She and Tres crossed the shiny terrazzo floor passing several retail establishments: a small café, a combination souvenir shop and newsstand, a barber. Huge posters boasting of great bargains for trips to faraway places papered the floor-to-ceiling glass walls of a travel agency. In the middle of these ads a colorful banner shouted for all to view, "Great Fun—Tejas Bonanza Resort and Floating Casino" as if it were already built and open for business.

Holly found herself frowning. She grabbed Tres' arm and pulled him away from the glass where he stood admiring his reflection. Not a single other person in the building's lobby had passed them without giving Tres a second look. Holly figured that might have something to do with his outfit: a pale yellow short-sleeved shirt whose elongated collar points winged out over the shoulders of his papaya-colored sleeveless knit vest atop what looked like flannel slacks in winter white.

At the end of the hall, scaly mesquite tree trunks framed the entrance to Barnes Bank. Surreptitiously, Holly passed her hand over one as she walked by. Though heavily sealed and varnished, it felt real enough. How much had that cost, she wondered? Deep red circular-patterned floor tiles seemed to be made of mesquite also.

Tres walked up to a receptionist filing her nails behind a blocky wooden desk. Holly wondered if it too was fashioned from mesquite. Holly supposed all the locally-sourced wood was supposed to give Barnes Bank that "hometown" feel, all the better to compete with—how had Noble put it?—some megalithic financial corporation.

The receptionist put down the file, ran her fingers through her long dark hair, and flashed a big smile at Tres.

Tres said, "We have an appointment with Mr. Barnes."

"He's ready to see you now," the receptionist replied. "I'll just buzz you in."

Holly jerked Tres's arm before they walked into Noble's office. "Let's get one thing straight. We're here to get my name on Clark's account to sign checks. We're not here to get you an installment on your allowance. So don't get any ideas. We have a lot of bills to pay and we need to settle his estate."

"Ah, Sis, I'm not after any money. I just think you should consider letting me sign checks too. It'll save time and I can help you get everything taken care of."

Holly stifled a laugh. "Sure. Like you've ever taken care of anything in your life. I don't think so."

Noble greeted them at the door. "Have a seat. How can I help you two?"

Holly and Tres sank into two comfortable, leather armchairs facing a massive rough-hewn desk. Its top, one enormous slice of mesquite with natural rather than finished edges, bore turquoise inlays. Behind the desk, floor-to-ceiling smoked glass gave Holly a view of the cars and people passing by on Shore Drive.

Noble Barnes seated himself in a chair that in keeping with the rest of the furnishings seemed to be made of mesquite. Blocky and boxy, it didn't look at all comfortable to Holly despite the leather cushioning but it certainly appeared to be solid. Maybe that was the desired impression.

She noticed that Barnes had a stack of pamphlets promoting the Tejas Bonanza Resort and Floating Casino with the same logo as the travel agency banner. The artist's drawing of the project's concept had an eighth-mile long retail strip positioned squarely where the Rivera's Playa Rico neighborhood stood. "The buyer wants the entire block," Cilla Esquivel had said. "The deal of the century." A restaurant occupied the spot currently occupied by the Rivera home. The development had all the appearance of a done deal. The nerve! Holly felt her frown deepen.

"Holly?" Barnes said.

"Oh, sorry. I need to put my name on a signature card so that I can sign Clark's checks," she told Barnes. "His bills are piling up and it's urgent that I start taking care of them before the electric company decides to cut our power."

Tres asked, "Don't you think I should sign, too? Two to pay the bills will get things done much quicker."

Holly scowled at Tres. "Tres, we discussed this."

Noble cleared his throat. "Well, Holly's the official executor. If she wants you as an endorser as well, that will have to be her decision. Neither of you can sign Clark's checks until the bank has a certified copy of his death certificate. Holly, have you brought one?"

"No, I don't know that I even have one." Holly wound her hair around her finger.

Barnes smiled gently. "Well, it shouldn't be a problem to get one. Just ask at City Hall. I'll have my secretary call over there now and make sure they can provide it for you this afternoon. I'd suggest getting several. You'll probably find other agencies will want one. When you get them, bring one back here and I'll have a signature card ready for you."

"Make that two cards," Tres said.

Holly glared at him. "Tres, I said we'd discuss this later." She stood and rushed out of Barnes's office so abruptly, Tres had to scurry to catch up.

CHAPTER 16—A CONSPIRACY OF SILENCE

Holly could hardly believe it. It was just as the tipster had alleged: the signature card had been doctored. Holly set down the magnifying glass. Could it really be that easy to do? Apparently so which made her wonder why this sort of thing didn't happen more often. Ah, the hard part had to be getting the original signature card in the first place. It had to be an inside job. Either the forger worked for the bank or knew some unscrupulous someone who did. Who could it be and how extensive was the fraud? How embarrassing this was going to be for Frisco First Financial but Holly didn't feel the least bit sorry for the institution that had often been accused of redlining...

Lost in thought, Holly rounded a corner and skidded on the slick polished floor to avoid colliding with Sidney Qownsill.

"Holly," Sidney Qownsill said. "What a surprise."

"Mine, too," Holly said, and tried not to stare at his hat. The knit cap clashed with the day's weather and Qownsill's tropical-weight suit. "What brings you here?"

Sidney jerked a thumb behind him. Floor-to-ceiling glass enclosed an office full of utilitarian gray metal desks manned by people talking on phones and pounding on keyboards. Gold letters across the glass read, "Third Coast Title." "My office,"

Sidney said. "Say, you look upset. I guess you've heard the news, eh?"

"What news?"

"Sam Hill was killed last night."

Holly felt a chill far in excess of the building's overly enthusiastic air conditioning. "Killed? How?"

"Car accident."

"Did they get the other driver?"

"There was no other driver," Sidney said. "Hill drove his Jeep off Shore Drive, out by the naval air station. Easy to see how it could happen, I guess. It was way foggy last night, and, well, everyone knows Sam drinks, eh?"

Everyone but me, Holly thought, twisting her hair.

"Hmmph. Not the most pleasant visit for you, Holly, first having to deal with your father's death, and now this news about Sam Hill. Guess you'll be glad to be heading back to San Francisco. Were you making flight arrangements?" Sidney nodded in the direction of the travel agency.

"I'm not leaving," Holly shouted.

A couple passing in the corridor gave Holly a wide berth.

"Well, okay, little lady," Sidney said. "No reason to bite my head off. So what are you two up to?"

Tres answered, "Holly and I were with Noble Barnes getting signature cards for Clark's account."

"Oh, so you'll be signing Clark's checks now?" Sidney asked, his brow furrowed.

He looked concerned and well he should, Holly thought. "I don't think so," she said with a glare for Tres. Tres pouted while Sidney's frown vanished with an audible sigh of relief. That Tres's reputation as a spendthrift was widely known didn't surprise Holly but why should Sidney Qownsill care? "So you're in the title business?" she asked him. "I thought that you were an attorney."

"Right on both counts. The title company is a sideline you might say. There are just so many hours in a day and an attorney can bill only twenty-four of them. Had to find some way to make some money."

Holly struggled for a diplomatic reply and finally gave up. "Title business, huh? You would know then. Are Clark's will and a power of attorney all I need to handle his real property assets?"

"That should do it. So, thinking of selling the old place after all? Beauty. You know, Cilla Esquivel's the perfect person to help you with that. You could leave it in her hands with complete confidence and be winging your merry way back to San Francisco."

"You don't say." Holly did her best to reign in her irritation. She twisted her hair so hard it hurt. "But I'm not ready to sell yet. Not by any means. First, I feel I owe it to my father's memory to check out the Rivera land grant he was looking into before he died."

Sidney snorted. "I doubt there's anything to it. Legends and fairy tales is all that is."

"Maybe so but it's our legend."

Sidney shrugged. "I could look into it for you if you want but if I were you I wouldn't let that hold me up. If I were in your shoes—and let me tell you, I wish I were because I could make a lot of money—I would sell with the rest of the neighborhood. It's a monster of a deal. Take the money and run is my advice."

"Thanks," Holly muttered. She took Tres's elbow and practically dragged him away. Once out of earshot, she grumbled, "What is it with these people? Why is everybody telling me to get lost?"

"Ah, Sis, I think you've got it all wrong. He offered to help, didn't he? He just figured you're anxious to get home."

"I'm not going anywhere till I get some answers. C'mon."

"Where are we going?"

"The police station."

Tres stopped and sighed. "Ah, sis—"

Hands on her hips, Holly said, "You can either drive us there or we walk. Either way, I'm going."

Tres gave an even deeper sigh. "Fine."

The building that housed the Bonafides Police Department was in what Holly thought of as the "legal" district because it was home to the county courthouse, county appraisal office, notaries, document storage and destruction companies, bail bondsmen, and attorneys who couldn't quite afford the swankier address of Shorefront Suites. It was only a few blocks from Shorefront Suites but they could have walked in the time it took Tres to navigate downtown Bonafides's labyrinth of one-way streets and find a parking space.

The BPD occupied an old downtown office building, a simple multistory rectangle with a grid of windows that made the structure look like a giant masonry waffle. Holly thought it odd to have the city jail in the same building, not to mention on the same floor, where people paid their parking tickets and got their vehicles out of impound. To her that somewhat trivialized being incarcerated but it had been that way for as long as she could remember.

The Bonafides Chief of Police who met them at the third-floor reception desk was not the bantam, sensible, straight-talker she remembered from her childhood years. The Year 2000 model seemed to have achieved his lofty position by dint of pushing the biggest beer belly and having the loudest voice. She hoped that the dead-looking yellow mat on top of his head was a rug and not his real hair.

"Tres, good to see you," the chief said. "And you, Ma'am. Obviously, you're his sister. You could be twins. Can't believe how much you favor each other. Your dad was a good man, well-liked and admired by many in this city. Come, we'll talk in my office."

Holly expected some kind of noisy bullpen such as what was usually pictured on television crime shows. Instead, the chief led her and Tres down a corridor past cubicles and small serviceable offices. The gray metal desks, matching filing cabinets, and task chairs combined with the gray industrial carpeting gave the police department the appearance of an insurance company. Acoustic tile ceilings kept the ringing of phones and the chatter of conversations to a muffled hum. Hard to imagine crime being actually fought here. More like efficiently managed.

As would befit a CEO, the chief's corner office was wood-paneled and more luxuriously carpeted than the staff's quarters.

The chief settled his bulk into a high-backed executive chair behind a huge walnut desk that held only a lamp, phone, and notepad. "Take a seat," he said, indicating the two guest chairs in front of the desk. "Tell me what the BPD can do for you."

"Thank you," said Holly. "Perhaps you could help fill in the details about my father's death."

"Details? I don't see how we could help there."

"Didn't you investigate it?"

"Investigate?"

"Isn't that what you do? Investigate crimes?"

"Was there a crime? I don't rightly recall." He scratched his head. His hair moved as a solid mass.

"Who would recall?" Holly asked, unable to keep irritation from creeping into her voice.

"Hmm," the police chief said. He punched a button on his phone and yelled, "Who was on duty...?" He turned to Holly. "What day was that, you said?"

Holly told him and the chief broadcasted it throughout the third floor. His interoffice intercom buzzed and he took the call. Over the intercom, a woman's voice said, "Detective Creaser, sir."

"Detective Creaser," the chief repeated to Holly.

"So I heard." Detective Ted Creaser. Interesting.

"Apparently he was on duty that day," the chief said. "He would have caught the case if there was one. Creaser," he yelled into the intercom. Holly put her hands over her ears. A couple of minutes passed. When no one answered the chief's bellow, he yelled again. "Creaser, on the double."

After an interval a lot longer than the urgency of the summons called for, Detective Creaser appeared in the entrance to the chief's office. If the chief was the CEO, Creaser was clearly upper management targeting the top job, or at least that's what his sharp dress-for-success shirt, tie, suit, and wing-tips said to Holly.

The chief tipped his chair back and put his feet up on his desk.

Creaser leaned against the door frame.

The chief picked up a mug and took a sip.

Creaser examined his nails.

"Excuse me," Holly said.

"Yes, well, this is Detective Creaser," the chief said.

"I'm acquainted with Detective Creaser," Holly said.

"Tres. Ms. Berry," Creaser said, with a nod of recognition for each of them.

"They have some questions about...what was your father's name, you said?"

"Clark. Rivera," Holly growled.

"Right. Clark Rivera. He died," the chief told Creaser.

"I know that. I was at the funeral," Creaser said. "Sir," he added.

"How nice for you. Well, this young lady—what was your name again, you said?"

"Holly. Berry."

"Right. Creaser, this is Holly Berry."

"I know Ms. Berry," Creaser said. "Sir."

"Good. Ms. Berry has some questions about the case."

"There was no case. And I'm busy," Creaser replied. "Sir."

The chief bolted to his feet so quickly his chair fell over. At full volume he said, "Creaser, I'm ordering you to help this woman now.

Creaser shrugged and started down the corridor.

"Go with the Detective, Miss—what was your name again, you said?"

"Berry," Holly said through clenched teeth. "Thank you."

She hustled after Creaser, Tres at her side. "How did that man get to be chief of police?" she asked in a rough whisper. "Probably in tight with the good old boys' network. There's a lot of that going on around here, always has been. I'll tell you, Tres, if I were an investigative reporter here I'd have a field day."

"Now, Sis, simmer down. Remember you're in Bonafides, not Frisco. Things work a little differently here."

"If they work at all."

They arrived at Creaser's cubicle. Despite the ban on smoking in public buildings, an odor of stale cigarettes permeated the space. Holly would have expected to see piles of paper and overstuffed in-boxes but a phone set seemed to be the only work-related item on the desktop. The rest was devoted to shallow dishes filled with Jolly Rancher candies, half-filled foam coffee and soft drink cups, and swag from Bonafides University's football team, the Fighting Crabs.

Creaser lounged in his chair leaving Holly and Tres to stand alongside his desk. "So?" he asked.

"The chief said you could show me the reports on the investigation into my father's death," Holly said, twisting her hair.

"Did he? That asshole. There ain't no report."

Holly felt herself blushing, not so much at the profanity but at the lack of respect. While the chief had not impressed her certainly he deserved a little deference from those under his command. "No?"

"Weren't nothin' to investigate."

"I told you, Sis," Tres said.

"Your father died of a heart attack. That's what the doc said."

"Heart attack? It looked to me as though he'd been hit in the head," Holly replied.

"Well, I don't know about that. Maybe he fell, hit his head in the process. Yes, I do believe the housekeeper told Dispatch she saw blood. Panicked and yelled for the police. You know how excitable these beaners can be."

"Excuse me?" Holly said, her face getting hotter yet.

Creaser continued as if he hadn't heard. "That must have been it, he fell and hit his head. F'in' pain in the ass. Because of the 911 call, I had to fill out a bunch of stupid paperwork anyway. If I'd gone out there it would have taken me all damn day. Fortunately, Doc Roberts headed me off at the pass. Heart attack, pure and simple. Your Dad may have bumped his head when he fell but he's turning up daisies from a bad ticker. No foul play. No f'in' mystery."

"But...but—" Holly said.

"You wanna see, go down to Records at the county courthouse and get a copy of the death certificate. Says the same damn thing. Now I got work to do."

Creaser sat upright but his chair back remained in the reclined position. He stood, buttoned his suit jacket, and without another word, walked out.

Holly stood alongside Creaser's desk, mouth agape. When she could get her voice working again she said, "Let's go."

"Home?" Tres replied.

She shook her head.

"I know, I know," Tres said. "Just don't ask me to move the car."

"We can walk," Holly replied.

At the courthouse, Holly checked the directory for the location of the County Records office. She noted with secret pleasure that Larry Pomposas' office was also in the building. Maybe she'd stop in to say "hi" before she left.

She started for the escalator. Tres hung behind.

"Aren't you coming?" she asked.

"I, uh, I'm gonna grab a smoke," Tres replied. "I'll step outside and meet you right back here."

Holly shrugged and stepped onto the escalator.

CHAPTER 17—NO GOOD DEED GOES UNPUNISHED

Time *was running out. Holly didn't dare waste a second to look at the clock or her watch. It was all she could do to scan the incriminating documents in the short time she had before someone returned and discovered her. She wished she had something like a discreet spy camera to capture the damning material but all she had was her memory. She hoped that she would recall enough facts to offer probable cause for an investigation. She redoubled her efforts to speed-read without overlooking any details when she heard footsteps...*

"Miss? Hello, Miss?"

Holly looked up from the document.

"So is that the certificate you wanted or not?" asked the Records clerk. The overhead fluorescents twinkled in the clerk's five pairs of small silver hoop earrings that to Holly made the young woman's earlobes look like they were spiral-bound.

"Yes, yes," Holly said. "I'll need copies. Five. No, make that ten."

"Pay the cashier, then bring me the receipt," the clerk said with a sigh.

Holly stood in a seemingly interminable line at the cashier, then in another seemingly interminable line at the clerk's counter before finally walking away with ten copies of her father's death certificate. She exited the Records office, walking slowly and reading the death certificate for the third time. Not that it was such fascinating reading. It was actually quite straightforward. Holly simply couldn't believe it. She scanned the words for a fourth time when suddenly the fire alarm shrieked like a demented banshee. The lights flickered and then the corridor went black, lit only by a small window at the far end. From the offices behind her, Holly heard screams, crashes, and the sounds of people scrabbling around in the dark. In a minute, they would stumble out into the corridor and mow her down in a blind rush to leave the building. They wouldn't be taking the elevator, they'd be heading for the stairs. She'd better beat them to it, get down the stairs, and be gone before she got stampeded.

Moving as fast as she dared in the dark, Holly felt her way along the wall toward the emergency exit's feeble red light. Her hands found the exit door. She pressed the crash bar, pushed open the heavy fire door, and stepped into a windowless stairwell even darker than the hallway. Just as she reached for the handrail, a hand hit her square in the middle of her back and shoved. Holly clutched at the handrail to keep from pitching headfirst over the rail into the void of the stairwell. She lost her footing and skidded down a flight of concrete steps edged with metal. Screaming, she grabbed the bottom railing to brake her uncontrolled descent, and ended up spread-eagled on the landing.

Behind her, the steel door banged loudly as it hit the wall, followed by excited voices.

Feet pounded on the stairs above her. A hand grabbed her collar and pulled her upright. "You okay?" Holly heard. "You poor thing, you almost went over!"

"Why couldn't you be more careful?" Holly cried. "You almost sent me over the railing."

"Not me," the voice replied. "I walked in to see you going head over heels down the stairs."

"Someone pushed me," Holly said.

"Now I know you're upset but I'm sure it was just an accident," said the disembodied voice in the darkness. "People were panicking, thinking we were having a fire drill."

With that, the lights came on.

"Well, looks like it was a false alarm," said her rescuer, a heavy man in a faded T-shirt, gym shorts, and flip flops. "Sorry you got pushed. No way to treat a lady but then some folks just don't care anymore. That old every-dog-for-himself attitude."

"I'm sure you're right, honey," said his female companion, a gray-haired woman in a patio dress. She straightened Holly's clothes and hair.

"Maybe so," Holly replied, though she was hardly convinced. The push was deliberate and with intent. Why? Who would want to hurt her? Who even knew she was here? "Either way, thank you very, very much."

She exited the stairwell and crossed the corridor to the escalator, her steps still unsteady.

"Holly!"

She looked across the crowded lobby to see her brother waving at her. He ran to meet her at the bottom of the escalator.

"Where have you been, I've been looking all over for you?" he asked. "And what the hell happened to you?"

"I was push—I fell down the stairs," Holly answered.

"I don't like the looks of that gash on your head."

"Gash?" Holly put a hand to her forehead. Tres gestured "other side." Sure enough, when she took her hand away it had blood on it. When had that happened? She must have hit her head on the railing somehow or maybe a step's metal trim cut her scalp. She excused herself, found the ladies room, and blotted the cut with a paper towel.

"Maybe I'd better get you to an emergency room," Tres said when she returned.

"Scalp wounds are always worse than they look," she said, or so she had heard. "I'll be all right."

"Still, I'm taking you right home."

"Actually, we need to make a stop. Is there an office supply store or an art supply store around somewhere?"

"A what? What are you going to do, Scotch tape your head back together?"

It took three stops for Holly to find what she needed. Xacto knives and blades were still in stock at the big-box office supply store. She found graph paper, art boards, and Rapidograph pens at a similarly huge arts-and-crafts store. She even found a knock-off brand of rub-down letters and a dusty coil of border tape in a clearance bin but forget about some kind of waxer. The clerks she asked just gave her a blank stare or suggested that she try a beauty supply house. Finally Holly admitted defeat. She would just have to use rubber cement.

Holly sat silent for the remainder of the drive. What she had learned, or not learned, about Clark's death this morning made no sense whatsoever. No police report, no death investigation? For a man who had his head bashed in? If one more person told her to get out of town she would have to do some bashing of her own. Speaking of bashed heads, the cut on hers did sting and she felt a headache coming on.

Tres pulled into the driveway of the Rivera villa. Holly looked to the right and left, fully expecting to see Cilla Esquivel lurking in the bushes, ready to ambush her.

"You sure you're going to be okay, Sis?" Tres said. "Give me a call later and let me know you're all right. If I were you, I'd go get my noggin looked at."

"Are you telling me to go get my head examined?" Holly replied.

Tres chuckled. "I just think with a head injury that you should see a doctor, that's all."

Maybe Tres was right, Holly thought. Perhaps she should see a doctor. And she knew exactly what doctor she wanted to see.

CHAPTER 18—BLOOD IS THICKER THAN WATER

"I think you're right, Tres," Holly said. "I should have this looked at. Would you please give Doc Roberts a call?"

Tres tried not show the sudden alarm that he felt. "Doc Billy Bob? Wouldn't you rather just go to the ER?"

"No, I wouldn't. I really don't think I could sit for hours waiting to see someone. Not the way I'm hurting." She tipped her head to one side, put her hand to the gash, and winced.

With a heavy sigh, Tres picked up the house phone, and dialed the free time-and-weather recording. "No answer," he said, hanging up the phone. "Guess Doc Billy Bob is out. On a call, probably."

"On a call?" Holly replied. "Don't be ridiculous. You yourself said he doesn't practice anymore, that he just came over the day Dad died to do you a favor. I'll bet he's in his backyard bird watching or something. Let's just drive over there and see."

"Aw, Holly, it's getting late. It's been a long day. And maybe you should rest."

"You're the one who said I should see a doctor. Now let's go."

Trying not to grumble, Tres helped his sister into the car. He dreaded this face-to-face. No way was Holly talking with Doc Billy Bob a good thing although fixated as she was about that death certificate, sooner or later she would be insisting on a confab. Sure, he had given the doc some money for his trouble but had it been enough to buy his discretion? If it hadn't and this meeting went badly, Tres would have to call Larry again and Larry would not like that. The man was already steamed. While Holly was in the County Records office, Tres excused himself for a cigarette break and called Larry to give him a heads up. Tres's report that Holly had talked to the police chief and Detective Creaser about Clark's death made Larry furious.

"Under no condition must she be allowed to pursue that line of questioning," he said.

Tres thought that his sounding the fire alarm and Larry's killing the courthouse lights might slow Holly down. His sister was so hard-headed even a tumble down the stairs didn't stop her.

Tres drove aimlessly around town trying his best to get lost. Foiled again. Despite his best efforts he found Doctor William Roberts's office right where Holly remembered it from childhood, attached to the man's home on Lynn Street. Equidistant from the county hospital and several other older hospitals, the once-upscale area had been the address of many of the city's professionals. When the city's population center had shifted east so had the newer larger hospitals and clinics, doctors, and specialty practices that made up the medical community. The end of Lynn Street in the shadow of largely-deserted office buildings looked old and seedy. The shingle outside Doctor Roberts's office was so faded it was nearly illegible.

Several times Holly knocked on the office door and waited, twisting a strand of hair, but received no answer. She turned and gave Doc Roberts's residence a thoughtful glance.

A cracked cement walkway cut a path through an untended yard to the front door of the house. A dry summer had allowed weedy Johnson grass to overtake the water-loving St. Augustine grass most homeowners used to give their landscapes golf-course-green lushness. Holly minced through the overgrowth, stopping every other step to pick sticker burrs out of her ankles.

When no one answered Holly's pressing of the house's bell she tried knocking.

Tres tugged at her arm. "C'mon, Holly, he's not home, just like I told you."

Just as Holly shrugged in defeat the door opened to reveal a shrunken, wrinkled man with uncombed white hair and a stubbly chin. His sleeveless undershirt was yellow with age and his faded twill shorts were ragged at the hem. A parrot missing most of its chest feathers perched on his shoulder. The man and the bird peered at the two callers.

"Sorry, I'm not seeing any new patients," said the man. "Not seeing any old ones, neither."

"Doctor Billy—Doctor Roberts," Holly said, pushing her way into the dark, stuffy foyer. "I'm not here as a patient. I'm here about a patient. Clark Rivera."

Oh, no, Tres thought, and felt suddenly chill despite the heat of the day.

"Open wide," the bird said.

Frowning, Doctor Billy Bob studied his bare feet housed in foam rubber flip-flops, then gazed the ceiling. Holly described her father. Roberts thought some more. Finally he said, "Clark Rivera. He wasn't no patient. He was dead."

"Yessir. He was. You pronounced him."

Roberts nodded. "Of a heart attack."

"This won't hurt a bit," said the bird.

"You're sure? You're certain that's what he died of?" Holly asked, twisting her hair.

"Course I'm sure. That's what you told me."

"Me?" Holly said. "I wasn't there."

"Were too." Doctor Billy Bob pursed his lips and nodded.

"You must be confusing me with my brother." Holly turned toward Tres.

The doc peered at Tres. "Well, I'll be," said the doctor. "Twins."

"Not exactly, but it's not important. So you didn't examine my father?" Holly asked.

"Nothing to examine. Right, Doctor Roberts?" said Tres. It was hard to sound cool and casual with his heart in his throat.

Doctor Billy Bob shook his head. "Uh, right. Didn't have to. He was dead. Nothin' I could do for him."

"Just a little stick, just a little stick," said the bird.

"But the cause of death, weren't you concerned about that?"

"Nothing to be concerned about. Right, Doctor Roberts?" Tres said.

"Uh, right. Man was dead. I pronounced him dead. Someone wanted to know what he died of, they should have asked the M. E."

"It'll be over in a minute," said the bird.

"But a heart attack? What about the big wound in his head?" Holly asked.

"What wound?"

Holly tapped her own skull. "Here."

The doctor squinted at Holly. "I don't see no wound, girlie. You got a little scrape there but it certainly ain't no big wound."

"Not me," Holly said. "My father. The dead man."

"Didn't see no wound there, neither," Doctor Roberts said. "When I saw the man, he was laying on the floor in his home office room. I didn't move him any. I just checked his heart and it wasn't beating."

"If the heart isn't beating, you've had a heart attack. Right, Doctor Roberts?" asked Tres.

"Right."

"Open wide," said the bird.

"You're sure you didn't see where his skull was cracked?"

"Sure I'm sure."

Holly propped her hands on her hips. "I don't believe you. It was plain as day."

Roberts made a face. "Hell, woman, the man was lying on his back."

"And you didn't even turn him over?"

"Open wide, honey, open wide," said the bird.

"What for? He was dead. I could tell that without rolling him all around the floor."

Holly groaned and threw her hands up in the air in frustration. She turned to go.

Roberts said, "Ma'am?"

"What?"

"Speaking of bumps on the head, that's one you got there does look nasty. If I was you, I'd have a doctor look at that."

"Open wide, honey, here I come," the bird cried, and let out a cackle.

"Let's go, Tres," Holly said, and headed for the car.

"Thanks, Doctor Roberts," Tres said. "Thanks a lot. You've been a big help, a really big help. I mean it." He fished out his wallet and handed the doctor a fist full of bills. "A token of my gratitude," he said.

"Appreciated," replied the doctor with a wink.

They drove back to the Rivera villa in silence. Holly sat brooding on her side of the Jag. Tres drove without a word, relishing the feeling of triumph and relief. The old doc had come through for him again and he wouldn't have to report another screw-up to Larry. Life was good.

Of course, life could be better. Tres still didn't have access to Clark's money and this latest *mordida* had left him broke again. He also needed a fix and some sugar. He could take care of all three needs with one visit to Larry. Just as soon as Tres dropped off Holly he'd get on the cell phone and take life from good to stupendous.

CHAPTER 19—THE BLIND LEADING THE BLIND

"Batten down the hatches, matey," said Joe Eddie.

Rusty Burger looked up from his bowl of snack mix nuts and twisted on his bar stool to see what caught the attention of the barkeep at the Marina Bar, Grill, and Bait Shop.

"Here she comes, making waves and all sails before the wind," Joe Eddie said.

Indeed she was. Holly Rivera Berry marched across the floor under a full head of steam. She was mad all right and for the life of him Rusty couldn't imagine what he did to deserve it.

The woman emphatically plopped her cute little butt on a neighboring bar stool and pounded a dainty fist on the bar. "Give me a double, Joe Eddie."

"A double what?"

She stopped, her mouth open, and looked puzzled. She turned to Rusty. "I don't know. What's good?" she whispered.

"Give her a Michelada," Rusty told Joe Eddie.

Joe Eddie looked at him sideways. "You sure?"

"She looks like she could use one." To Holly he said, "Upset about Sam Hill, huh?" and then he was sorry he had said anything as her expression went from peeved to aggrieved.

"Oh, Sam," she said. "He was about the only bright spot about being back here. I saw him yesterday. I'm afraid that I scolded him about his drinking. He said it was just an act but apparently not. His drinking turned out to be the death of him." She frowned. "What?"

"What 'what'?" Rusty asked.

Holly shook her head. "Your expression. This was supposed to be where you say, 'Yeah, poor Sam. I guess he really was hitting the sauce too hard.' But you didn't."

Rusty bit his lip. "Sam told you it was an act and it pretty much was. People liked to think that they were putting one over on him and he let them. It was just easier than butting heads but he was paying attention all the time."

"Looks like he wasn't paying enough attention last night, not to his driving at any rate."

"I dunno. I drove by that section of Shore Drive this morning. Lots of skid marks where he went off the road." Rusty would love to get a look at the police report and the M.E.'s report not to mention Sam's Jeep. Getting to see the reports would take some doing but Sam's Jeep might be in the realm of possibility.

"You know that's not the safest road on Bonafides, especially in the dark. No guard rail and—" Holly's purse emitted a muffled ring. With a grimace, she rifled around in it and withdrew a cell phone. "Excuse me," she said and put the phone to her ear. Her expression became only more pained. She latched onto a strand of hair and twisted it around her finger. Whoever the caller was, he was doing all the talking. Holly's end of the conversation was limited to "Yes, sir," and "No, sir." Finally she ended the call and stowed the phone back in her purse. "My boss," she said in a tone that spoke volumes. "Barkeep, where's that drink?"

"Coming up, ma'am," Joe Eddie replied.

"So who put a burr under your saddle?" Rusty asked, grateful for the interruption. The *Daily Breeze* had pretty much painted a picture of a drunken driver who went off the road but Rusty wasn't so certain that was the complete story. If he had to venture an opinion he'd guess that Sam hadn't been completely at fault. Still, he wasn't ready to share his suspicions, not yet.

"Oh, everybody." Holly ticked them off on her fingers. "My boss, the police chief, the detective, the doctor, my brother for Pete's sake."

"So what's new? Even more interesting, who used you for a punching bag?"

"What?" Holly asked.

Rusty dabbed at her head with a bar rag. "You're bleeding. What did you do, fall or something?"

"I believe falling is your stock in trade."

Rusty felt his face grow warm. He didn't know which worse: being taken for a drunk or a klutz. Neither was true. Mostly he was simply distracted, had something on his mind, and not watching where he was going. Okay, sometimes he did overdo it in the beverage department. "You should get that looked at."

"Damn it, not you too. Everyone wants to tell me what to do."

Rusty held up his hands in self-defense. "Hey, forget I said anything. Here, drink your drink."

Holly lifted the bottle of Tecate beer. Salt rimmed the opening which was plugged with a lime wedge. She removed the lime and took a healthy swallow.

"Yep, that should do it," she said in a strangled voice, clutching at her throat.

Clearly the hot sauce Joe Eddie had added to the cold beer had made an impression. Rusty suspected Holly struggled not to choke and admired the game effort. "So, you want to tell me now how you got that knock on your noggin'?"

"Someone tried to kill me," she said calmly.

"Get out of Dodge."

"Seriously. I was in the courthouse—"

"What were you doing there?"

"Trying to get a certified copy of my father's death certificate. Detective Creaser said if I wanted one I needed to go to County Records."

"What were you doing talking to Creaser?"

"The police chief said Creaser—"

"The chief? What were you doing talking to him?"

"Noble Barnes said—"

"What were you doing talking to Barnes?"

Holly propped her hands on her hips. "Do you want to know how I got hurt or not?"

"I asked you, didn't I?" Rusty replied.

"Then stop interrupting me and let me tell the story."

"Fine. Tell it." Rusty shoved a handful of snack mix into his mouth and crunched it with a vengeance.

Twisting that strand of hair, Holly proceeded to relate how she had just left the county records office when the building's fire alarm went off and the corridor went dark. "I was trying to use the stairs to get out of the building and somebody pushed me. I could have been killed. Tres said he thought I must have imagined it, what with everybody rushing to get out of the building."

Rusty traced a water ring his beer bottle left on the bar. "Let's see. Just before you were pushed, you talked to Creaser, the chief, Noble Barnes—"

"And Sidney Qownsill, while we're counting heads. Ran into him outside of Noble's office."

Rusty nodded. "See, that fall was no accident. Any one of those sonsabitches could have done it."

Holly set down her drink. "You mean you don't think I imagined it? Everyone else does."

Rusty shook his head. "Little lady, you spent the day running up against the entire cartel. That fall was no accident."

Holly scoffed. "The famous cartel again." She looked at him sideways. "No accident, huh?"

"No accident."

"Well, at least someone believes me."

"Which is why, at the risk of you reaming me out again, I urge you to stop poking around and asking questions about how Clark died."

"So you think someone killed him."

Rusty shrugged. Not just Clark but maybe Sam Hill as well, he thought but didn't say.

"But why?"

Rusty sighed and took a swig of beer. "The Rivera land grant."

"That old saw? Why would anyone kill me or my father over that silly nonsense?"

"Because, Ms. Rivera, if the land grant has substance, and I believe it does, your father—well, now you and your brother I guess—own land the cartel wants to develop for the Tejas Bonanza Resort and Casino."

"You're talking about more than just the house, right? The house Priscilla Esquivel keeps leaning on me to sell."

"Of course she's leaning on you. The cartel wants that whole street, and they already have most of it. All your neighbors have agreed to sell. And if that sale goes through, Cilla's the agent of record. She stands to make a bundle. But nothing's going to happen if you don't cooperate. It's all or nothing. The cartel can't possibly develop it commercially with a private house sitting in the middle of it."

"I see." Holly took a slow sip of her drink.

"But I'm talking about more than simply your house. I'm talking a big chunk of Isla del Tesoro."

"You think I own it."

Rusty nodded. "Clark certainly thought that he did. Oh, he didn't at first. Like everyone else, he thought that was just an old family myth. Then your mother died and all the Riveras sort of rallied 'round your father, while Taffy's kin kind of ignored him."

Holly could imagine. Her distant great aunts, black-garbed *madrazas,* would have wailed and cried and pretended as if they really mourned Taffy, although when she was alive she was "that *gringa"* Clark had married. Secretly grateful to have her out of the picture, they would have fussed about Holly's father like he had been orphaned.

"It sort of got him re-interested in his heritage and he decided to look into the Rivera land grant. All those guys—Barnes, Qownsill, Priscilla Esquivel—were happy to help him with it. They made lots of noise but nothing really seemed to be happening. At the same time, they offered to buy the land."

"Land they kept saying my father had no clear title to?"

Rusty nodded. "They offered him sort of a quitclaim kind of deal. Clark got suspicious."

"I don't blame him," Holly said.

"He did a little digging around. Found out they were all investors in this Gap development and Clark began to suspect that they didn't have his best interests at heart."

"I'll say." Her face pinched in anger, Holly looked around as if for a dog to kick or something to throw. She settled for twisting her hair. "Wait a minute. How can that be true? All of my father's accounts are still at Barnes' bank. If Dad suspected a conflict of interest, why would he continue to do business with Barnes?"

"Couple o' reasons," Rusty said. He took a big gulp of beer to whet his whistle. Storytelling was thirsty work. "Some of his money was tied up in time accounts. Your father was a sensible man, after all. He realized cashing out some investments prematurely would cost him as much or more than Barnes. Mostly he didn't want to tip off Barnes and the other guys that his allegiance had changed. He was biding his time until he had all the ammunition he needed. Meanwhile, he hired me to look into substantiating the land grant."

"And why you, if I may ask?"

"Well, I am an attorney. Okay, was an attorney. Mostly 'cause not only could I do the work, I was someone Clark felt he could trust. He wanted someone who absolutely was not tied in with that bunch." He pointed at Holly's beer bottle, which was empty. She nodded and he called for Joe Eddie to fix her another.

"I see your point." Holly started in on her second drink.

Seemed to Rusty like the hot pepper sauce was going down pretty easy.

"OK, let's assume that there is something to the land grant. Why shouldn't I sell the land? This Gap development looks to be the up and coming thing. If the land is that valuable, I stand to make millions."

"You do. Then you too can be complicit in irreparably damaging a natural resource." Rusty took another swallow of beer to wash out the bitter taste the idea had left in his mouth.

Holly shrugged. "I don't know about that. From what I've read, the Army Corps of Engineers thinks it's a sound idea."

"Ah, the Corps." Rusty nodded. "The fine folks who brought us the rape of the Florida Everglades. Oh, and the New Madrid Floodway Project. That one is an open gap that someone thought ought to be closed." He took a swallow of beer. "It's still open, by the way."

"Hmm," Holly said.

"Look, I understand where you're coming from. A couple of years ago, I would have said the same thing. Growth, jobs. Progress has to be a good thing, right? But since my suspen— my career change, I've spent a lot of time out on the water there. I developed an appreciation for this area that most people don't have." He clasped his hands and stretched his forearms toward her across the bar. "Come out on my boat and I'll show you."

Holly slammed her fist on the bar. "I'll do it."

Rusty thought it might be Holly's two Micheladas talking but found to his surprise that he didn't really care why, he was just pleased that she wanted to come. Now why should that be? Probably it was because if she gained confidence in him as a boat captain, maybe she'd trust him as a lawyer. He'd get another chance proving the validity of the Rivera land grant, at stopping the cartel. Yeah, that was it.

CHAPTER 20—MUDDY THE WATER

Holly stood in the shadow of the boathouse. The vessel she was about to board didn't look fast and furious enough to be used in gun running although that's what was alleged. It barely looked seaworthy. So disreputable was its appearance in fact that she was disinclined to get on it. But board she must if she was going to expose the villains involved in this deadly trade—

A sea gull at her feet squawked and startled her out of her reverie. She glanced at her snazzy brand new Tissot sport watch and groaned. It was already eight-fifteen and no sign of Skipper Rusty Burger, crew, and other guests. So much for leaving promptly at eight a.m. A gust blew her hair across her face. Smoothing it back behind her ears she caught a few strands and vigorously wound them around her fingers.

Holly sat on the worn and scuffed wooden dock, threw her bare legs over the edge, and regarded the vessel before her: Rusty's so-called fishing boat, "Miss Conduct." Misconduct, indeed. She hoped they'd make it back safely.

She looked back down the pier. Four men lumbered towards her loaded down with equipment and dragging huge ice chests. Either they have plans to catch a load of fish or they are bringing enough provisions to mollify any disappointments, she thought. One of the men had a large bird on his shoulder and carried only a fishing rod and tackle box. Oh, no, it was Doc Billy Bob. Why was he going on this trip? Too bad for him. He wouldn't get much fishing done. Holly planned to spend the entire trip picking his brain.

"Hi, Holly," Rusty said. "Sorry we're late. Doctor Roberts was delayed. He had an urgent phone call or something. Let me introduce you to everyone. This is my First Mate and only crewman. His name's Delmiro Reyna but he goes by Miro."

Holly stood, smiled, and shook Miro's hand. "Nice to meet you, Miro," she said. Such an elegant name for the little fellow. He was shorter than she, with a lopsided but friendly grin and wore spotless jeans and a white T-shirt.

"You already know Doctor Roberts and his noisy bird, Forceps, I see," Rusty said. "This is Doc's fishing buddy, Willy."

Holly noticed that Doc Billy Bob looked somewhat better than the last time she had seen him. He still had a stubbly chin but at least he had combed his white hair. His jeans were about as faded as the shorts he wore on Tuesday, wrinkled and ragged at the hem. Another yellowed T-shirt hung over the top of his jeans and sagged across his sunken stomach.

"Good to see you again, Doctor Roberts," Holly said as she shook his hand.

"Open wide, open wide," squawked Forceps.

Willy's white hair stuck out at sharp angles from under his blue and grey Dallas Cowboys ball cap. His ruddy complexion seemed to indicate he was Doc Billy Bob's drinking buddy as well as a fishing crony. His attire was the same as the doc's. Apparently, jeans and a T-shirt were the uniform of the day. Someone should have told her. Holly had gone back to the Finders Keepers boutique and spent a bundle on her ensemble: the watch, gleaming white shorts, Adriennne Vittadini cabled sweater vest and cardigan, and new Sperry Topsiders. Fear of apprehension by the fashion police clearly was not uppermost in Rusty's mind. He had on his usual now-sleeveless faded red plaid shirt but he wore a white T-shirt underneath. Holly suspected that as the heat of the day wore on, he would shed the plaid for comfort's sake.

"Hey, what the hell have you been doing?" he asked. "Have you been cleaning fish all week?"

"Huh?"

Rusty picked up one of Holly's hands. Several of her fingers bore Band-Aids over the paper and knife cuts she'd gotten pasting up the paper by hand. "I've been working on the newspaper," she said.

"I thought you were a writer," he replied. "Your hands look like you've taken up professional corn-shucking instead."

Rusty jumped onto the boat and reached out to help Holly board. Miro hoisted gear from the dock to Rusty. Within a few minutes everyone and everything was on board and Holly heard the engine choke a few times before it finally roared to life. Holly looked around. "Miss Conduct" was a twenty-foot boat in desperate need of refinishing. Flakes of its chipped white paint dotted the deck. The engine room was the main cabin in the center of the boat. Storage benches wrapped around either side of the cabin. Across from the benches on the sides of the boat, gadgets spaced about a yard apart held fishing rods. A wooden table stood at one end of the vessel. Stains and scratches suggested that it was used to clean and gut fish. It had a stainless steel sink on one end to rinse and clean away the blood.

Holly stopped at the other end and leaned out. The wind pushed her hair away from her face and she wiped tears from her eyes. "That air sure is salty," she said.

"Yeah, but the breeze will help keep us somewhat cool," answered Miro. "I'll be glad to bait a line for you when we get to fishin'."

"Thanks, Miro, but I'm just along for the ride. I'm not much of an angler although I do love a good fish dinner," said Holly.

"Willy and the Doc like to troll for sailfish in the Gulf but we'll probably stay in the bay and cast for redfish. Past Cuda Smith Park we'll slow down and they can cast for reds or snapper. Snapper swim near the bottom," said Miro.

"I heard my name. Are you talking about me?" asked Doc.

"This won't hurt a bit," added Forceps.

"Miro was just asking if I wanted to fish and he was telling me that you like to go for sailfish," replied Holly. "I told him that I didn't fish and was—"

"Whatcha mean you don't fish?" Doc asked. "Why are you here? I sure hope it's not to bug me about Clark's death. I've been badgered enough about that mess, I tell you what. Why just this morning I...uh, never mind about that."

"Just a little stick, just a little stick," said the bird.

"I knew you were trying to hide something," Holly said. "What about this morning? Rusty said you had gotten an urgent call. Who from?"

"None of your business. You should be paying more attention to that bump on your head. Maybe you should be more careful."

Rusty came up behind them. "What's none of her business?" he asked.

"It'll be over in a minute," said the bird.

"Nothing." Doc Billy Bob scowled. "I just want to get out to the Gulf and snag a few big ones. Keep her away from me. I'm sure she'll scare off all the fish. I've paid you a good fee and I want to enjoy myself. I'm going to grab a cold one to get me in the mood."

"Open wide," said Forceps.

Rusty took Holly's arm. "Let's not get his goat, Holly. He is a good customer and I can't afford to lose him."

"I'll try not to get in his way," said Holly. "But I can't help feeling that he's hiding something." She twisted a strand of hair.

"Miro," Rusty called out, "take us down around the Crane Islands a little ways so Holly can see her house."

"Aye, aye."

"Here's the Playa Rico pocket park. Ever seen it from this side?"

Not since she was a kid, Holly had to admit.

"And there's your house," Rusty said. "When was the last time you had this view of the back side?"

Holly smiled in appreciation. Clearly the architect had had this vantage point in mind when he designed it. The back deck that she had renewed her affection for definitely looked inviting.

Rusty turned her to face the water. "Look over there."

"Where?"

"Straight across, at Isla del Tesoro's intracoastal shore. See those little birds? Crested cannonbirds."

"So? They're just funny little shorebirds."

"They're endangered funny little shorebirds," Rusty said. "The more coastlines get developed, the more their nesting sites get destroyed. They're virtually gone from the Atlantic coast. We have some here now but once the dredging starts they'll be gone too so you might as well enjoy them while you have the chance."

Her cell phone played its signature ring tone. She rummaged in the bottom of her jauntily nautical Ralph Lauren canvas tote purchased especially for the trip and dug out the phone. "Good morning, sir," she answered.

"Berry," her boss said. "I got the paste-ups you sent and I—"

"Gimme that damned thing." Rusty grabbed the phone from her.

"Hey!"

With a curving overhand pitch, he tossed the phone overboard.

"My phone. What have you done? That was my boss." Calling to compliment her on a job well done, she prayed, and not to talk about do-overs.

"Oh, shut up," Rusty said.

"I beg your pardon."

"Shut up and listen."

His right arm around her waist he pulled her against him and put his left hand against her mouth. His palm was rough but his hand was warm, gentle, and smelled of sea salt and a pleasantly herbal cologne. Against her back, his belly was soft and cushy but the chest that supported her shoulders was firm enough.

"Listen to that. Hear it? Hear the wind? The birds? The water? Isn't that better than some goddam phone?"

For a moment all Holly could hear was the blood boiling in her ears. When that died down, though, she could indeed hear the wind and the sea gulls. Spotting the flying cell phone and thinking that Rusty had thrown them an edible treat they swarmed above the boat and begged for more with loud shrieking caws. Holly felt like shrieking herself. The nerve of him. Still, the longer he held her, the more she felt as though a weight had been lifted from her shoulders.

She watched the little crested whateverbirds for a while as they flew, pecked around for food, argued, and flirted with one another, apparently unaware that they were doomed. She envisioned the shore lined end-to-end with buildings, swarming with people instead of skittering little birds. She realized that the image irritated her and she turned away.

"Rusty, look. There's another boat. What are they doing here?"

"Damned if I know. Ahoy," Rusty hollered. "Where y'all going?"

"Out to the Gulf." The shouted reply was almost lost in the wind.

"You took a wrong turn. You need to stay in the Intracoastal until you reach Turtle Point."

"We're taking a shortcut through The Gap."

"Stupid tourists," Rusty muttered. "Should have hired me to show 'em around." He yelled to them, "You can't get there from here. It's silted in."

"It looks open on the map," came the shouted reply.

The other boat seemed headed for the short overpass that carried the state highway over The Gap and down Isla del Tesoro "Uh, oh, Rusty, I think they're going to go under the overpass. I don't know much about boats but I don't think they have enough clearance."

"Fools," said Rusty. "Turn about. Turn about." To Holly he said, "You're right, that's a BayCruzer. They don't have enough clearance." He hollered to the other boaters, "Turn about, turn about. You can't make it under the bridge."

The other boater replied, "We don't need much draft."

"It's not the draft that'll get you, it's the height..."

Rusty's warning was cut off by a loud crunch as the top of the boat's cabin collided with the underside of the overpass. The BayCruzer digging into The Gap's soft bottom made a grinding noise. Startled, Holly jumped, Rusty grabbed her, and they both fell against Miss Conduct's side. Their momentum nearly pitched them over the boat's low side wall.

"Rusty, you almost pushed me in."

"Me? You almost pulled us both in," said Rusty. "Miro, slow us down. We need to see if these folks need any help."

Rusty leaned over Miss Conduct's side and hollered, "Can we help you?"

"We've already radioed for help and some friends are on their way," replied the sailor. "Thanks for the offer. I guess I've got a lot to learn about these waters. I didn't realize how low that overpass really is."

Rusty leaned over a little further to hear him, lost his balance, and fell into the muddy water of The Gap.

"Miro," Holly yelled. "Rusty fell in. Get a life ring. Get a rope or something." The Gap wasn't deep enough to drown in but Holly couldn't see how Rusty could climb back into the boat without some assistance.

Miro poked his head out of the cabin "He'll be fine, Holly. This isn't the first time that he's fallen into the drink."

Rusty got to his feet in the hip-deep water.

"Are you okay?" Holly called.

"Hey, look what I found." Rusty held Holly's cell phone aloft. He shoved it in his pocket, sloshed to the boat's rear, and used the outboard motor as a ladder to clamber back in. "Man, that water is nasty. I'd better hose off." Holly's phone beeped balefully and he handed it to her. "Here, I believe it's for you," he said. Holly covered her mouth to stifle a giggle.

Rusty peeled off his wet plaid shirt, opened a jug of fresh water, and poured some over his head. "Here, gimme that," he said, and took her phone.

"Hey, you're not going to toss it overboard again, are you?"

"No. I'm gonna fix it." He took out the battery and poured some of the fresh water over the case.

"What are you doing? You'll ruin it."

"Trust me," he said. "I've had a lot of practice. I end up dunking mine all the time. You may have noticed I sometimes take a little tumble?"

Holly chuckled. She followed him to the cabin where he popped the lid of a small plastic container.

"I rinsed the salt out and now we're going to dry it." He blew on the phone and then buried it in a bed of white grains. "Rice," he said. "Works pretty well most of the time." He snapped on the lid and handed her the box. "Tomorrow morning, should be good as new."

Gosh, I hope so, thought Holly. Having blown her budget on her yachting ensemble she had little left for a new phone. "Those poor boaters," Holly said. "I guess if The Gap is going to be dredged the bridge will have to get raised too."

"Like that will ever happen," Miro replied. "They'd have to re-engineer not only a state highway but a county road. You no sooner come off the overpass but you hit that traffic light at the intersection with the Livingston Freeway to downtown Bonafides. All that would have to change if the bridge was raised."

"Oh." Holly imagined the machinations Bonafides would have to pull off to get the cooperation it would need from the state and county.

"Oh, listen to 'em gripe," said Doc Billy Bob. "Some people just don't like change. Dredgin' The Gap is gonna be a big help. The water in the Lagoon will be fresher. Boatin' and fishin' will be better and easier. A two hour trip to get into the Gulf will take two minutes. I say let's get that ditch dug."

"Won't hurt a bit," squawked Forceps.

CHAPTER 21—DON'T KILL THE MESSENGER

"I'm going to punch up the engine again," said Miro. "We'll be getting to Striker Cove before too long."

Miss Conduct moved quickly as it paralleled Isla del Tesoro, easily handling the chop where Bonafides Bay met the Intracoastal.

Rusty felt somewhat more comfortable having shed his shirt and rinsed off the mud from The Gap. He joined Holly and handed her a pair of binoculars. "From here you can practically see across Isla del Tesoro to the Gulf. You remember Cuda Smith Park, don't you?"

A stretch of Gulf-side beach not much different from any other on Isla del Tesoro, it had gained popularity largely because of its location. Its access road was the first that drivers from Bonafides encountered once they hit the island. Cuda Smith Park was considered a "park" by virtue of once having had a wooden bench with a lattice shade *ramada*. The bench and *ramada* had long since been appropriated to feed a beach campfire. The "park" got its name from Oscar "Cuda" Smith who in the 1970's was a Bonafides surfer destined for greatness. Smith acquired his nickname not, as many people assumed, from having the moxie of the fearsome fighting fish. He earned the moniker from his "woodie," a beater Plymouth equipped with a surfboard-toting roof rack. Cuda's promising career was cut short at a surfing competition in Hawaii when he went into fatal anaphylactic shock from eating poi. Since poi is eaten without deadly results even by babies who are allergic to other foods, many suspected that Smith's meal was tampered with. However, no investigation was made and nothing was ever proved.

"Of course I remember Cuda Smith Park," Holly replied. "I practically grew up on that beach. It was so easy to get to. I even did a little surfing when I was younger. It was like a party every weekend. Just pile everyone into a pickup, park on the beach, build a bonfire—oh, wait. That's not far from The Gap. What will happen to that beach if The Gap is dredged all the way to the Gulf side?"

Rusty gave her a rueful grin. "You're catching on." He found he didn't relish being the bearer of bad news but Holly Berry was beginning to look like she might actually be an ally. She was after all the executrix of Clark Rivera's estate. If he could get her interested in the Rivera family land claim, get her on his side... He eased his persuasive line out a little bit to see if she would take the bait. "Once the dredging starts that will be gone too," he said.

"But that can't be," she replied. "That's a major park for beach goers around here, not to mention all those tens of thousands of Spring Breakers. Where will they go if not Cuda Smith Park?" She twisted her hair.

Where would they go indeed? Sure, Florida and Cancún in Mexico got a big chunk of Spring Break business but so did Texas. Most of the Texas-bound 'breakers headed for South and North Padre Island but Isla del Tesoro got its fair share. For a week the beach was lined shoulder to shoulder with tents, campers, shade canopies, propane grills, and barbeque smokers. Teenagers and twenty-somethings liberated from the burden of keeping their grades up took advantage of Texas's "open beaches" law and drove up and down the sand, flirting with each other from open-bed pickups. The festival of drinking, beach-going, sunbathing, drinking, partying, barhopping, and drinking was a big moneymaker for the local merchants.

Rusty twisted the proverbial knife. "The developers want to make the resort's stretch of beach private. No driving."

"What? That's crazy. They can't do that."

Rusty pretended he hadn't heard and added another twist to the knife. "The Spring Breakers will have to go further up the beach, near where the crested cannonbirds nest."

Holly narrowed her eyes. "You know, this dredging thing is sounding worse the more I hear about it. I really didn't care in the beginning but I'm starting to see why my father was so against it. You can put a hotel anywhere but there are only so many places like this."

"What did I tell you?" Rusty replied, emboldened by the ammunition he gained as her outrage grew.

"He didn't tell you the whole story," said Doc Billy Bob, scowling. He grabbed a beer from the cooler. "Once they dredge The Gap, we could get out to the Gulf just that quick. I could catch me a sailfish, maybe even a shark, like I wanted to today, 'cepting Skipper here's too busy trying to hit up the lady. I gotta admit, I sure gotta do a double-take. From the back I'd swear that you were Tres. With that ponytail it's hard to tell you two apart."

"Here I come," said the bird as he flew onto Holly's shoulder.

Holly threw her hands up and shoved Forceps off of her. "Get him away from me."

Forceps cackled and flew back to the Doc. "Open wide, open wide," said the bird.

"Maybe he thinks you're Tres too," said Doc Billy Bob. "Tres likes him."

Holly turned to Rusty. "Can't we travel the Intracoastal and go out through the ship channel at Turtle Point?" Holly asked.

Rusty opened his mouth to answer but Doc said, "Takes too long and uses too much fuel fightin' them bay currents. Now, you dredge The Gap, we could scoot right out just like them tourists who crashed into the overpass wanted to. Gulf water flowing in would freshen up the Lagoon, too. Make it smell better." He waved his hand in front of his nose. "As it is, we're stuck here in the Bay fishin' for reds. Which it's almost too hot for now, anyway." Doc walked off grumbling.

"Is that true?" Holly asked.

"What, that it's too hot to fish for reds?" Rusty shrugged. "We're out here, aren't we?"

Holly glared.

"Okay, okay. Fishin's better when it's a little cooler."

Holly shook her head. "That's not what I'm asking."

"Oh, you mean about quicker access to the Gulf? That's true enough. My question would be, 'at what cost?'"

"No, no. Is he right about Gulf water flowing into the Lagoon."

Rusty shrugged. "Depends on who you're asking."

"I'm asking you."

She was, wasn't she? Well I'll be damned, Rusty thought. He'd almost forgotten what it was like to have someone interested in his opinion on anything except what bait to use. "I don't think it will make much of a difference. The Gap's too long, too shallow, and too winding. Even if there is some inflow, I don't think the effects will be very far-ranging."

She frowned. "It's confusing."

"Not to me," he replied. "What do you say we get some lunch while Doc and Willy are fishing? We've got some sandwiches and chips in the cabin. You can have Coke, water, or beer to drink."

"Coke sounds good," answered Holly. "I'll stay away from the beer, though."

Holly settled on a bench in the cabin and Rusty got beverages from the cooler. Holly popped open her soda. "Where's Miro?" she asked.

"Helping Doc and Willy haul in their catches. Miro's job is helping to land the catch and keep them on ice.

"Good," said Holly. "'Cause I've got something to ask you. Sam Hill told me that you'd help and I guess I could use it. Too many things are just not adding up or making sense. How could Clark have died from a heart attack with a big gash in the back of his head? Who tried to push me down the stairs at the courthouse? What is Doc Billy Bob covering up? And did Sam really have an accident? You don't think he did, now do you? What about the land grant angle? Why is Priscilla Esquivel badgering me to sell the house and..."

"Whoa, whoa, girl." Rusty laughed. "You've got more questions than a detective and you are not one. This is not the time or place to discuss this. I agree with you. There are too many unanswered questions. Me, I'd like to start with the land grant thing. I think Clark and I were on to something. In fact, I'm thinking about making a trip to San Antonio to check out some leads."

"Great. I'll come along."

"Like hell you will."

"Why not? Do you think I'd get in the way or slow you down?"

"It's not that. It's just that—"

"Or maybe you're afraid that as an experienced journalist, I'd be better at digging up clues than you."

"You wouldn't but that's beside the point."

Miro poked his head in the hatch. "Rusty, they've caught their limit, yours and mine, and I think they're almost out of brew. Punch up the engine and head back home."

"Look, I don't have time to argue about this now, Holly," Rusty said. "When we get back why don't you make a quick trip to your house, shower, change, and meet me for a drink?"

"Why? Are you saying I stink or I'm not dressed good enough for that sleazy dive at the Lagoon?" replied Holly.

"No, of course not. But I do and I'll need some time to rinse off the boat and stow everything once I get rid of the fishermen. Besides," he said with a grin, "I was thinking of someplace with a more varied beverage selection than the Marina Bar and Grill. Do you know where El Gato Negro is?"

CHAPTER 22—BETWEEN THE DEVIL AND THE DEEP BLUE SEA

So as not to call attention to herself, Holly avoided making eye contact with anyone and focused on her drink as if it were the most fascinating thing in the room. Every now and then, however, she slid her eyes to the right or left or risked glancing at the mirror behind the bar, trying her best to make it all look very casual. In this dimly lit cocktail lounge with its many deep, darkly shadowed booths it was hard to see anything outside the pools of yellow light cast by the pendant lamps above the bar and over the tables. However, the last time she dared to steal a peek, the two men were still here, so involved in their conversation that they had...

"...hardly touched your drink," Rusty said. "Don't you like it?"

"It's fine." Holly took a sip of her Fog Cutter. Rum with several fruit juices sounded good when Rusty described it but the murky concoction turned out to be the color of the Lagoon on a bad day and had a lot more alcohol in it than she had expected.

It kind of fit with the whole back-alley ambience of the El Gato Negro Lounge. The bar, tables, and chairs were mahogany, the upholstery of the booths and bar stools black. The dark-paneled walls were hung with paintings and posters of black felines with glowing, hooded eyes, all of whom seemed to be harboring a secret of some kind. Even the cocktail napkins were black emblazoned with neon-green cats' eyes.

"So, we're agreed. I'll pick you up at nine a.m. tomorrow," Rusty said.

"Agreed." Holly raised her Fog Cutter and Rusty his beer for a toast when her cell phone warbled from the depths of her purse.

Rusty frowned and wiped beer foam from his upper lip. "Is that your phone? I can't believe it. That thing still works after the dunking it got this morning?"

"Apparently so," Holly said.

"Thing's made of tough stuff." Rusty grinned. "Good ole' American technology." He snapped off a salute.

Clearly he hadn't noticed the phone's Nokia logo. "Uh, you've got that right."

"You'll excuse me if I don't sit here listening to you suck up to your boss." Rusty slid off his stool. "I'm going to go hit the head."

"You're excused," Holly replied. She unearthed a plastic container from her purse, snapped off the lid, and excavated her ringing phone from its bed of desiccating white rice. She flicked off the few grains sticking to the case. For a change, the call wasn't from her boss but she didn't want Rusty listening in just the same. "Hello, Larry," she said into the phone.

"Hi, Sweetness. Have I got the deal of the century for you. That is, if you're free tonight."

Deal of the century? Wasn't that what Priscilla Esquivel had offered her? Or had that been Sidney Qownsill? Hard to keep up with the plethora of wonderful deals these thoughtful, generous people offered her. "I don't have any plans," Holly said. Yet. She twisted a strand of hair.

"The Tejas Bonanza Corporation is hosting a shakedown run on its gambling barge tonight for its investors."

Gambling indeed. About this floating casino that was part the plans for the Tejas Bonanza development...wasn't gambling illegal?

"I've been invited along and I can bring a guest," Larry said. "Interested?"

Hmm. Sounded like a late night and she had just made plans with Rusty to leave early in the morning for San Antonio. "Don't these things usually go on into the wee hours?"

"They do. But not to worry, love. I won't keep you out too late."

"Then I am interested," Holly said. She could kill two birds with one stone: spend some more time with Larry and check out the members of this so-called cartel that Rusty Burger was always going on about. If such a group existed, they sure ought to be aboard. "It's a date," she said and managed to set a time and place before Rusty returned from the john.

*****

Holly shoved her arms through the sweater sleeves. Dressing for this date had presented a challenge. Her serviceable skirt and blouse had seen so much wear on this trip they weren't fit to donate to Goodwill. Nothing else that she had brought for what she had assumed would be a brief stay would do. She didn't want to wear the same outfit she wore for dinner with Larry at the Pilothouse.

That left the spangled sheath Cilla Esquivel chose for her at Finders Keepers. Would it be appropriate? Holly didn't have a clue as to what was suitable for an evening of gambling on a boat. Honestly, how many occasions did call for pavé sequins? She didn't need the Adrienne Vittadini cardigan she had bought for the "cruise" on Rusty Burger's boat for warmth but it would at least tone down the disco dress's wattage.

Sparsely distributed streetlamps offered a few brief glimpses of the landscape on either side of the road as Larry's convertible carried them along. A black ribbon down the middle of Isla del Tesoro, the highway stretched ten miles to Turtle Point and the Nuevo Puerto marina. She chuckled thinking about the marina's "New Port" name. It was indeed a relatively new port, a deep water ship channel carved out of a much narrower shallow natural pass that had been as silty and shifting as The Gap.

Just over the dunes to the left was Bonafides Bay, to the right was the Gulf. She remembered the land mass as acres and acres of sandy scrub but now condos, subdivisions, and golf courses lined the highway. Why was it that the streets in the old Hispanic neighborhoods had names like Oak and Washington while all the new subdivisions had Spanish names like Casa Fina or Hacienda Bonita?

A medallion Larry wore on a gold chain around his neck winked as they passed under the streetlamps and his white shirt gleamed against his tan. He pulled her back into the curve of his shoulder and chuckled softly.

"What?" she asked.

"Nothing important," he replied. "Just thinking I could get used to this. Notice how we fit together? Like a hand and glove. Must mean we were destined for each other."

She replied with a small murmur as she cuddled closer. She could get used to this, too: cruising down the island road in a leather-lined convertible with Larry Pomposas. He was handsome. The blond hair, the swimming-pool-blue eyes. Very aware of it, obviously. The blue sweater vest he'd chosen complimented his eyes and hair color perfectly. Good looks, intelligence, ambition—he could be the next governor. Wouldn't she make a great First Lady? Whoa, way too soon with those thoughts. She hardly knew the man. Hadn't even been to bed with him yet although she bet he'd be great. Something told her that she could find out if she wanted to.

Her concerns about her attire evaporated the minute he had picked her up. "Wow, girl, you do a man proud, being seen with you."

The generous lighting of the Puerto Nuevo marina glowed like a beacon in the distance. Larry turned into the parking lot and Holly could barely contain her surprise when he pulled into a "reserved" parking space. At the dock a large yacht gleamed as brightly white as a full moon. Several young men dressed in red-and-white striped T-shirts and white trousers lounged on the afterdeck. Crew? They didn't seem concerned about impressing anyone with how hard they were working until Larry stepped aboard. Then they jumped to their feet. Holly thought she saw one of them salute. Larry grinned broadly.

"I thought we were going aboard a gambling barge," she said. "Where is it?"

"It's anchored offshore a ways. Once The Gap is dredged and the rest of the development's complete it will be moved out into international waters. Right now it's been more convenient to have it moored near the Puerto Nuevo ship launches so workers can get to it. For now, the yacht shuttles guests back and forth to the barge. Later, when the operation is in full swing, it'll use water taxis to ferry people from the resort hotel."

Holly pictured the Gulf beach near The Gap choked with sprawling buildings and ablaze with garish neon. "So where is everybody?"

"Oh, they've been on board for hours. The yacht's already made one trip for the evening but for you, a special crossing."

"How'd you pull that one off?"

"The yacht belongs to the Tejas Bonanza Corporation. They owe me, so I use it for special occasions. You, my love, qualify as a very special occasion. So you see, we're totally independent. When you've had enough fun, we can leave, go relax at my place. Sound good?"

The nerve. He had it all planned out. Unfortunately, she couldn't make any sincere objections since it all sounded great. Delaying an answer to the question she said, "Quite a boat." Even in the misty half-light the varnished wood deck and paneling gleamed, the brass rails shined, and the beveled glass in the portholes sparkled like gems.

"Yes, it's a beaut." Larry gave the steward their drink order as they boarded the yacht. Holly bristled that Larry didn't ask her what she would like but she could hardly argue with his selection this time. No Cutty Sark; the steward brought them a couple of crystal flutes and Montrachet in a champagne bucket. Glasses in hand, they settled in the comfortable lounge chairs on the deck. "To us, my love," Larry toasted her.

Avoiding a quick reply, she smiled and took a drink of her wine. Slow down, boy. There is no "us"—yet. Let me maintain some shred of dignity, she thought. She aimed to keep the conversation light and casual, no commitment for now.

They hardly finished their second drink when they pulled alongside the gangplank of the gambling barge. The vessel appeared to be about three stories tall. When the sea mist briefly parted she observed quite a few people engaged in what appeared to be skeet shooting on the rear deck. Could that be done at night? Apparently so. Almost in unison they pivoted and faced the open sea. She wondered what had distracted them.

A speedboat moved very fast in their direction, really kicking up spray. Moonlight sparkling off the phosphorescent foam must have been what caught the attention of those on deck. The boat looked like a contestant in a powerboat race, unlike the dark hulk of a freighter sitting motionless further out to sea. As she and Larry climbed the gangplank, Holly noticed the speedboat pull alongside their yacht. She wondered if the speedboat had carried visitors from the freighter to the barge, just as the yacht had brought her and Larry.

There appeared to be an exchange of life vests with the yacht. What was that all about? Some kind of safety drill? Images of the *Titanic* filled her mind and she was glad the staff was so safety conscious.

The gambling barge's decor contrasted sharply with that of the yacht. Weathered barn board wainscoting, heavy beamed ceilings, and plank flooring gave the corridor they were in a ranch house feeling heightened by the wall-mounted trophy deer, bear, and javelinas. The accusatory stares she got from the stuffed animals as she walked down the hallway with Larry gave her the creeps.

The corridor took them past the dining room.

"Hungry?" Larry asked.

Rows of buffet tables crammed with food filled the room. Steam trays held beef bourguignon, chicken cordon bleu, and teriyaki grouper. Vegetable crudités, mango slices, strawberries, and pineapple chunks in the shapes of hearts, spades, diamonds, and clubs were arranged on platters like playing cards. Gilded wire baskets of breads and crackers surrounded huge crystal bowls piled high with peeled shrimp. People crowded the aisles between the tables and stacked food on their plates to overflowing.

"Maybe later when it's not so crowded," she replied.

Larry chuckled. "I don't think there will be a 'later.' I imagine it will be this way all night."

"Who are all these people?"

"Invitees. It's a chance for the investors to thank all the people who have been helping them along the way, and at the same time take the barge on a dry run, work out all the bugs."

"I see." She also thought she saw Noble Barnes elbow to elbow with Sidney Qownsill at a display of cheesecakes and Key lime pies. No surprise to see them aboard. They were both obviously supporters of the project's development. No doubt Priscilla Esquivel was here, too. Holly resolved to keep a sharp eye out for the woman who she was sure wouldn't miss a chance to pester her about selling the house.

Passing the dining room she and Larry stopped at the cashier's window. She noticed row after row of slot machines, a regular Las Vegas on the sea.

"Isn't that Doc Billy Bob over there?" she asked. "Got to be—I see the parrot on his shoulder," Holly said, answering her own question as they headed for the blackjack table. The shorter doctor hung between two much larger men. "Looks like he's having quite an argument with those two men."

"Well, he gets quarrelsome when he's had too many drinks, which is most of the time. You probably didn't know they serve free drinks to the gamblers. Serving old Doc free drinks is equivalent to spitting in the ocean. Hardly noticeable except he gets mean and loud."

"I don't give a damn who's listening," Holly heard Doc yell. "You SOB's owe me more money and I want it now. I saved your asses, don't forget that." The two men took hold of Doc's arms and moved him quickly through the casino.

"I saved your asses, I saved your asses," said the parrot.

The doctor hollered "Take your damn hands off me or I'll tell the whole world what—"

"Take your damn hands," echoed Forceps.

The rest of the conversation was lost as the doctor was escorted into a distant room. Just before the doors closed, Holly thought she spotted Detective Creaser. What was he doing here? Could he be an investor? Did city cops make that much money? Maybe he was working off-duty, helping with security.

"I don't get it," Holly said to Larry. "I thought gambling was illegal."

"Oh it is," Larry replied. "Tonight's just pretend. It's all for charity. You know, like casino night at a church fundraiser, until the boat can be moved."

"And when might that be?" she asked, trying to hide her derision.

"Ah, the lady likes the high life. Be patient, my love. It's in the works but these things take time."

Looking around the room, Holly saw Tres at a poker table. Tres, an investor? Was that what he wanted Clark's money for? He appeared to be in heated conversation with the dealer. His table was just distant enough that she captured only an occasional word.

"Sorry, the boss said no more." the dealer said.

"Hey, I don't need your crap. You get your boss over here."

"Won't do any good. I've got my orders: no more."

Strange, Holly thought. Sounded like Tres was being refused credit. Which meant he was in over his head. He was taking it pretty hard for someone who was playing with Monopoly money.

CHAPTER 23—FEELING COMPLETELY AT SEA

Not much of a card player, Holly didn't pay much attention to how the game proceeded. Instead she busied herself by taking in the ambience and the appointments of the social hall, transformed for the Mission Tradition Casino Party. Just4Fun was a wildly profitable event planner used by many of San Francisco's largest charities to organize fundraising Casino Nights for them. Holly could see why they were so popular. The staff had done an amazing job. They had turned off the hall's harsh overhead fluorescents and set small flood lights on the floor. They shined up on huge posters arrayed around the room's perimeter picturing playing cards, dice, chips, coins, and large denomination bills. Gaming tables set close together discouraged the crowd from circulating so nearly everyone in attendance sat at some game or other. Servers threaded their way around keeping the players provided with drinks. But just what was that one server's problem? It seemed that she had to lean in just a little more closely than necessary to place cocktails on the table. Now wait just a minute! Was she picking the man's pocket? Was larceny the key to Just4Fun's brilliant bottom line? Holly was about to move in closer to get a better look when one of the bettors bolted up from his chair, patting his pockets and shouting...

Before Holly could figure out why her brother was so upset, a cocktail waitress came to take their order.

"Champagne," Larry said. He turned to Holly. "The perfect drink for an occasion like this, isn't it?"

"Sure," Holly replied, although she would have preferred being consulted first.

Larry took her elbow and led her to a gaming table. The cocktail waitress trailed close behind with a champagne bucket and glasses. She uncorked the bubbly with a loud pop that drew curious glances from the others at the table. Larry beamed, accepted a glass, and took his time about deciding if the beverage was acceptable.

Drinks served, Larry placed a bet. The dealer had only started to deal cards when a steward leaned over Larry's shoulder and whispered in his ear. Holly could hear only a few of the steward's words: "said it has to be handled" and "come right now."

Larry excused himself to Holly saying "Sorry, I'll only be gone a minute" and followed the steward out of the room.

Bored with sitting at the blackjack table by herself, she roamed through the room. She had expected typical Las Vegas casino wear: the men in shorts, dark socks, and Hawaiian shirts, the ladies in flower-patterned patio dresses and mules. Seemed the rule in Sin City was the larger the lady, the more vivid the dress. However it was diamonds and denim for the Tejas Bonanza crowd. The men sported their best Western-style formal wear: string ties with sterling and gold tips, Stetsons, and Luchese boots. Holly recognized the brand of the world-famous King Ranch Saddle Shop on the leather holding some of the looks together. Just to make sure no one took them for ranch hands or roughnecks, the men wore gold-nugget rings. Every woman seemed to have on something fringed, was draped in gems, and carried a clutch or bag decorated with bling. Holly felt right in step with her bejeweled dress.

She went off in search of Larry. Following the direction she thought she had seen him take, she found herself at the end of the casino where the two men had led the loudly protesting Doc Billy Bob. Double doors led to another room yet unexplored. She no sooner put her hand on the knob when the two men who had escorted the doctor appeared.

"Sorry, Miss, you can't go in there," one of them said.

"But I want to see Larry Pomposas. I'm his guest."

"Sorry, Miss," the man repeated in a tone that brooked no argument.

"Well. In that case, tell him he can find me in the dining room." Maybe while she waited for Larry she'd get a bite.

At one table, the biggest jumbo shrimps she had ever seen draped the edge of a huge crystal bowl filled with ice. Between her and the shrimp stood a woman who from the back looked suspiciously like Cilla Esquivel. Holly decided she didn't want shrimp that badly and edged back when Cilla turned and spotted her.

"Why, Holly Berry, what a pleasant surprise to see you here. So this is what you needed an outfit for." Cilla winked. "Looks better on you than on me, Sugar."

Holly doubted that was so. Cilla was herself poured into a little—very little—black dress, a Donna Karan maybe. Holly swore she had seen some movie star wearing it on the Academy Awards red carpet. "Thank you. It was a terribly generous gift. How are you, Cilla?" Holly asked with little enthusiasm.

"Why fine, Sugar, just fine as frog's hair. Couldn't be finer. Unless of course you're going to tell me you will sell that little old house of yours."

"I'm still living in it, in case you hadn't noticed."

"Well, don't let that stop you. I'm sure we can arrange some kind of leaseback arrangement. The buyer would be ever so grateful."

"If it's that valuable, maybe I should just keep it," Holly said.

"Oh, no, honey, it's not that valuable. Only to this one person, that's all. Look, come with me. I've got some friends here who can explain it much better than little old me."

Before Holly could spear a shrimp Cilla had her by the arm and dragged her across the room to a table where Noble Barnes, Sidney Qownsill, Edison Pulitiz, Senator Candy Schultklopfen, and a man Holly didn't know sat chowing down. "Look who's here, boys," Cilla said.

"Holly." The men all half rose and reached across their plates to shake Holly's hand.

"What are you doing here?" asked Senator Candy.

"Senator," Holly acknowledged. Meeting and making a good impression on Candy Schultklopfen couldn't hurt. "Larry Pomposas invited me."

"Ah, Larry," Candy said with an approving nod. "And where is the next governor of the Lone Star State?" Candy put a hand to her mouth. Long shiny red fingernails nearly scratched the tip of her nose. The woman laughed loudly. "Oh, perhaps I shouldn't say that like it's fait accompli. Especially not with an esteemed member of the fourth estate present."

"Heh heh," Edison Pulitiz laughed, and well he might, Holly thought. The man wouldn't know a good story if it paraded naked in front of him.

"Holly needs a little encouragement about selling the old Rivera place," Cilla said.

"Oh you definitely should, dear," said Noble Barnes. "As executor of Clark's estate, it's your responsibility to act in the estate's best interest."

"I believe I am doing just that," Holly replied. "I'm beginning to think that selling the house is the last thing my father would want." She twisted a strand of hair. "In fact, not only was he planning to hang onto it, I think he was about to assert his rights to the other land we own."

"What land is that?" Cilla asked.

"Isla del Tesoro. The land granted to the Riveras by the Mexican government."

Pulitiz snorted. "Oh, that. That old legend. The ravings of an old geezer."

Holly propped her hands on her hips. "Who are you calling an old geezer?"

"Oh, not your father. His father, Don Gabriel."

"I'm no longer certain he was raving," Holly replied.

"Well I am," said Sidney Qownsill. "I told you I'd look into that title claim and I have. Nothing to it."

"We'll see about that. I'm going to San Antonio tomorrow to do a little digging around."

"You won't find anything," Sidney said.

"Why spin your wheels?" Candy asked. "Sell the house. You'll make a tidy profit. Surely you don't want to stand in the way of progress."

"Progress, huh," Holly replied. "Razing the habitat of already endangered wildlife is progress? Replacing a popular public beach with an exclusive private resort is progress? I don't think so."

"Honey, you really must look at the big picture. Sure there'll be changes, there's some sacrifices involved, there always are. But the city has to move forward. In the end, everyone in the area will benefit from an investment of this type."

"The trickle-down theory? Like I believe that fairy tale."

Holly didn't know what was making her so contentious. Maybe it was the two glasses of wine she'd had on the yacht washed down with the champagne, all on an empty stomach. Holly Rivera Berry, she told herself, you are cut off for the night.

"Really, I would have thought Larry of all people would have explained this to your satisfaction. Speaking of Larry, where is the boy?"

"The steward wanted to see him about some problem or other. I think maybe it involved Doctor Roberts. Anyhow he went to some room. There were guards. They wouldn't let me in—"

No sooner had the words left her mouth than the entire throng at the table jumped up and rushed from the dining room.

Something I said? Holly wondered, and went to see where they had gone. As she passed the exit door she noticed a crowd out on the deck leaning over the railing. She picked up part of the excited exchange as she went out the doors.

"Ohmigod, that poor man fell overboard," someone said.

"Not sure about that. I saw some men with him before he fell. Looked like they might have helped him go overboard," came another comment.

"Please don't. I'll keep quiet. Too late. Too late. Please don't. I'll keep quiet. Too late. Too late," someone squealed in a raspy voice.

Holly looked up and found the source of the shrieking. Forceps, Doc Billy Bob's parrot, screeched from its perch on the stair railing.

"What's up?" Larry asked as he appeared beside Holly. He put his arm around her shoulder.

"A man fell overboard. I think it must be Doc Billy Bob. There's his parrot up there."

"In that case the doc must be around here somewhere. Maybe passed out under a table. You saw how he was putting it away."

"I don't know. There's quite a commotion at the rail. Look, I thought I saw Detective Creaser earlier. Maybe he—"

"You did? Creaser's here?"

"Yeah, in that room." Holly pointed to the doors behind which Doctor Roberts had earlier disappeared.

"Oh, I'm sure you're mistaken."

"No, really, I saw him," Holly insisted. "Maybe he could help look for Doc Billy Bob."

Larry smiled. "Let me see what I can find out."

Tres took Larry's place at Holly's side. "They're saying someone went overboard and that it was Doc Roberts." He looked more concerned than horrified.

Holly said, "Larry went to see." She twisted a strand of hair. Then she turned and glared. "Meanwhile, little brother, you and I have some talking to do. About this little gambling habit it appears you have."

"You mean just now? Holly, it's just play money. For charity. You know."

"I know it seemed more serious the way you were acting."

Tres staggered back and stepped on someone's foot.

"Hey, watch where you're going."

"Uh, um, I can see you're upset, Holly. Let me get something to calm your nerves."

Before Holly could get a word out he had disappeared into the crowd.

Larry returned and said, "It's a good bet that it is Doc. No one seems to be able to find him."

"There were two men with him. I thought maybe they were taking him somewhere to sober him up."

"Well, yes, apparently they had. That's, uh, what the steward wanted to talk to me about earlier. He was concerned about the company's liability if Doc got abusive. I suggested they keep him on ice till he settled down."

"Then why did they let him loose? They should have kept an eye on him. Sure, he may have been old and a drunk but he didn't deserve this."

"If it does turn out to be him, I'm sorry. We all are. You saw how drunk the old boy was. Still, it's a tragic accident." Larry put a comforting arm around Holly's shoulders. "I can see you're upset. C'mon, let's leave. This is not at all what I had in mind for our evening together."

CHAPTER 24—THE ENDS JUSTIFY THE MEANS

Larry looked through the sliding glass doors to his condo's balcony. On the other side stood Holly, her back to him, her hair fluttering in the breeze. If not for the sweater over her shoulders and her sparkly dress, she could easily pass for Tres. Larry frowned. Not because Holly looked so much like her brother. That, actually, was a bonus.

Nor did he frown because he was upset that she had gone out on the balcony. He could hardly blame her for that. It was one of the condo's best features, one of the things that made it so exclusive. It commanded a great view of Bonafides Bay. From here he could see the Treasure Island Bridge that carried motor vehicles over the Intracoastal from Bonafides to Isla del Tesoro. The sight was more spectacular when lights outlined the bridge's iconic bell-curve shape. That the bridge had been dark for some time was a popular gripe in letters to Edison Pulitiz's *Daily Breeze*. The grumblers wondered why the city could afford to dredge The Gap but couldn't light a bridge that was a signature of the cityscape.

They simply didn't understand the intricacies of municipal budgeting. They didn't get that replacing the Treasure Island Bridge light bulbs was an expense, whereas dredging The Gap was an investment, one that would bring in millions of dollars in federal matching funds, courtesy of Candy Schultklopfen.

Dimwits, Larry muttered, thinking of the naysayers. If they kept up their grousing they would ruin everything. That, however, wasn't his most pressing problem. At the moment he was more concerned with getting the balcony sliding doors open which he could hardly do with a champagne flute in each hand.

He willed Holly to turn, see him, and open the doors. When she didn't he resorted to a gentle kick at the metal frame which got her attention. She slid the doors open and he joined her on the breezy balcony.

"Were you standing there long?" she asked. "I didn't hear you."

"Still thinking about what happened on the barge? It was tragic but it was an accident," Larry said.

Holly sipped her drink. "I'm not sure it was." She paced the balcony, twisting a strand of hair. "I'm not sure any of it was."

"Any of what?" Larry asked, hoping she would mistake his tone for concern rather than apprehension.

"Sam Hill's death. My father's death. That incident in the courthouse. I'm not certain someone isn't behind all of them."

Larry felt his pulse quicken with anxiety. Rash acts, all. None were part of the plan but desperate times called for desperate measures. At least no one would be able to tie them to him.

Talk about death wasn't going to get Larry where he wanted to go. He'd given Holly plenty of drink tonight but it only seemed to make her moody and morose. Maybe he should give her some coke. That always did the trick with Tres. If she wasn't into drugs though he could easily blow—he chuckled silently at the pun—the whole thing by offering her some. That left only one other option and not an objectionable one at that. He stepped into Holly's path to stop her restless pacing.

"Ugly talk for such a beautiful night." He put his palm on her cheek. "For such a beautiful lady." Before she could say another word he kissed her.

After only the slightest hesitation, she returned the kiss. Encouraged, he pulled her in tighter. Their amorous explorations became less tentative and more passionate until finally he was able to lead her from the balcony.

What approach would she like? he wondered as he steered her across the living room. For him to tear her clothes off and jump her bones as though he was inflamed with passion for her? Or would she prefer the slow strip? It was so important to get it right, to impress her with his perceptiveness and sensitivity. Quickly he weighed her reaction to his impulsive kiss under the mistletoe at the funeral reception. She had been startled but not offended. So, she was attracted to him. That was a plus. However she had waited for him to make the next move. Which he had, out there on the balcony. To which she had responded. She was willing, as long as it looked like his idea. Too much of a lady to want to appear eager, aggressive? Fine. He'd treat her like a lady. She wanted to be seduced? Fine. He would seduce her. He liked that. That appealed to him.

As he led her into the bedroom he pictured himself as a cowboy gentling a skittish wild colt into the corral. He removed each item of her clothing painstakingly, giving her ample time to approve or disapprove each step of undressing her. He placed her hands on his shirt, waiting for her to buy into the proceedings by undoing the buttons herself. Finally, as a piece de resistance, he lifted her up and laid her on the bed, thanking those hours in the gym for the strength to do it without rupturing something. The colt in the pen, harnessed, its spirit tamed, he mounted her.

As she writhed under him he thought, yes, Holly Rivera, got you right where I want you. Right where they all end up one way or another. Under my control.

And it wasn't unpleasant. Not at all. In fact, he genuinely enjoyed himself. To the touch, she was oddly similar to her brother Tres: the texture of the hair, the length and breadth of the body felt almost familiar. Yet she was definitely a woman. It was like making love to two people at the same time, which heightened his own pleasure. First Holly, then Tres. Holly...Tres. Oh, Holly. Oh, Tres. Oh, Holly.

"Oh, Tres."

The words were out of Larry's mouth before he realized he'd spoken them aloud. Fortunately, Holly didn't seem to have heard. He carried on.

****

Though it was way past the hour when he should have been getting ready for work, Larry lingered in bed. It was a fun night but a long one, made even longer by the drive to The Island to take Holly home, then the drive back to his Bonafides condo.

The champagne flutes on his nightstand brought a smile to his lips. He pressed his face into a pillow that still bore a little of Holly's scent. He leaned back, ran his hand through his hair, then slowly down his body, lightly brushing his nipples on his way down to the real McCoy. He closed his eyes and mentally relived the events of the night before. His growing excitement quickly deflated as reality intruded. Houston, we have a problem. Which would it be? Holly? Tres? Holly? Tres? Should he flip a coin? Hell no. What he needed was to figure a way to have both.

Larry reached for the phone and punched in the familiar number. He let it ring at least seven times, knowing it would take that long for the phone to be answered.

"Hello. Who the hell is calling at this ungodly hour? It better be who I think it is."

Larry smiled, shifted the phone to hold it between his shoulder and chin. "Hello, Romeo. Was just thinking about you. Was that some maiden voyage on the gambling barge?"

"I wouldn't know," Tres replied. He sounded angry. "I spent most of it alone."

"But sweetness, you know that couldn't be helped. Duty called. You know I love you like there's no tomorrow. Next time we meet, I'll prove it beyond a shadow of a doubt. Hugs and kisses, maybe a special treat."

He heard Tres sigh. "When?"

"I have to get to work, so we won't visit now. But soon. Very soon." Larry grinned. He had that dog on its leash.

He pressed the switch hook, then dialed another number. After two rings, a recorded voice said, "*Bueno*. This is Clark Rivera..."

Larry frowned. It was eerie hearing a dead man speak. Why hadn't anyone put a new message on the Rivera home answering machine? Where was the dear girl at this hour anyway? Quickly he prepared a short speech. "Hello there, precious one. Just wanted you to know how much I enjoyed our evening. In fact, both the evenings that we have had: dinner and you know the other one. I think I could get used to you, given the chance. Talk to you soon."

Larry put the phone down and smiled. Now he had all the chess pieces right where he wanted them. He smiled. He'd have checkmate soon.

CHAPTER 25–WHERE THERE'S SMOKE, THERE'S FIRE

Mata Hari-like, she sidled back and forth across the balcony, pretending to be lost in thought but keeping an eye on the subject all the while. She knew that the moonlight would make her hair gleam like polished wood and put stars in her eyes, silhouette her body against her diaphanous clothes. The wounded, fragile female act would disarm all of the subject's defenses until at last he would be telling her all his secrets...

An electronic buzz sounded and Holly bolted up from a dream. What was that noise? The phone? Which phone? Who could be calling her this early? Probably Rusty telling her he was on his way.

No, it was the reminder alarm on her cell phone. Ohmigod, it was almost eight-thirty and she was supposed to meet him at nine. She would have to get washed and dressed in thirty minutes and hope he didn't notice that she just threw herself together. Knowing Rusty, it was a good bet he wouldn't.

The face that greeted her in the bathroom mirror was that of a woman who had had too much to drink and stayed up way too late the night before. Three drinks—or had it been four?—weren't that much, were they? Certainly not enough to explain her behavior. She recalled the seductress dream she had been having before the cell phone's alarm woke her. Seductress, my ass. Who had ended up seducing whom was debatable. She had gone out with Larry on the gambling barge fully intending to get some answers. Every time she got the conversation steered around to the subject at hand he was called away or thought of something he had to do. She had gone with him to his condo only to continue her thwarted interrogation but there he stopped her from firing questions at him by keeping her mouth busy with something other than talking. Had that been deliberate or had he simply succumbed to her abundant charms? Speaking of abundant charms, Larry proved to have charm in abundance. Okay, Holly, settle down now.

She hoped she'd have another chance at Larry Pomposas. It didn't seem too unlikely that she would have a problem fulfilling that wish. After all, he hadn't gone through three condoms because he found her company repugnant.

Damn, now some other electronic device yammered for her attention: the phone. She rushed to grab it hoping that it was Rusty calling to say he was running late as he had on all other occasions.

"Hi, Sis. When are you going to pick me up for the San Antonio trip?"

"Pick you up? Tres, I never said anything about you coming along."

"I really think I should go with you, Holly. I know you said you wanted to get to know Rusty better but a trip up there without me isn't the way to do it. I hear he is quite the ladies' man."

Holly rolled her eyes. If Tres were concerned about some man sullying his sister's honor it was Larry Pomposas he should be worried about. "Tres, I told you yesterday and again last night, I didn't want you to go on this trip. You know I think something is going on. Rusty will talk to me more without your being along. So that's the end of that. I will call you when I get back if you want."

"That's the least you can do. I am not happy about this. I'm just trying to take care of my sister. It's a macho thing. You know how we Spanish men are."

Macho? Spanish? What did Tres take her for? His only interest in his Hispanic heritage was the possibility that a Spanish land grant could mean money for him. As for looking after his sister, the only person Tres cared about was himself. What was it about this mission that really had him concerned? "I've got to go. I'm not quite ready and Rusty is in the driveway honking. I'll call you when I get back. Bye." She tucked her limp white blouse into the white shorts she had worn on Rusty's boat and dashed out the door.

Rusty looked fresher than she felt. Crisp jeans and what looked like a new blue denim shirt. Nothing cutoff and not a bit of plaid in sight. Roper boots with—glory be, could that be a shine?

"Sorry I have been running a little late. Tres called, wanted to go along. I told him no deal."

"Good. This is a venture that doesn't need any extra help. Get in, let's get going."

"In that?" Holly frowned at Rusty's transportation.

"Not good enough for you?" Rusty said. He smiled but his tone was resentful.

The Lexus SUV had probably once been a handsome vehicle but was in need of a bath if not a paint job. Fitted to the front bumper white PVC tubes for holding tall fishing poles obscured the grille.

Holly regretted having offended him. "I just meant that rather than staring at PVC all the way to San Antonio we might have a better view in my rental. It's got cruise control, air, entertainment system, all that good stuff."

Rusty walked slowly around the PT. He grinned. "Do I get to drive?"

"We'd have to run by the rental place so I can add you as a second driver."

"I don't want to take the time to stop. We're late as it is. Just give me the keys. I promise I'll be careful."

"Well, all right," Holly said, against her better judgment.

He was careful, for about as long as it took them to get to the Treasure Island Bridge. He gunned the engine and climbed the bridge at top speed. On Livingston Freeway he drove about 15 miles per hour over the limit, weaving in and out of traffic, cutting off urban cowboys in their Ford 150s and Ram dualies.

"Uh, not to be critical, but don't you think being pulled over for a traffic violation will put something of a dent in our day?" Holly asked, winding a strand of hair around her finger.

"Was I speeding?" Rusty replied.

She couldn't tell if he was kidding or not but he did decrease his speed.

"You said something about an entertainment system," he said. "Got anything to play in it?"

She hadn't brought any of her own tunes from home. Who knew she would be here long enough to need them? But she had scooped up a couple of her father's CDs. She slid one into the drive.

"What's that?" Rusty asked.

"Linda Ronstadt. *Canciones de mi padre—My Father's Songs.*" Holly could understand the disc's place in her father's collection. In the '80s, the pop-rock star had returned to her Hispanic roots and put out a recording of Mexican folk songs. Holly had found that her father also had an extensive selection of Vicki Carr's Latino recordings.

"Not exactly what I had in mind for road tunes," Rusty said.

"My father's stuff. And you would have preferred...?"

"ZZ Top? Robert Cray? Kenny Wayne Shepard?"

Holly winced. "Roadhouse blues. Texas honk tonk. I think you've been spending too much time in the Marina bar."

Rusty laughed. "Had I known we were going Tejano I would have picked some of the local talent. We've got some Tejano Hall of Famers who call Bonafides home. Well, whatever. Decision-time. You want the scenic or speedy route? We can stay on I37 or take 77 to 181."

The so-called scenic route would put them on a two-laner to world-class destinations like Zunkerville and Poth. "Let's just get there," she replied.

"Darn and I was so looking forward to stopping at the Dairy Queen in Skidmore. Okay, little lady, speedy it is." Rusty set the cruise control.

"Where exactly are we going?"

"The Institute of Texan Cultures. I have been working with a young man there. He got real interested when Clark showed him his copy of the land grant. There are a lot of these grants floating around. Mostly the Anglo judges ruled against them as being too far-fetched. Your dad didn't feel that way and thought he had found a lead that would validate his claim. This young man, Gilberto, offered to help."

"Do you think Dad really thought he had a chance to prove his claim?" Holly asked. "When I was young he never indicated any interest in his Mexican heritage."

"Guess he changed his mind," Rusty said as Linda Ronstadt wailed plaintively in Spanish.

"And then I have to wonder why someone would want to kill him."

"My personal theory is he was getting too close to proving he owned the land that the cartel wants to develop. Of course, murder is a rather extreme method of slowing him down."

"Is our land that valuable?"

"Honey, does a boat float?"

Holly distinctly remembered telling him not to call her "honey," but found it no longer bothered her enough to mention. "I know this: everyone is trying to get me to sell quick and vamoose back to California. Even Tres seems to want to let the place go. Although, after watching him at the gambling tables last night, I wonder. Maybe he's been doing some illegal betting and got in over his head."

"Gaming tables? Where?"

Holly gave him the for-publication version of her night aboard the Tejas Bonanza barge.

Rusty said, "I figured you'd be home getting a good night's sleep. That place isn't even officially open for business. You have to know somebody to get aboard. Oh, don't tell me. You went with Larry Pomposas. I saw him putting the moves on you at the funeral reception. Holly, I warned you about him. He is up to no good, that I can promise you. Look what he did to me."

"Yes, I did go with Larry. I was doing a little scouting on my own. I just want to see what all those people think they have going. I met a bunch of people last night. Some I knew, some I didn't. All any of them could do was to tell me how great this development was going to be for Bonafides and the whole area." Holly debated whether or not to tell Rusty about Doc Billy Bob going overboard. She decided it would just add strength to his argument, an argument that was increasingly making her anxious. "Anyway, it's really none of your business whom I spend time with."

"No, I guess it's not," Rusty muttered.

They rode in silence for miles. Holly stared out the window at seemingly endless cotton and sorghum fields crisping in the summer heat. She twisted her hair into a knot as she pursued lines of thought that all terminated at dead ends.

After a while, Rusty started humming. Holly looked over at him. He smiled, then broke into full song, harmonizing in perfect Spanish with the CD. Holly would have joined in but she didn't know the words.

Finally they neared Highway 1604, the outermost of the roads that looped the city of San Antonio. Roadside pastures with horses, cows, and sheep gave way to RV parks, then industrial complexes, shopping centers, and civic buildings. Traffic which had been light to non-existent became increasingly congested. They passed Loop 410. At the intersection with highways 10, 35, 87, and 90, Holly sent up two prayers: one of thanks that she didn't have to negotiate the confusing stack interchange, the other that Rusty would manage it without wrecking the PT.

Signs gave directions to the Alamodome ahead and to the right but Rusty veered off to the left and turned into HemisFair Park, site of the 1968 Texas World's Fair.

"The Institute's over there, past the Tower of the Americas," Rusty said. They parked the car and proceeded on foot through the water garden, past wading pools and waterways that flowed into rushing falls. The splashing sound alone made Holly feel cooler in the midday heat.

"Come back here, *hijito,*" came a woman's voice behind them. Holly no sooner heard the patter of little runaway feet when a youngster intent on escaping parental supervision plowed through between her and Rusty. Knocked off balance, Rusty stumbled and seemed headed for a plunge into a nearby pond. Holly grabbed his arm and pulled him back toward safety. The inertia flung him into her arms. She pushed him off and tried to regain her composure.

"What is it with you?" she asked. "You see a hole in the ground, you've just got to fall in?"

"Holes aren't the only thing I'm falling in, I think."

Let's not go there, Holly thought, and said, "Try to stay on your feet this trip, will you?"

"I'll see what I can do. Ah, here we are."

They stood in front of a long skiff-shaped white building surrounded by dozens of colorful international flags. Rusty said, "Let's go inside and see if Gilberto has something for us. Bet he thought no one was coming back. I doubt he knows about your father being gone. It'll be a shock for him."

The darkness of the institute's cool interior provided a complementary backdrop to the colorful exhibits on food, clothing, music, and festivals of different ethnic groups: Filipino, Belgian, Japanese, and Swiss, as well as the expected Spanish, Mexican, and Native American. All of them at one time or another, and some of them still, called Texas "home." Near the Swedish exhibit, Rusty stopped and waved at a young man. Slight in stature, his gleaming blue-black hair was darker than his suit, and his shirt's white collar glowed ultra-bright against toast-colored skin. He spotted Rusty and the smile that spread across his face was that of someone greeting a long-lost friend.

"*Hola,* Rusty. Haven't seen you for a long time and I wondered what happened to you. Where is Carlos—I mean,

Clark? Did he get the information I sent him? I was surprised I did not hear from him."

"Gilbert, I hate to tell you, but Clark is dead."

"Dead? How? Why? Had he been ill? That would explain why he did not contact me."

"Officially it's a heart attack. This here is Holly, Clark's daughter. She is here from California to close the estate."

"Holly, please accept my condolences. I am pleased to meet you. Clark spoke of you so fondly."

Holly was surprised to hear that her father had spoken of her at all. "Hello, Gilberto. I certainly am interested in anything you might have found. Dad always thought there was something to the old land claim but I just passed it off as a pipe dream. Still, Rusty tells me that others have been successful in some of these claims."

Gilbert nodded. "Yes, there have been a few successful challenges mounted in the courts. It takes much work, much research, much cooperation. I have received some assistance from people at the Mexican Cultural Institute here in the Park, from the Mexican Consulate, and from the Mexican American Cultural Center. They are tied to the Church, where they provide pastoral education and language studies. The Church has many good records as you can imagine. Better, sometimes, than the state or even the *Federación*. I told your father all this."

"I don't remember him saying anything about it," Holly replied, twisting her hair.

"Well, not 'told,' exactly. I mentioned it in the material I sent him. Did he not receive it?"

"He might have. I haven't had a chance to go through all his papers. What would I be looking for? A large envelope? A FedEx package?"

"A facsimile," Gilberto replied. "Several of them. I sent the first to tell him not to give up hope, that I would send him more information in a few days, after I had met with Ramos Sandoval of the Institute and Father Marquez Martinez de Noyola from the Center. Father Noyola told me about a bequest the Center had recently received. Besides money there were numerous heirlooms. Artifacts, really, several hundreds of years old. Among them were some documents. Sandoval believes they date back to the days of the de la Garza Falcón expeditions."

"No," cried Rusty, his eyes sparkling.

"Is that good?" Holly asked. The name of de la Garza Falcón sounded familiar from her grandparents' stories but she couldn't remember what de la Garza Falcón was famous for.

A family of tourists jostled them to get to a nearby exhibit. Holly had to wait for her answer until she, Gilberto, and Rusty got repositioned out of the flow of traffic.

"The brothers de la Garza were charged by their superior officer, José de Escandón, with colonizing New Spain," Gilberto said.

"The Falcóns, Captain Blas María, and his brother, Captain Miguel, established settlements all along the coast, from the San Antonio River to Tampico, maybe even as far south as Veracruz," Rusty added.

"We—Sandoval, Father Noyola and I—believe these documents to be *auténtico*."

"What documents?" Holly asked, excited without knowing exactly what she was excited about.

An overactive toddler on a leash wrapped himself around Rusty's leg and the conversation was interrupted while Rusty, Gilberto, and the little boy's mother got Rusty untangled.

"Maps," Gilberto said finally. "Censuses and ledgers. Correspondences with many of the Spanish kings of the periods."

"So?" Holly asked.

"So there may be documents showing that one of the de la Garzas, or Escandón, or even the king, deeded land to the Riveras. Your Riveras, Holly." Gilberto grinned, his white teeth gleaming almost as brightly as his eyes. "Such documentation would bolster your argument in court. Challengers laying claim to the same land would have to produce records legitimately documenting a sale or transfer of title. If they could not..." Gilberto gave a grand shrug.

"Wow," said Holly.

"Wow is right," Rusty said. "So, let's see the documents."

Gilberto's smile dimmed. "Ah, there is one *problema*."

Rusty sighed. "There would be."

"The documents are in tatters. Faded, crumbled, water-spotted. They must be restored. There are several experts—archivists and preservationists—working on the project, including documents regarding the Rivera land grant."

"Why would they work so hard on that?" Holly asked.

"They want justice for their people," Gilberto said. "But it takes time. I told your father all this in the faxes."

"I haven't seen these faxes," Holly said. "Of course, I haven't been through all his papers, but if you sent them recently, I would have thought he would send me copies, or that they would at least be on the top of the pile in his office."

Gilberto lifted his eyebrows in an expression of helplessness. "They should be there. I took extra care to send them to the special number he gave me."

Holly frowned. "What special number?"

"In his reply to my first fax, about how we had what Rusty likes to call a 'hot lead,' your father instructed me to send further correspondence regarding this matter to another number."

"I don't get it," Holly said. "There's only one fax machine in the house and it's on a dedicated line. It's not as if he has a commercial office."

"Maybe he wanted it sent to someone he trusted. An attorney or banker?"

"I thought that 'trusted attorney' was me." Rusty pouted like a jilted lover. "And I don't know anything about this."

"Maybe the geniuses at the Ridge Pack 'N' Mail screwed up," Holly said.

"Could be, although they're usually pretty good. What was the number you used, Gilberto?"

"I do not know it from memory. Let us go to my office and I will look it up."

Holly and Rusty followed the young man downstairs.

"Gilberto, when my father died, I inherited the house he owned near The Gap. Several people have been encouraging me—"

"Pressuring you, you mean," Rusty said.

"Whatever. To sell it. I guess in the light of all this, you'd say I should hold on to it."

"Of course I cannot advise you on real estate," Gilberto said. "But if I were you, I would not sell until the *gorda* sings."

"The *gorda?*" Holly frowned.

"The fat lady," Rusty said. He chuckled. "Boy, if that doesn't lose something in the translation."

They reached the Institute's lower level. "Here we have additional exhibits but for the most part this floor is for offices, workrooms, and storage. Here is my office."

The room wasn't much larger than a closet. Books, files, and portfolios stood in stacks from the floor virtually to the ceiling and one wall was lined with metal file cabinets. Gilberto opened one and removed an overstuffed accordion file.

"My 'Clark' file," Gilberto said. He thumbed through the file and produced a sheet of paper. Rusty grabbed at it and Holly looked over his shoulder. The message thanked Gilberto for his efforts and as he had said, requested that he send further communications to another number.

"Not the Pack 'N' Mail," Rusty said. "I know all those numbers by heart. This isn't any number that I recognize."

"Nor me," said Holly. "But I do recognize the number in the header." Small numbers across the top of the page showed the phone number from which the fax originated. "This was sent from our house, from Clark's study. She twisted a strand of hair. "I think I smell a rat, and I think that rat's name is Tres."

Rusty chuckled.

"In the future, Gilberto, please send your faxes, and anything else, to Rusty. I think that will be the safest."

"Not to Clark's home? Excuse me, now your home?"

"Noooo. Better send it to Rusty. If that's okay with you?"

"Of course," Rusty said. "You'll let us know as soon as you have anything definitive."

"Certainly. In fact, I can send you away with one small item which I hope is a sample of more to come." Gilberto pulled another document from the file. "This is but a photograph. However, Father Noyola has the original in a very safe place."

Holly took the paper. "Why it's the map. The map you faxed to my father, Rusty." She gave it to him.

"Not exactly," he said. "This one has something that didn't photocopy well." He pointed to a marking in the corner.

In the center of a circle, Holly could see faint markings of what looked to be initials surrounded by scroll work. She thought she could make out a tiny hand holding a pen. "What is it?"

"You can see it clearly on the original," Gilberto said. "And Rusty, you will be pleased to know that it has been authenticated."

"Will somebody please tell me?" Holly felt like shaking somebody. "What's authentic?"

"The seal. It's the seal of Raoul Elena Cordoba, cartographer to King Charles the Third of Spain."

CHAPTER 26—POT CALLING THE KETTLE BLACK

Holly tipped back her high-backed leather executive chair and propped her sandaled feet on her Empire desk. The Stuart Weitzman high heels she had worn on the first few days of her elevated new status lay abandoned under the matching credenza. She gazed out over the City of Bonafides. Holly had to admit: she may have tired of dressing to broadcast her success but she never tired of her view of the Bay from her penthouse office. Tough day today; she was wiped out. Who knew that having all this money would be this much work or make life so complicated? Once she returned to Earth from the high of finding the Isla del Tesoro pirate treasure Holly had to confront the enormous challenge of what to do with her new riches. She had spent a little on herself but a girl can do just so much shopping. She had no shortage of prospective advisors who wanted to tell her what to do with the rest. So many causes appeared to be worthy and their proponents made such persuasive arguments. The question was whom to trust. Of course Larry Pomposas had suggested that she help to finance his gubernatorial campaign. "Money and power, Holly," he said. "We'll be unstoppable." True enough and she was been tempted. She had been surprised as anybody to find herself turning for advice to, of all people, Rusty Burger...

"Rusty? No way," she said and then realized that she was thinking aloud.

"Huh?"

"Sorry. Never mind," she stammered.

Rusty took Gilberto's hand and shook it. "You'll keep us posted?"

"Certainly."

"Before we head back to Bonafides, why don't we get a bite to eat, celebrate a little?"

"Sounds great," Holly said. "Gilberto, may we buy you a late lunch?"

"Some other time perhaps. I really should get back to work. But if you are going to celebrate may I suggest Mi Tierra?"

"Good idea but we don't have a reservation," Rusty said.

"I could make a call."

"You can do that?" Rusty said.

Holly was impressed. Larry Pomposas was probably the only other person she knew with enough influence to get into the famous and immensely popular Mexican restaurant on a moment's notice.

"Next time. When you're with us," Rusty said.

"It will be my pleasure."

"Thanks again, Gilberto," said Holly.

They left the cool of the air conditioned Institute and headed across the park which despite the many shade trees simmered in the afternoon heat.

"You walk on the inside of the path," Holly said. "I'll walk next to the waterways. We don't want to risk a dunking this late in the day."

Rusty smirked. Then his expression turned serious.

"What?" Holly asked.

"I've just been thinking. Whoever was getting Gilberto's faxes knew as much, no, more really, than Clark did about the legitimacy of the Rivera land grant claim. I have a feeling that if we find the person who's been getting these faxes, we'll find the person who ran Sam Hill off the road."

"What? What makes you think—?"

"Oops." Rusty slowed, then stopped. "I wasn't going to say anything." He sighed. "I got a good look at the rear of Sam's Jeep and there's a lot of recent damage there."

"And just how do you know that? According to the newspaper, his vehicle ended up in the Bay."

"It did. It was fished out and impounded until the cops ruled it an accident, closed the case, and notified the registered owner that he could have it back."

"Well, that would have been Sam. I don't understand."

Rusty smiled. "Oh, quite some time ago he gave me power of attorney. I've been collecting his mail, trying to keep things organized until his relatives can take charge. I got his Jeep out of impound and had it towed to my place. I dunno, I don't like the looks of the damage."

Holly recalled Sam telling her that he had given Rusty power of attorney. She started walking, her thoughts racing ahead faster than her feet. "C'mon, Rusty. You're no crime scene tech. It's a Jeep. It was pretty banged up to begin with from what I could see. Couldn't some of that damage be old dings and dents?"

Rusty shrugged. "It they were old there'd be corrosion in them, wouldn't there?"

"True," Holly admitted.

"There wasn't. The exposed metal was bright. See, I think someone forced Sam off the road. And I think someone pushed you down the courthouse stairs."

"And shoved Doctor Roberts off the boat?"

"What?"

Holly told Rusty about the incident aboard the gambling barge.

"I told you it was dangerous to hang with Pomposas."

Despite the scolding, Holly felt better that Rusty knew about the doctor's suspicious drowning.

Rusty scowled. "Yes, I'll bet the same person or persons are behind all of that. Not to mention who killed Clark."

In spite of the midday heat, Holly felt a chill pass over her. She twisted her hair. "Well, that certainly popped my party balloon."

"Sorry," said Rusty. "We really did get some good news from Gilberto. And I know just the place to celebrate. It's close enough that we could walk it if it weren't so hot. You drive, I'll navigate."

"All right," Holly said. In San Francisco, she didn't drive very often, preferring to use the city's excellent municipal transportation system, so she was a little nervous about negotiating midtown San Antonio. On the other hand, she mused as she took the wheel, she had seen Rusty drive. She didn't know which was the lesser of two evils.

"No, not that way," Rusty said. "Market's one way going the wrong way. Take Durango to St. Mary's."

"What's there?" Holly asked.

"You'll see."

They passed the Mexican Consulate and Rusty took the opportunity to give the high sign to their unseen, unknown confederates within. "OK, start looking for a place to park."

That turned out to be "Mission Impossible." After Holly drove around in seemingly endless circles Rusty suddenly said, "Here. Turn in here."

Rusty directed Holly into the parking garage of La Mansion del Rio. With its white stucco walls and wrought iron gates, the elegant hotel made Holly think of a grand hacienda. Graceful archways granted a peek at shaded courtyards beyond. Visions of a crisp salad, warm tortillas, a chilled shrimp cocktail, and a cool citrus-garnished goblet of Sangria filled her head.

"We're eating here?" Holly asked, pleasantly surprised. She hadn't thought of Rusty as the La Mansion type.

"Nah, we're not eating here, we're just parking here. Where we're headed's just over that bridge."

The passage was one of the many footbridges over the Riverwalk. Lined with cypress trees, palms, flowering shrubs, and tropical plants, gift shops, art galleries, and restaurants, the Riverwalk wound its lazy way for miles through San Antonio's midtown. Holly looked at the water with misgiving.

"Hurry," she said. "Let's get across before you fall in."

"Don't worry," Rusty replied. "Got it under complete control." As if to prove it, he flung a leg over the stone railing.

"Rusty, quit fooling around."

"Okay, okay, let's get to lunch. Anyway, we're here."

Dick's Last Resort was further from La Mansion than just a few city blocks. In terms of ambience it was light years away. She followed Rusty into a dark, smoky bar lit by the garish red and green of neon beer signs and decorated in what she imagined was supposed to be Early Texas Roadhouse. Blues on the PA competed with noisy patrons to see who could be the loudest. Located in what had been the basement and morgue of an old hospital, it had all the charm of the Marina Bar, Grill, and Bait Shop, minus the bait. At least Holly hoped minus the bait.

"We'll sit outside," Rusty informed the hostess.

"Suit yourself," she said. "It's no skin off my nose."

Pretty surly for a hostess, Holly thought, although sitting outside proved out to be a good idea. It wasn't as smoky or noisy and the San Antonio River gurgled just on the other side of a low block wall.

"Pull up a chair," Rusty said.

"A chair" turned out to be a seat at one of the rough picnic benches under a corrugated tin shed roof. Holly had no sooner seated herself when a blue-jeaned and T-shirted waitress appeared.

"Know what you want?" she asked.

"No," Holly replied. "I haven't looked at the menu. I don't even have a menu, as a matter of fact."

"Well, hurry it up. I ain't got all day," the waitress said, and vanished into Dick's dark interior.

"Well, I never—" Holly said. "How am I supposed to order without a menu?"

"Get the ribs," Rusty said. "That's what I'm having."

Holly frowned. What was it with the Bonafides men that made them so ready to decide for her? Holly liked ribs all right but always felt like she needed a bath afterwards. Her white-with-white outfit would attract the dark red sauce like a magnet. She tried to picture holding up her end of the conversation while wresting sticky-sauced meat from stubborn bones with her teeth. "Do they have a salad?"

Rusty laughed. "How about peel-and-eat shrimp? Shrimp's good here. Crab legs?"

Again, food that had to be manhandled. "A sandwich?"

"Catfish?"

"Catfish it is," Holly said.

The waitress appeared with two frosty, salt-encrusted margaritas.

"We didn't order that," Holly said although given the chance she might have.

"Yeah, well you should have," the waitress said, setting down the drinks. "Are you ever gonna order?"

"Ribs and catfish," Rusty said.

"It's about time," the waitress replied, and marched off.

"They really should give their wait staff some training," Holly said.

"Oh, they do, they do," Rusty replied with a chuckle.

For all the waitress's attitude, their order arrived fast and hot. Between bites and sips, Rusty painted colorful pictures of the Rivera vs. Tejas Bonanza land claim trial, with him as the starring counsel.

"The Riveras' claim goes back to the seventeen-hundreds, Your Honor," he intoned. "Can opposing counsel produce a similar claim?" To punctuate his point he waved a half-gnawed rib bone, flinging barbecue sauce into the air.

When they were nearly done with lunch, Holly said, "If we're going to be hitting the road soon, I better wash up first." She stood and headed for the interior. "You wouldn't know where the lady's room is, would you? Never mind, I'll just ask the waitress."

"No, Holly, don't ask—"

"Excuse me, where is the ladies' room?"

In a voice that could be heard over the chatter and the music, the waitress announced, "This woman wants to know where the ladies' room is."

Waiters, waitresses, and bus boys rushed to Holly's side. "I'll show her." "No, I will." "Come with me." Surrounded, Holly found herself paraded to her desired destination, serenaded with

"We're going to the potty" and accompanied by the applause of the other diners.

Holly returned to the table where Rusty sat grinning.

"What are you laughing at? I've never been so embarrassed!"

"I told you not to ask." Rusty stood. "What say we stretch our legs a little before we get back in the car. Care for a walk?"

"As long as we're walking away from here," Holly replied.

They strolled along the Riverwalk. Birds chirped in the lush foliage and river barges drifted slowly past. Holly thought the scenery could easily make her forget she was in the middle of a bustling city. She eyed the river with concern, though. No wall or railing separated the water from the pedestrian walkway.

"Want to take a boat ride?" Rusty asked.

"With you? You want to risk another dunking?"

"Nice," he said with a smirk. "Speaking of barges, uh, you said you were on the gambling barge last night. Learn anything?"

Not while she was on the barge exactly, Holly thought, but she wasn't about to tell him where she had spent the remainder of the night. "Just that everybody wants me to sell that house."

"That's not news."

"No. Tres has a gambling problem."

"That's not news, either."

"It was to me."

"Oh, I thought you knew. You probably don't know he has a little drug problem, too."

"Tres?" Holly stopped in her tracks and propped her hands on her hips. A startled passerby collided with her and gave her a dirty look before moving on. "You would know."

Now it was Rusty's turn to glare at her. "I don't have a drug problem and you know it." A young woman approaching with two little kids in tow took a couple steps back and then cut a wide circle around Holly and Rusty. "But Tres does have one, I'm sorry to report."

"You're just saying that because you don't like him."

"I don't like him, I admit it. He's lazy and manipulative and he sure takes advantage of you. That doesn't mean it isn't true."

"How do you know?"

"You forget. I'm alleged to be a former user myself."

A young man passing by gave Rusty a thumb's up. "*Former* drug user. Way to go. Stay straight, man. Right on."

Holly narrowed her eyes at him. "You told me that wasn't true."

"It wasn't. But I learned a lot in the process of defending myself. Tres does coke. So does Larry. I think they share their stash. They sure are chummy."

"Larry? Coke? He does not. You're jealous of him, that's all."

"Jealous of Pompous Ass? Get out of town."

"Watch your language, Mister," scolded an older woman strolling the Riverwalk with an equally elderly male companion.

"Someone put that coke in my Lexus," Rusty said. "It was Pomposas or someone he got to do it."

"Like Tres? I don't think so."

"I didn't say it was Tres. I was thinking Creaser. He does a lot of dirty work for Larry. People don't want to see it. All they see is a good relationship between the police and the DA so they look the other way."

"Hmph." Holly started walking again, skirting a young couple window-shopping in front of a jewelry store.

"Hear me out. What happened on the boat last night? Doc Billy Bob went overboard, right?"

"Yes..."

"You thought there was something hinky about that. Like he was pushed. Who pushed him, do you think? Larry?"

"Not Larry!"

"OK. How about Tres?"

"Not Tres, either."

"Creaser, then."

Holly had no retort to that because Rusty had just voiced an unsettling suspicion she had had since the accident. She sighed. "But why?"

Rusty stopped walking and ticked off points on his fingers. "Your father died under suspicious circumstances. Doc Billy Bob pronounces him dead of natural causes. You dig Clark up, start asking questions. Who's got answers? Doc Billy Bob. Suddenly, the man goes for an unscheduled midnight swim."

"But why kill Doc Roberts? I'm the one asking questions. Why not kill me?"

"Maybe they've tried. Your spill in the courthouse? Maybe you don't kill so easy. Maybe it's easier to push an old man overboard."

"Or drive one off the road? Like Sam Hill?" Holly asked, feeling her eyes tear up.

"You said it."

"But why kill Sam? He didn't know anything."

"Maybe because he was your ally. Maybe they felt if you had no friends in town, you'd leave before you stirred up too much trouble."

"Great. Blame it on me." Holly felt suddenly weary. "It's getting late. We should head back."

"There's another bridge up ahead."

They crossed over without incident and headed back to the car, walking west. Sun-blinded, Holly couldn't help bump into other people. She shaded her eyes from the blaze with her hand.

"You know, there was one other odd thing that happened last night." She told Rusty about the speedboat from the anchored freighter, and the exchange of life jackets between the speedboat and the yacht.

"I've seen that freighter," Rusty said. "It hardly ever moves. It certainly never comes into port that I know of. I've always thought there was something fishy about it, no pun intended."

"So what do you think is going on?" Holly asked.

"I don't know but I mean to find out."

You and me both, Holly vowed. Up ahead beckoned the colonial facade of La Mansion del Rio. Almost there, she thought. I can't believe we made it past all this water without Rusty falling in. She quickened her step.

From behind, someone yelled, "Heads up" followed by a grunt, a "Sorry, man, sorry," and a sound Holly had been dreading all day. She stepped to the side as a man on Rollerblades whizzed past her and she turned, hoping the splash she had heard had been made by a flying fish. She sighed. "Looks like Coleridge had it right: 'Water, water, everywhere, nor any drop to drink.'"

Standing chest deep in the San Antonio River, Rusty sputtered, "Stop spouting poetry, woman, and help me out of here."

CHAPTER 27–BUTTER WOULDN'T MELT IN HER MOUTH

Holly eyed the jewelry in the glass showcase. Her informant had tipped her off to a scam being run by one of the San Francisco's oldest and most respected jewelers: they were passing off glass as precious gems. She could bust this scam wide open if only she could get a sample to a certified gemologist. On her salary, there was no chance of her being able to buy anything. So how was she going to get her hands on some evidence...?

"Now this is a real stunner, don't you think?" Larry Pomposas pointed to a pair of earrings in the glass showcase. "Let's see those, Dmitri."

The tall, elegant jeweler opened the case and handed the earrings to Larry. Larry stepped in close to Holly, so close that she could feel the heat radiating from his body. He held the earrings up to her face. "I like the way the stone complements the color of her eyes without competing with them."

"Hmmm," the jeweler replied.

Was that a cravat he was wearing around his neck? Holly wondered. She'd only seen them in pictures, movies, and plays. Did real men actually wear those?

"The stone's perfect but I'm not so sure about the setting," said Dimitri. "Given the chance, I'd love to design something special for the lady, something that would better suit the size and shape of her face."

Holly tried not to squirm. It was odd being talked about in the third person as if she were a child or a pet, even if the context was flattering.

"And you'd do a swell job too, I know," Larry said. "Except that Holly's not going to be in town much longer—"

I'm not? Holly thought.

"—and we were really looking forward to getting something today."

We were? That shouldn't present a problem, she thought. At the moment she and Larry were the only customers in the shop that was so quiet she could almost hear the jewelry sparkling. She looked around the stylish shop. The warm wood and pristine glass of the cabinets glowed. The showcases were the brightest objects in the shop whose ambient lighting was somewhat subdued. Holly looked closely at the showcase light fixtures. Tiny flood lights shone down on colored and clear stones in their gold and silver settings. Were those halogen lights? she wondered. What was it about jewelry store lighting? For some reason, gems didn't seem to gleam quite as brightly anywhere else.

"Tell you what, Dmitri. Why don't we take the necklace for now? You work on the earrings. When they're done, let me know." Larry turned to Holly. "I'll fly out to San Francisco and personally put them on. How's that?"

He would do that? Holly felt not only warmth flood her cheeks but a little sexual sizzle as she pictured that scene. "Oh, Larry, you don't have to get me anything." What was she saying?

"I know I don't have to. There really aren't too many things in general that Larry Pomposas *has* to do. This is something I want to do. This will look so nice on you, especially in the moonlight on our next date." He drew the chain around Holly's neck and fastened the clasp in back. His fingers brushed the nape of her neck and sent a tingle down her spine.

"Uh, about that—" She'd been eager for another evening with Larry when he had first proposed it but after her disturbing conversation with Rusty she found herself just the teeniest bit uncertain.

"Thanks, Dmitri. Put the necklace on my tab and get started on those earrings." Larry slipped his arm through Holly's elbow and led her from the store saying, "Ready for lunch? Do you like Thai food? Of course you do. Who in San Francisco doesn't eat Thai food? There's a splendid Thai restaurant right here." He pointed to the low, tree-shaded masonry building across from them. Large plate-glass windows framed linen-draped tables in a shop book-ended by smart boutiques.

"I'd love to, Larry," Holly said, somewhat awed with the idea of a man running a tab at a jewelry store. Rather a far cry from running one at the Marina Bar, Grill, and Bait Shop. "And it seems rude not to, after you bought me this. But I really can't. I've got to get some work done."

"Work?"

"I've got another edition of the paper to paste, er, work on and there's still a lot to do on my father's estate."

Larry hung his head in a show of disappointment. "I'm sorry to hear that but I understand. I know you're eager to get home and you've had to stay in Bonafides a lot longer than you planned. That's what I told myself yesterday when you said you were too busy to get together. You were working then, too?"

"More or less." Holly debated whether to tell him just exactly what she had been doing. She decided she might as well. He would probably hear about it from Tres. "I was in San Antonio all day, chasing down a lead into the Rivera land grant."

Larry snorted. "Talk about a waste of time."

Holly stopped in her tracks. "A waste? Is that how you really feel about it? I'd almost think you weren't interested in helping me."

Larry turned on the full wattage of his smile. "You're totally wrong about that. I only want what's best for you. And what I want is for you to have a nice lunch before you buckle down to work." He pushed open the door to the restaurant.

A dark-haired woman in a sky-blue silk sheath hurried to greet them. "Larry," she said with a warm smile. "Would you like your usual table?"

"Yes, Irene. And my friend and I are in something of a hurry."

"No problem," said Irene. "I have just the thing for you. Our sushi sampler. Think of it as Thai fast food. Not fast to prepare, just fast to serve and eat."

"That will be great, Irene," Larry said.

Holly winced. She hated sushi. She didn't like to admit it as it seemed almost sacrilegious for someone coming from San Francisco. She certainly wasn't going to mention it now. Larry clearly did not take "no" for an answer to anything.

Irene seated them at the center window table, a "see and be seen" spot if there ever was one, and brought them tall glasses of a pink iced drink. "Our iced tea of the day," she explained. "Passion fruit."

"Perfect," Larry said, waggling his eyebrows at Holly.

Irene hustled off to the kitchen as fast as anyone could hustle in a body-hugging cheongsam and returned with a large boat-shaped serving dish. "I brought you some spring rolls, too."

"Thank you, Irene. You're good as gold to me."

"There's no being too good to you, Larry," Irene said before leaving them alone to their food.

Larry expertly snagged a California roll from the platter with his chopsticks, utensils Holly had never mastered much to her chagrin. She speared a spring roll with her fork.

"I don't know, Larry. It's like you're trying to dissuade me from pursuing the claim altogether. I've got to tell you: after my trip to San Antonio, I've begun to think we really might have grounds for a legitimate claim and ought to bring suit. I'd like to force an examination of the claim in a court of law."

"You would?"

"Yes, and I'd like your input as to how to go about it."

"My input would be to forget it." He swallowed some tea. "Why can't I seem to persuade you that the development will be good for the city and the area and in particular, good for you?

The developer is prepared to offer you a much better price than your property is worth just to wrap up the deal. You know they have all the land they need except for yours."

"So I've been told. Many times. By Cilla Esquivel. Now you, too. Why do I get the distinct impression that you want me to walk away from pursuing the claim?" Holly asked.

"Because you're not likely to prevail. It would be very expensive for you. Meanwhile, the action would impede the progress of The Gap development. The feds won't kick in their share unless they think the community's behind the project one hundred percent."

Holly put her food down uneaten. "If my claim puts a stop to the development so much the better. I'm not sure I really approve of what they are going to do to the area. Messing with the environment and all for the benefit of private developers at taxpayers' expense."

Larry frowned. "That's not you talking, dear one. That's Rusty Burger talking."

"And what if he's right?"

"But he's not. Consider the source. You know he doesn't have a very good reputation: drugs, disbarment—"

"He wasn't disbarred, he was suspended," Holly said, surprising herself with the heated defense she was putting up for that buffoon. It was a good thing Larry hadn't been at the Riverwalk when Rusty fell in. That clumsy goofball would never hear the end of it.

"Still, I hate to see you getting more involved with him. Not someone you should spend a lot of time with or put much stock in. The people who oppose development in The Gap are wrong. Most of them are nuts and gadflies. They oppose anything that looks like change or progress. Sure, it looks like it's all for the benefit of the select few. And yeah, they stand to make some money, but they should. They're taking all the risk. Meanwhile, this project is going to put Bonafides on the map and that will be good for everyone."

"Except the people whose land was stolen right out from under them." Holly crossed her arms defiantly. "Larry, I thought you supported me on this."

"I do. Darling, I just don't want to see your time and money go up in smoke on a pipe dream. No one, and I mean no one with half a brain, thinks any of those Spanish land grant claims are worth a hoot. That may not include your friend Rusty. But then again, I said no one with half a brain. They're just chasing their own tails and don't have enough sense to know it."

They finished their lunch in silence. Holly was too steamed to make conversation and Larry was too busy eating. He polished off the sushi, apparently oblivious to the fact that Holly hadn't eaten a single one. When the platter was empty, he called to Irene to put the lunch on his tab, walked around, and pulled Holly's chair out, nuzzling her ear as he did so. "You know I hated it that our maiden voyage on the floating casino ended so poorly."

Holly frowned. Ended poorly? That was an understatement. A man died that night.

"Want to give it another go tomorrow night? My friends are going to take the yacht to the barge, have one more night aboard before it's open to the public. Later, when we've had enough fun, we can go back to my place."

Holly found it a little difficult concentrating with his tongue in her ear. His attentions were certainly pleasing but it didn't make her forget that her request for help with the lawsuit had gotten the brush-off. Didn't anyone tell the truth anymore?

She had to admit, she never had a lot of illusions about Larry Pomposas. One didn't get far in politics with too much honesty but it looked increasingly like she had just gotten broadsided. No help there.

Holly eased herself away from Larry. A little more of that tongue action and they would be tumbling into bed again. It wouldn't take much persuasion because that sure sounded like a much better way to spend a Sunday afternoon than pasting up another edition of the *Mission Crier*. Larry did make her feel great but she was no longer sure his interest in her was genuine. The dinners, the jewelry, the sex...was it all just a big distraction play? And if so, a distraction from what exactly?

CHAPTER 28–WHEELS WITHIN WHEELS

"Grady *Norson here, and this is* Good Morning, America. *I'm with Holly Rivera Berry, investigative reporter for the* San Francisco Informer. *Ms. Berry is credited with exposing—bad choice of words, there, huh, Holly?—the illicit affair between councilman Jonah Blackley and a production intern for* KHUE-TV. *Tell us, Holly, how did you uncover—oops, there I go again. Sorry—the affair?"*

"Well, Grady," said Holly, "I noticed that KHUE *was giving the councilman a lot of press. None of the stories were falsehoods but they were little stories. Dog bites man, that sort of thing. Nothing we here at the* Informer *would bother to cover. It started to look to me like an equal-time violation. He's running for reelection, you know. He got a lot of air time and favorable air time at that."*

"And you learned that the intern produced her own stories and slipped them into the broadcast, is that right?"

"You make it sound like that was easy to discover, Grady," Holly replied with a gracious smile.

"Oh, I know it wasn't, and after this commercial break we want to hear all the details. But I can see how it would be tempting to a production intern to take advantage of her position..."

Slowly, Holly lowered her Xacto knife onto the top of her father's desk and gazed out the study's window overlooking The

Gap. Silly little fantasy, but wait. Why she hadn't thought of that before? Yes, that would be tempting indeed and not hard to pull off. With her left hand, she twined a strand of hair. She could do that: slip a little story or two into the *Mission Crier* from time to time. Nothing untrue, nothing controversial. Just some little tidbit that would showcase her writing abilities. Her boss would never notice but someone else might. An editor from the news desk of *The San Francisco Informer* maybe or for that matter, even KHUE-TV. She rubbed her right index finger against her thumb.

"Ouch!" She looked with dismay at the thin red line spouting along her finger. Her mind had wandered so far from her task she had cut herself with the sharp Xacto blade.

She tore off a piece of scrap paper and wrapped her finger in it so she wouldn't bleed on her work. She pasted down a syndicated story on "Fifteen Creative Things You Could Do with Plastic Wrap," then tackled the classifieds. "Egyptian cotton towel set and king-size 500-thread count bed linens. Wedding gift, never used. A steal at $100. Monogrammed NPT. "

Holly chuckled. Yup, that would be a fantastic deal if your initials happened to be NPT. She wondered what happened. Wedding canceled? Monogrammer made a typo?

She shook her head, pasted down the item, and tackled the next: "IBM Model M keyboard, $80. Best in the world, hard to find. Backspace key doesn't work."

It was true, the clicky keyboard was a joy to use. Holly herself liked it. It made such a satisfying clatter. Her boss always assumed she was feverishly hard at work when he passed by. Also true was its scarcity since production of that model had all but ceased. While eighty dollars was a good price for the increasingly rare item, this particular one would be of practical use only to someone who never made mistakes.

She found herself gazing out the window again. Somehow making sure the *Crier* got out on time so the Bay Area could know all about a great deal on a used tombstone didn't seem all that important at the moment.

Blood threatened to ooze through her improvised bandage. The cut was deep and ragged. She needed a Band-Aid and obviously she already needed new blades for her Xacto knife. Next time she was out she had better get some replacements.

Since it didn't look as though she would be leaving Bonafides any time soon she was going to have to get serious about finding a way to lay out the paper digitally. Too bad Edison Pulitiz appeared to be involved with the "cartel," as Rusty Burger liked to refer to it. She probably would have been able to make some kind of arrangement to use a workstation at Putlitiz's paper.

With another sigh, she left her father's desk and went in search of a Band-Aid. When she returned, her eye fell on the pewter cross, still poking out from where it lay atop a stack of books under the divan. She really should get it and those books out from under the divan and put them back where they belonged. Shelve the books, clean up this office, and put her father's papers in order. And yes, she should hang the cross back on the wall. She vowed that she would as soon as she got the paper off to the publisher. Meanwhile there was something that bothered her about that cross.

She stood in the doorway and stared at it peeping out from under the divan and willed the feeling of unease to solidify into something she could analyze.

At last it came to her. She had imagined that it had simply worked itself off its nail and then slid behind the divan. If that was what had happened, why wasn't it lying on the floor? How had it gotten on top of the stack of books?

Probably nothing to it. No doubt her father, or Artemisia, the housekeeper, had fished it out from under the divan and then, like Holly, had been too lazy or too preoccupied to re-hang it.

Then why not simply leave it on the divan or a table? Why shove it under the furniture?

Holly, she told herself, you're just procrastinating. Stop woolgathering and get back to work. The sooner you finish, the sooner you can sneak onto that gambling barge.

Until she put it into words, she hadn't been aware that she seriously considered doing just that. Now that she'd verbalized the intent, she realized she'd been thinking about it ever since she turned down Larry's invitation to go aboard a second time.

She had to admit that her immediate reaction was that she would learn more eavesdropping on the cartel than she would by sitting down to dinner with them.

The only question left was "how?" How to get aboard without any of them knowing?

She pasted down the "Used Tombstone: Cheap!" ad and tackled another for "Savings on Gift Rapping." Shoot, that had to be a typo. Oh, apparently not. The ad was for a contemporary spin on a singing telegram service.

Her mind drifted back to the floating casino. Could she ferry over to it on the Tejas Bonanza yacht? She could drop Larry's name and maybe the crew would remember her from the other night. Really, who could forget the lady in the disco ball dress? No doubt Larry and the cartel planned to use it though. Unless she beat them to it, they might have it tied up to the barge. If she somehow got to it before they did, the crew might say something to Larry.

No, she would have to find another way.

She needed a boat. Sailboats and yachts could be chartered, she knew, but at the last minute? Doubtful. Didn't charters require a day or two's notice?

Where could she get a boat?

As she pasted down the remaining strips she answered her own question but the answer presented problems of its own.

Rusty had a boat. Oh, she so hated to ask him. He would lecture her for sure about the folly of her plan. There seemed to be no help for that. Now, how to get a hold of him? It wasn't like he kept regular office hours. He didn't even have an office in which to keep regular office hours. Did he have a home phone? Did he even have a home?

The proprietor of the Ridge Pack 'N' Mail might know. Holly had to go there anyway, to get the newspaper layout off to San Francisco. There was a Walmart near the Pack 'N' Mail. While she was out, she could stop and get more Xacto knife blades. As a reminder, she stowed the knife in its protective plastic sheath and tucked it into the pocket of her jeans.

She climbed into the PT Cruiser and chided herself. The car had gotten pretty darn dirty on the drive to and from San Antonio the other day. Instead of lunching with Larry yesterday she should have cleaned it. She'd stop at a car wash and get that taken care of too. There was one on the way. It wasn't fully automatic, just one of those self-service operations that took a fistful of quarters in exchange for the use of a power sprayer but it would knock off the road dust and dead bugs.

Riprap Ridge was a mere half hour's drive but it felt like a world away from the tidy lawns, neat oleander hedges, and trimmed palm trees of her Playa Rico neighborhood. In Riprap Ridge, sunbaked weedy lots held short-term rentals and motels that weren't much for looks on the outside and undoubtedly were even less attractive on the inside. Their owners knew there was no point in putting any money into them. The clientele was mostly people here for fishing vacations. They didn't plan to spend any more time in their motel room than it took to shower and sleep.

Holly hit the car wash and managed to get as much soap and water on herself as she did on the PT. Slightly damp, she headed for the Ridge Pack 'N' Mail. The shop occupied one suite in a slump-block strip that held a *taqueria*, a dollar store, a pizza place, and a liquor store.

Carla, the clerk, gave Holly a blank look when she asked how she could get in touch with Rusty quickly.

"Have you tried his 'office'?" Carla said.

"His...oh, right. Silly me," Holly replied.

The Marina Bar, Grill, and Bait Shop wasn't far and sure enough she found Rusty hard at "work" at the bar.

"Didn't think I'd see you today, little lady," he said. "Join me for an early dinner?" He waved his hand at the food in front of him.

Holly eyed his repast. "Dinner? It's a sack of pork rinds," she said.

"Too hearty for you?"

"Are you kidding? That's junk food," she scoffed.

"Is not," he said around a mouthful. "Pork rinds are nearly all protein, something not widely known. Check the label." He held out the bag. "Read the Nutrition Facts."

"Yeah, right."

"Seriously. Think about it. Once they render off all the fat, what's left?"

She shuddered to contemplate. "I'll pass just the same. Anyway, that's not what I wanted to talk to you about. Can I borrow your boat?"

"What for?" he asked.

She told him her plan.

"Absolutely not," he said. "Too dangerous."

"Sailing alone at night. Hmmm, maybe you're right. Okay, you take me."

"Not on your life, little lady," he said. "If we get caught not only will I never get my license back, Larry will probably find a way to take my boat away from me not to mention put me in jail."

"But how else are we going to find out what's going on aboard that barge?"

"I've been thinking about that," Rusty said. "I have a suspicion and I have a plan. Leave it to me."

"What are you going to do?" Holly asked.

"The less you know about it, the better."

Oh, thought Holly, so we're back to sell-the-house-and-skedaddle to Frisco, are we? We'll see about that. She crunched with all her frustration on a pork rind which turned out to be quite tasty although she wasn't about to tell Rusty that. She turned on her heel and left in a huff but she didn't go far. It was a challenge to find a place where the bright red PT would be unobtrusive. Figures she had just washed it. Left dirty, it would have blended in better. She managed to stash it partway behind a huge pickup. She could see the road through the forest of fishing poles secured to the pickup's front bumper. Even with all the windows rolled down and an offshore breeze blowing through, it was a steam bath in her car and a stinky one at that. The Lagoon smelled of salt and rotting organic matter. Luckily she didn't have to wait long. Rusty ended his "business day," climbed into his Lexus, and turned toward the freeway.

Tailing someone was a lot harder than it appeared on TV especially when the pursuit vehicle was bright red. Holly hung back several car lengths to avoid detection. She had to watch not only Rusty but the traffic around her. She didn't want to be caught in the left lane if Rusty suddenly decided to exit. With their characteristic contempt for such niceties as obeying speed limits and signaling lane changes her fellow motorists didn't make it any easier. Fortunately Rusty was kind enough to signal and divulge his intentions so Holly was prepared when he left the freeway. She was not prepared when he pulled into the first big shopping center just the other side of the freeway, parked, and strode into the Walmart.

Now's a fine time to go shopping, Rusty Burger, Holly thought. Don't you remember we have a mystery to solve?

She followed him into the store. He didn't stop to collect a cart so neither did she.

Despite the fact that it was a Monday afternoon the store was jammed. It was odd. From a quick glance at passing carts it seemed that everyone bought the same stuff: cases of SPAM, Vienna sausages, and canned tuna. Jars of peanut butter, instant coffee, boxes of cookies. Canned sodas. Dry milk and granola bars.

Blue light special? Now, wait, wrong store. That would be Kmart. Okay, some big sale maybe, but why the huge jugs of water? The carts overflowed with flashlights, multi-packs of batteries, and portable radios. And ice. Bags and bags of ice.

The answer so stunned her she stopped in mid-aisle. Hurricane preparation. June 1 was the official start of hurricane season. The locals stocked up on supplies in case a storm came ashore. Was a hurricane headed for Bonafides? Must be, given the degree of mild frenzy the shoppers exhibited. What was going on in the tropics? Holly realized she was so preoccupied of late she hadn't read the paper in days and had no idea what was happening in the outside world. Not that the Bonafides newspaper would have helped. In its previous life as *The*

Intelligencer the paper's weather page gave details about storm systems brewing in the Atlantic and the Gulf well in advance. *The Daily Breeze's* weather page reported little more than the temperature ("hot" and "hotter") and the chance of precipitation ("none" and "greater than none.")

Holly had to weave through crowded aisles and dodge unruly children to stay on Rusty's tail. Fortunately his red hair was easy to keep in sight.

Finally he came to a stop at the sporting goods counter. Holly stayed back where she hoped she was concealed by the fishing poles. She was too far away to hear what was being said but she didn't dare move closer. What if Rusty turned suddenly and saw her?

He said something to the clerk behind the counter. Whatever Rusty had asked for gave the clerk some pause after which he went behind the counter into the stock area. When he emerged he came out from behind the counter and he and Rusty started toward Holly's aisle. She scanned for a place to hide. A barrel of basketballs took up a large space at the end of her aisle. She stuck her head deep into the barrel, pretending to be a shopper looking for just the perfect one which of course had to be at the bottom. After a couple of minutes when she thought she might die from vinyl asphyxiation she raised her head. Rusty and the clerk were deep in conversation over a fishing lure. Holly sidled around the end of the rack. Her body was hidden but she could keep an eye on Rusty in a fish-eye mirror suspended from the ceiling. The concave surface gave a distorted fun house mirror reflection. She saw Rusty select a couple of lures. Then the clerk handed Rusty what appeared to be a small clear envelope with something white inside.

Ohmigod, Holly thought, stifling a gasp with her hand. Drugs? Cocaine? It was true, then. Everything that Larry said and Rusty denied was true. He had been a user then and still was.

She had no more time to lose. She didn't know what plan he had for revealing what the cartel was up to out on the Tejas Bonanza. Hell, for all she knew he was part of it and his protests were just one big cover-up. If she was going to find out what was going on, she would have to do it herself.

She still needed a way to get on the barge. She could call Larry and tell him that she had changed her mind and would go aboard tonight after all. No, that wouldn't work. The cartel members would never speak openly in front of her. Besides, even in the face of Rusty's duplicity, she realized that she didn't quite trust Larry either. Part of this mission would be to unveil his true colors.

Looked like it was back to Plan A, flawed as it was. Somehow she was going to have to get the yacht to take her over.

Before she started for the Puerto Nuevo marina she would have to change. Holly ran a mental inventory of the clothes she had on. Hmm, her dark-brown leather sandals and jeans would do but the *Mission Crier* tee-shirt she had put on this morning wouldn't. It was bright gecko green; the screen printer had an oversupply of shirts in that color and gave her boss a discount. Holly was certain the shirt would glow in the dark. Apparently she was going to have to do some shopping. She looked around at the unkempt, overflowing shelves and crammed clothing racks. Walmart wasn't her usual purlieu, but given the circumstances it would have to do. Normally, she wouldn't be caught dead in a Jaclyn Smith ensemble but that was okay. She didn't plan to get caught, period.

CHAPTER 29–ALL AT SEA

Holly twisted her hair and ground her teeth in utter frustration. Damn, she had just missed them, the scallywags. The dark sedan was halfway down the street with its passengers, the corrupt pharmaceutical executive and the crooked DEA agent hidden behind its blackout windows. The vehicle was just far enough away that she couldn't make out the license plate. No way that she could run fast enough to catch up. In desperation she looked around but not only were there no taxis, there weren't even any other cars nearby. Damn, how was she going to get the goods on these scoundrels now...?

Holly stood on the dock at Puerto Nuevo and sighed. It was just as she had feared. The yacht had long since left, was in fact pulled up to the barge. The barge itself had not yet been moved to international waters. Still, it was some distance offshore. How far? A hundred yards? Two hundred? Three? It didn't appear to be much farther offshore than the Gulf oil platforms. How far out where they? She recalled that there were anglers who would kayak out to those platforms to fish so how far could that be?

The question was moot as no one had left a kayak conveniently lying around.

"Darn," she muttered, twisting her hair. She supposed she could wait. Maybe the yacht would return and she could prevail upon the crew to take her over. Maybe...

"Something wrong, Miss?"

She turned to face the speaker, a darkly-tanned shirtless young man in a ball cap, well-worn khaki shorts, and deck shoes, all damp.

"I missed the boat," she replied. "I really mean it, I missed the boat." She pointed at the yacht.

"No you didn't," he said. "That place isn't open for business yet. Those people, that's a private party."

"I was supposed to be part of it," she said although she doubted she looked like it in her hastily-assembled stealth outfit. Blue jeans, sandals, and the only dark T-shirt she could find at Walmart that didn't have some Day-Glo-bright screen printing on it. On a clearance rack she had found a brown shirt with the black *Grizmo* logo, swag long left over from promotional efforts for the wildly-popular animated film.

In the interest of saving time, she spared a stop at the house to change. After her impromptu shopping trip she drove to a nearby McDonald's. She switched out her top for the T-shirt in the ladies' room and sped off to the Puerto Nuevo marina. Parking her car a distance from the dock, she shoved her purse under the seat; her car keys were all she would need for this cruise. When she pocketed those, she discovered the Xacto knife she had stowed away when she had set out this morning. Damn! Walmart had replacement blades. Wasn't getting some her original intent when she first set out? She'd have to make another trip. In her own defense she had not been thinking about art supplies then nor was she now. Laying out the paper was not Job Number One at the moment. Getting aboard the gambling barge was.

"I'm, uh, supposed to help with the, uh, catering staff. But I got here late and I guess they left without me." She screwed her face into an expression that she hoped conveyed sufficient anguish. "Gee, I'll probably lose my job."

"Oh, that'd be a bummer," he said. He lifted his cap and ran a hand through damp spiky hair. "Well, I could take you over there. I just got off work, cleaning the yachts." He waved his hand at the cabin cruisers tied up in the marina. "Was gonna go out on my own boat and do a little fishing myself. I could give you a ride."

"Would you? That would be great."

She followed the young man to his vessel which was little more than a rowboat with an outboard motor. She waited patiently while he loaded up his fishing gear then climbed aboard and they put out to sea. From the dock the water hadn't looked all that rough but the ride in the small low-sided skiff was bumpy and wet. Holly had been on horseback rides that weren't this bouncy. She gripped the boat's sides to steady herself on the seat which was punishing her bottom.

As they neared the barge, she said to herself, "Nice going, Ms. Rivera. Now, how do you propose to get back?"

"Well, Ms. Berry," she answered, "I'll do my sleuthing then I'll sneak aboard the yacht and get a ride back when everyone leaves."

"Hm," said Ms. Berry. "Not a bad plan."

"Thank you," replied Ms. Rivera.

Her young chauffeur pulled up to the yacht's boarding ladder and grabbed the lowest standoff, steadying the skiff somewhat while Holly mounted the ladder. "Thanks for the lift," she said. She grasped the side rail and with her right hand, patted her side looking for her purse, then remembered she had left it in her car. She gave the young man a sheepish grin. "I was going to give you a little something for your trouble. Looks like I left my bag behind. I'll have to owe you."

"Not a problem. You can usually find me around the marina," he said, and with a little salute, motored away.

Holly clambered over the side and quickly flattened herself on the deck. The yacht appeared deserted but who knew who might be inside the cabin or salons? Crouching below the level of the various portholes and windows, she skulked around the side but didn't encounter a soul. Either the crew was aboard the barge or Larry and company had piloted the yacht themselves. Just as well, Holly thought. There'd be no pesky crew to worry about later when she stowed away for the return trip.

Quickly but quietly she scurried up the gangway ladder onto the barge. Below her, ghostly white disks floated close to the water's surface like fat globules in a bowl of greasy soup. Something leaking from the barge? No, they were hordes of jellyfish. She couldn't remember ever seeing so many in one place. Was there something about the barge that made them congregate there? Had the storm that brewed in the Gulf driven them in?

The sound of a motor interrupted Holly's ruminations about the jellyfish. The noise grew louder as a speedboat came around the barge and pulled up alongside the yacht. Holly hustled up the gangway, stood in the shadows of the entrance, and watched as two men stepped off the speedboat and onto the yacht. Her heart pounded as she realized how close she had come to being discovered.

The two men stood close to the yacht's sides as other men handed them packages from the speedboat. The packages that the two men stacked on the yacht's deck appeared to be wrapped in plastic. They gleamed in the twilight. The two men on the yacht opened hatches, pulled out all the life jackets, and proceeded to stuff the plastic-wrapped packages in what seemed to be gussets in the life jackets.

Holly stepped back deeper into the shadow, breathless with astonishment. She and Rusty had been right. It was about drugs. That had to be what was in the plastic packages. She'd seen enough news coverage of drug busts to recognize them. Holly put the racket together piece by piece. The freighter, a depot for the drugs, brought them close to shore, but not close enough, because the freighter stayed in international waters. That's why it seemed never to move, never came into port, as Rusty told it. The speedboat ferried the drugs from the freighter to the yacht, anchored oh-so-innocently at the barge, where they were stuffed into the life jackets. When the yacht docked in the marina, the life jackets were brought to shore. There they no doubt were relieved of their secret illegal cargo and returned empty to the yacht to be refilled the next time the yacht was moored at the barge. She imagined a future gambit when the barge would be in operation as a gambling casino. Scores of innocent people in drug-stuffed life jackets ferrying back and forth in water taxis, unwitting mules.

Holly took a deep breath. As profitable as gaming was, she wouldn't be surprised to find the drug smuggling produced more revenue. In fact, the barge might just be a front for the smuggling operation. She shook her head. Larry, Larry, Larry, are you a part of this? He was no stranger to the drug business. After all, if Rusty were to be believed, it was Larry who planted the incriminating drug evidence that got Rusty suspended.

Rusty! Holly's heart stopped as a sudden gust of wind blew the cap off one of the dark-clothed men on the yacht, revealing a head of curly hair that was unmistakably red, even in the fading light. Oh, Rusty, not you too?

Ouch, Holly nearly yelled out loud. She had been twisting her hair so hard she had almost pulled it out of her head. She let go of the strand and gnawed on her knuckle instead. What to do now? She should just jump aboard the yacht, sail back to shore, and call the cops. And she would, if she had a clue how to pilot the damn thing. Well, then, she should stowaway on the yacht and after Larry and crew had ferried her back she could call the law.

Except that if she left now she would leave still not knowing anything about how her father died. Nor might she ever learn the truth if the guilty parties were serving time on other charges. No, she would go ahead with her original plan.

Now where was her quarry? she wondered as she crept down deserted halls. Whom would she find aboard and were they eating, drinking, or talking?

All three at once, she decided as she neared the room where the casino had been held the other night. Apparently they were gaming still. She heard the clink of china, the whir and rattle of the roulette wheel, laughter and conversation but she wasn't close enough to make out what was being said. What she needed was a parabolic microphone. Or failing that, a drinking glass. She tiptoed to the dining hall and snatched a tumbler from the buffet. Then she returned to the corridor outside the gaming room and positioned herself roughly opposite where she remembered the roulette table had been. She put the glass to the wall and her ear to the glass. She had seen this done in a movie once. There was no time like the present to find out if it worked.

Actually, it worked fairly well. The voices were somewhat more distinct. She recognized Noble Barnes's resonant bass. Holly couldn't hear every word but she could make out some and figure out the rest from the context.

"Very well, thank you," he said. "We're doing lots of portfolio loans and since we charge one hell of a lot of interest they've been very profitable. Given the way the megabanks are regulated it's business they can't touch."

"'Course, we wouldn't want to look too closely at the 'portfolio' the loan money is coming from," said someone else. Sounded like Edison Pulitiz.

"The people we're making the loans to aren't asking any questions, let me tell you," Barnes replied.

"Like Tres Rivera?" The new voice belonged to Sidney Qownsill.

Tres? What did Tres need a loan for? Oh, he was a spendthrift all right but how much money could even a clotheshorse like Tres need? Unless...? Rusty had said Tres was into gambling and drugs. Could it be true? Could Holly believe Rusty?

Just how could Tres get a portfolio loan anyway unless he had mortgaged his condo? Holly wouldn't have thought he had that much equity in it. Had Tres put up the Rivera home in which Tres had no equity at all? Or had Barnes accepted a personal guarantee? No scenario made any sense. Holly felt a headache coming on.

"Are you kidding?" Barnes asked. "Tres can't get his hands on it fast enough the way his debts keep mounting."

"Opening this casino may make gambling convenient but it won't make it any less expensive," said Sidney with a laugh.

"Not if you play the way Tres does," said Barnes.

"Or have the misfortune to get one of Sidney's special dealers," said Pulitiz.

"Trained in the trenches," Sidney said.

Holly could almost picture his self-satisfied smirk. So, Sidney Qownsill was running some kind of illegal gambling operation? And now these shifty shufflers would be working the Tejas Bonanza tables to make sure that the house always had the advantage.

"Even without the gambling debts, he'd be on the hook for drug money," said Sidney.

"If Larry didn't just give him the stuff," Barnes said.

Larry? Gave Tres drugs? Holly thought she was going to be sick. Ohmigod, maybe Rusty was right in suspecting that Larry planted drugs on him.

"Don't do that, Larry," said Pulitiz.

"Yeah, it's not like you have to pay him for sex."

"Are you kidding? Larry Pomposas has never had to pay for sex."

Ohmigod, Holly thought. Larry...and Tres? LARRY AND TRES? Here she'd been fantasizing about moving into the Governor's Mansion with a man who was screwing her brother. Her brother, for God's sake.

Tres was gay? No way Holly could have said how she felt about that, she was simply too stunned. How could she not have known that about her own brother? Holly felt dizzy and forced herself to take deep breaths.

She had heard enough. How much could a girl take? So she was leaving, even though she hadn't learned anything about what had happened to her father...

The next few words made her hesitate.

"Poor Tres. He was doing a lot better when Clark was alive. At least then Tres had his dear old Dad to sponge off of." Pulitiz.

"He was banking—no pun intended—on his inheritance from Clark," Barnes said. "But now that Holly's taken over the estate..."

"Holly." The spite in Sidney Qownsill's voice was unmistakable even through the primitive listening device. "Cilla Esquivel has done everything in her power to get that house away from that girl. I tell you what, Cilla's madder than a hill of fire ants in a rainstorm. First Clark refuses to sell, now Holly. We were in a much better position when Tres was calling the shots. I wouldn't put it past Cilla—"

A hand on Holly's shoulder was a distraction she didn't need at this, the most crucial point in the conversation. She brushed it off.

CHAPTER 30–NO TIME LIKE THE PRESENT

Below decks, it was noisy and dark. Engines clanked and it smelled of rust and petrochemicals, salt, mold, and damp metal. Holly could hear only muttering communicated by a through-deck fitting to the room above. Soon though it would be safe to proceed to the upper decks and position herself where she could comfortably eavesdrop on the perpetrators. She didn't want to miss a syllable of what was coming next...

The hand returned and this time it clamped her shoulder hard and spun her around, bringing her face to face with Detective Creaser.

"You'll hear much clearer inside," he said. His big hand on her arm gripped as tightly as a tourniquet. He dragged her inside the gaming room. "Look who I found listening in," he said.

Edison Pulitiz, Noble Barnes, Sidney Qownsill, and Larry Pomposas looked up from the card table, open mouthed.

"I—I wasn't listening in. I—look, Larry invited me. I'm just late."

"Holly," Larry cried, "how'd you get here?"

"Umm, hitched a ride, so to speak."

"How much do you think she heard?" Barnes asked.

"Any of it would be too much," said Sidney Qownsill.

"I heard it all," Holly said, hoping a brave front would disguise her abject terror. "I heard that—Sidney, you're running illegal crooked gambling. Barnes, you're loan-sharking. And you, Larry, you dopehead two-timing bisexual manipulative sonofabitch—you're screwing my brother."

"'Son of a bitch'? Hey, I resent that," Larry said.

Holly tipped up her chin defiantly.

Larry looked stricken. "Holly, you don't understand."

"I think she understands a little too much," Sidney Qownsill said. "Now what are we going to do about it? Ted?"

Holly didn't like the look in Detective Creaser's eye nor the way he fingered his service revolver. He shoved her into one of the upholstered game-table armchairs and cuffed her hands behind the backrest with what looked like a plastic cable tie. It didn't appear all that formidable at first but Holly found as she wriggled her wrists that the restraint was plenty tight. It wouldn't take too much squirming for the plastic to cut into her skin.

"Holly, dear, I wish you hadn't gotten involved," Noble Barnes said.

"But she has," Sidney Qownsill said.

"Holly, don't fight us. Join us," Larry said.

"It's too late for that," Sidney said. "Anyway, I don't trust her." He shuffled his playing cards. "She could fall overboard," he said in a speculative tone.

Creaser shook his head. "Been there. Done that."

"Doc Roberts," Holly said. "You did push him over the side."

Creaser shook his head. "Me? I'm an officer of the law. I investigate crimes, I don't commit them."

"What do you call this?" Holly hiked her hands up the back of the chair, then quickly lowered them when the cuffs pinched. "This is unlawful imprisonment. This is kidnapping." She wasn't about to mention the cold-blooded murder they seemed to be considering.

"I'm just taking a trespasser into custody pending further investigation. Now Doc Billy Bob, he was drunk. He was becoming abusive. We were concerned he would become violent.

We detained him but he got away. He probably tripped and fell. It's unfortunate. Had he remained in our custody he might still be alive."

"But you didn't feel a need to investigate." Holly didn't know which she felt more strongly, anger or fear.

Creaser simply shrugged. "Looked like an accident to me, plain and simple."

"Like Sam Hill driving off the causeway? Just another accident that didn't bear further investigation?"

"In my opinion, yeah," Creaser said. To the others he said, "It would look suspicious as hell, two 'man overboards' in a row. That I'd have to investigate and that would delay the opening of this tub."

"We can't have that," Sidney said.

A new voice spoke up. "OK, it's all loaded. We're taking off."

Everyone turned to the speaker who had just entered the room. It was one of the men who had been stuffing drugs from the speedboat into the yacht's life jackets.

"What is he doing here?" Edison Pulitiz asked. He turned to the others. "He's not supposed to be here. We're supposed to be anonymous. Now he's seen us." To the smuggler he said, "If you're done, get the hell out of here."

The smuggler had his shirt collar turned up and the bill of his cap pulled down low, but there was something familiar about the set of the shoulders. Holly felt dizzy with shock and despair. Was there no one in Bonafides who could be trusted, no one to whom she could turn for help?

"You two-faced lying traitor," she said and strained against her bonds.

The smuggler frowned at her and shook his head vigorously.

"You've been part of this all along. I knew it," Holly cried.

"You know him?" Noble Barnes said. He leaned forward to get a better look at the man. "Hell, I know him. We all know him." He pulled off the man's cap. "It's Rusty Burger."

Detective Creaser moved quickly and pinned Rusty's arms behind his back.

"I don't understand," said Holly. "Isn't he one of you?"

"What are you talking about?" asked Larry.

"He's one of the smugglers. I saw him. He was on that speedboat. He helped unload the drugs and stuff them in the life jackets."

"You're one of them?" Creaser asked Rusty.

Larry shook his head. "Figures. Seems I was right about you all along, Burger. You're just a doper. Oh, Holly, if only you had listened to me."

"I dunno," said Sidney Qownsill. "I don't trust him."

"You don't trust me, you don't trust him. Whom do you trust?" Holly asked.

"I don't think you're in a position to criticize," he replied.

"There's an easy way to test his loyalty," Creaser said. He yanked Rusty's arms. Rusty winced. "We've got a little problem here, Burger, maybe you can help us with it.

"And that would be...?"

Creaser waved his service revolver at Holly. "This little missy has become a liability. Remove her for us. Permanently."

"How?"

Creaser shrugged. "That's up to you. But don't spend all night thinking about it."

Rusty shrugged off Creaser's grip and paced for a few steps. Finally he said, "Look, the speedboat's waiting for me. Let me take her with me back to the freighter. I'll do her there. The boys on that freighter, they haven't been near a woman in a while. They'll be happy to help."

Holly would have gulped in horror if her mouth and throat weren't completely dry.

"I don't know," said Sidney Qownsill.

"No, it's a good plan," Rusty said. "That way she won't be connected with you guys. You heard her. She got a lift over here. Someone knows she's here. If something happens to her here, well..."

"He's got a point," Noble Barnes said.

Sidney Qownsill said, "All right but I'm following them at least to the gangway. I want to make sure they both get aboard that speedboat."

"Me, too," said Edison Pulitiz.

Creaser snipped Holly's restraint, pulled her to her feet, and quickly bound her wrists with a fresh cable tie.

Rusty grabbed her upper arm roughly. "C'mon, Holly, let's go."

"I'm coming too," said Noble Barnes.

Ultimately they all insisted on ushering Holly to the gangway, reminding her for some reason of the potty parade at San Antonio's Dick's Last Resort.

Rusty hustled her out of the room and down the corridor, hurried steps ahead of the rest of the escort.

"Hey, what's your rush?" she asked.

"Shut up," he hissed.

"What?" She could barely hear him.

"I said shut up and listen," he breathed. "I'm trying to help you. When I say 'jump,' Holly, you jump," Rusty said in a voice barely above a whisper.

"Hey, what's all the chit chat?" Sidney Qownsill asked as he caught up to them.

"The girl was trying to bargain with me," Rusty replied. "No deal, honey," he said sternly to Holly.

They neared the end of the corridor. Ahead, the gangway entrance framed the dark night sky and phosphorous-flecked water but the gangway no longer bridged the yacht to the barge. Instead it dangled off the side of the yacht, one end uselessly under water.

"Hey!" said Sidney Qownsill. "What happened to the gangway?"

"The speedboat, it's gone," yelled Creaser. "Rusty?"

"Now, Holly," Rusty hollered. "JUMP!"

His arm threaded through her elbows he launched himself onto the yacht and pulled her in with him. She managed to get out one scream before she belly-flopped on top of Rusty.

"Get down," Rusty said as if she weren't already as down as she could get. "Take cover." He rolled over with her underneath him. No sooner had he spoken than she heard an ominous pop from behind her. Something whizzed past her ear and slammed into the deck sending fiberglass shards flying.

"Let's move," Rusty yelled. He ran at a crouch around the far side of the cabin and dropped down into the cockpit. Holly scrabbled as fast as she could behind him.

"Yes," he cried. "Over-confident bastards left the key in the ignition. Holly, away all lines."

"Huh?"

"Get us loose from the mooring buoy." Rusty cranked the engine.

"Rusty, I can't. My hands, they're still cuffed."

"Oh shit." Rusty spun her around and tugged on the cable tie binding her wrist.

"Ouch, you're hurting me."

"Damn this thing is tight."

"You're telling me. I've tried worming out of it but I can't. Don't you have scissors, a Swiss Army knife, something?"

"I did but I was told I damn well better not bring any weapons on that speedboat. Shit, there must be something I can cut with aboard this boat somewhere. Stay here, I'll go—" Another volley of bullets interrupted his speech and his plan and they both hit the deck. "Damn, we have got to find a way to get loose and get out of here before they fill us full of holes. Keep your head down, I'll go find some kind of blade."

Blade. Blade? Blade! The Xacto knife she had tucked away when she left the house this afternoon. "Rusty, come back," she yelled. "I've got a knife."

Rusty skidded to a stop and turned on his heel.

"In my pocket, my jeans pocket."

Rusty's patting her down was a frisking she didn't mind under the circumstances. He found the Xacto knife and with some effort sawed off her restraints. "OK, I'll get the engine started, you release that mooring line."

"The what?"

"The rope tied to the anchor buoy. The...that mushroom-looking-like thing in the water. At the bow."

At a crouch, Holly started for the back of the boat.

"The bow, Holly, the pointy end. And keep your head down."

She didn't have to be told twice. Ducking and dodging bullets, she ran back to the bow. In the water she saw what indeed looked like an oversized mushroom connected to the boat by a rope. She struggled to unwrap it from its cleat and finally got all the rope unlooped. "Go, Rusty, go," she yelled, then dove for cover as a bullet slammed into the deck where she stood.

The yacht took off with a lurch that knocked Holly on her butt. She crab-walked to the back of the boat where Rusty frantically turned the wheel and flipped the throttle, taking them on a jouncing, zig-zagging course toward the marina.

"Shit," he said.

"What?"

"I think they're launching lifeboats. Those have got outboards on them; they'll catch up with us."

"What's the problem? They can hardly come aboard if we're moving."

"No, but they sure have more firepower than we do." He turned to her and asked, "Can you swim?"

"What are you talking about?" Here they were speeding away from a roomful of people hell-bent on killing her and he was asking about her athletic ability?

"We're not that far from shore. A few hundred yards, maybe. I want to send this puppy out into the Gulf, without us. Let them chase this rabbit. Meanwhile, we'll swim for it. Go get a life jacket. Get two, now."

No problem there. She knew where they were stored, having watched the speedboat crew stow them away.

"I don't understand," Holly said as she pulled on the jacket. "Why are you helping me?"

"You really do think I'm one of them," he replied.

"But I saw you with the smugglers."

"I infiltrated the group so I could check out my theory. I figured there was some kind of smuggling going on, that the barge and the freighter and the speedboat were all connected. I just didn't know how they were doing it." Rusty struggled into a life jacket. "I saw you sneak aboard and figured I'd better stick around to make sure you got away okay. I saw Creaser nail you and when I heard them talking about how to get rid of you I knew I had to do something. Just didn't have much time to figure out what."

"You're doing all right so far." Over the sound of the water splashing against the hull, Holly heard the distant sound of another engine. "You were right. They're coming after us. Seriously, can they travel as fast as we can?"

"Maybe not but they can certainly shoot farther. All they need to do is hit a fuel tank or a line and we're dead in the water. Literally." Rusty turned the yacht's bow towards the open water. "This is it. I've got it on autopilot headed for, I don't know, Mexico or something. Everyone into the pool." He dived off the side. "C'mon, Holly, there's no time to lose."

"Ohmigod, Rusty, we can't. Jellyfish. The water's full of them."

"To hell with the jellyfish," he called back to her. "Watch out for the bullets."

So she clambered down the ladder, pitched herself into the water, and swam, faster than she could ever remember or would have even thought possible in cloying jeans and leather sandals heavy with seawater. She thought about shedding them but she couldn't stop swimming long enough to wriggle out of them. Besides, they protected her from the jellyfish. For some reason, the number of jellyfish seemed to decrease. Perhaps the gunfire scared them off or it may have been Rusty's and her fevered splashing.

Their frantic efforts finally took them out of shooting range. Holly thought that the engine sounds had become fainter. Relieved, she slowed her pace only to find the jellyfish were back. Her jeans protected her legs but the creatures' tentacles seemed to home in on her bare arms.

She caught up to Rusty. "The jellyfish are killing me," she said, trying not to whimper.

"You'll be okay. They're moon jellyfish. The stings are irritating but they won't be fatal. Can't say that about the crew if they catch us. Keep swimming, Holly. We've got to get to safety before they reach us."

So she kept swimming but reaching safety looked to be an impossible task. In the distance, the lights of the marina glittered like faraway stars. "A hundred yards" hadn't sounded like much but with every stroke the marina appeared to get further away instead of nearer and Holly was already tired. Though the water wasn't cold, the lack of rain in April and May had left it painfully salty. Her eyes and lips were raw. "I'm not going to make it, I've got to rest."

"We're almost there. Look, there's a channel marker up ahead," Rusty said. "From there it will be only a little bit farther. We'll rest there for a minute but then we've got to keep moving. We can't stay in one place."

They swam to the channel marker and clung to its slippery side.

"OK," Holly said between gulps of air. "So if you were just trying to get the goods on the smugglers then tell me what you were doing buying dope in the Walmart?"

"Dope...in the Walmart? Hey, were you following me?"

"I had to know what you were up to. I had to know if I could trust you. So if you weren't buying dope, what was in that little plastic package?"

"My fishing license. I had to renew it. Thought I might have to use my boat for this little bit of espionage. Didn't want to be caught out in a fishing boat with an expired license."

CHAPTER 31–THE TIES THAT BIND

"This is Ken Lagroso, KBON-TV, Bonafides's leader in first-on-the-scene reporting."

Lagroso had the youthful, barely-out-of-journalism-school look and all the zeal of the small-town TV personality, Holly thought.

"I'm here somewhere on the Isla del Tesoro with Holly Rivera Berry who claims to have at her own great personal peril uncovered the biggest scandal Bonafides has seen since it was revealed that Grandma's Homemade Tamales are made in a factory in Billings, Montana." Lagroso turned to Holly and aimed the mic toward her. "Ms. Berry, you're all wet."

"I am not. I have proof, you silly ass cub reporter."

Lagroso ran a finger across his throat and screamed "Cut, Cut" to the videographer. Lagroso took a deep breath and somewhat more calmly said, "We'll edit out that 'silly ass' part in post. Okay, let's start rolling again." To Holly he said, "No, I mean, you really are all wet." He turned back to face the videographer and said with great gravity, "Ms. Berry hasn't even had time to dry herself off having just minutes ago reached shore after swimming to safety, dodging bullets and jellyfish—"

"Don't forget sharks."

Lagroso said, "There were sharks in the water?"

"In the boat," Holly sputtered.

Feeling something like a landed jack fish, Holly lay on the sand and gasped. Though she needed air, each breath tortured her nose and throat, already raw from salt water. At last, though, her breathing slowed to normal and wasn't quite so painful. She turned slowly on her side and reached out. Her hand touched something warm. She cracked open a swollen, stinging eye. Rusty lay on his back beside her. The moon and stars didn't cast much light but from what she could see they were alone on the beach.

She listened for the sound of engines, gunfire, or people but all she heard was Rusty breathing in long slow gasps. Too much booze, and maybe too much life, he clearly wasn't a contender for any Ironman marathon. She didn't draw her hand back, though. Instead she rolled closer, let her arm fall across his chest, and touched him gently.

"Rusty, we're alone. We're safe. We're alive, thanks to you. I didn't know whom to trust and I'll admit I didn't trust you either."

Rusty grunted, turned his head away from her, and coughed. "I guess now you know you can. Both of us are on their must-destroy list. No time to play anymore. We got to go all the way." He turned to Holly, inched closer, put his arm around her, and pulled her into an embrace. "You can trust me. I'll take care of you. I want to keep on taking care of you."

She didn't resist or move away. Instead, she put her head down on his chest. Reaching up to place her hand on his cheek she said, "I don't think I have ever wanted to be taken care of. I like to think I've been doing a pretty good job of taking care of myself."

"You couldn't use a little help?" Rusty's voice was soft.

She stroked his face, then his chest. It felt so good to have his arms around her. She reached up and kissed his lips. This was kid stuff, making out on the beach but she felt turned on, tingly all over. It occurred to her that might just be irritation from jellyfish stings.

Too soon he said, "This is great, Holly, but we really should get off this beach."

"You're right. We need to get out of these wet clothes and I am dying of thirst. I could use some water. Or hell, a drink. How about you? Or would you rather have something hot?"

"Honey, I already have something hot and you won't believe how much I want us to get out of these clothes, wet or dry. But I'm thinking we're too easy a mark on this beach. Let's find a car and get to some shelter."

"Yours or mine?" she asked. "My car's parked at the Puerto Nuevo marina."

"Better leave it there. If Larry and his pals see it's still there, they may decide we're still lost at sea. If they see it's gone, they may figure we're okay and hiding out somewhere and come after us. My Lexus is in the lot at the county beach park. It's a lot further but..."

"You're right. It's probably worth the extra walk."

"About a mile. It's not too bad. I walked it to meet the speedboat guys at the Puerto Nuevo launch. Then I think we'd better go to my place. Your house is the first place they'd look for us."

He had a place? This she had to see. Somehow she couldn't picture him anywhere but the Marina Bar, Grill, and Bait Shop. Holly picked herself up and made futile attempts to brush off the damp sand. "Ready?"

"You don't know how ready," he replied.

Under other circumstances, the starlit stroll along the beach might have been romantic but romance was far from Holly's mind. The salt drying on her skin made her itch and irritated the jellyfish stings. Her sticky sandy jeans rubbed her thighs and her soggy leather sandals raised blisters. She tried walking barefoot but the sand chafed her feet. She was dehydrated and exhausted from the effort of swimming with a life jacket which, while it helped to keep her afloat, made stroking through the water harder. When they finally reached Rusty's vehicle she crawled into the passenger seat and collapsed.

Now, sunlight streamed through partly-closed vertical blinds. Holly came full alert with a start. Where was she? The redheaded man next to her in the strange bed was her first clue. Apparently they had made it to Rusty's apartment. She didn't even remember the drive there.

What she did remember was that upon reaching his apartment, despite having spent half the night ducking gunfire, swimming desperately through jellyfish-infested waters, and hiking along the beach to where Rusty had parked his Lexus they had summoned up enough reserve energy from who knew where to make inordinately satisfying love in the entryway, in the shower, in the bedroom...

"Rusty, wake up. We've got to do something quick before the cartel comes after us."

Rusty reached over and pulled Holly into his arms. "We will. I've got it all figured out but first things first." He stroked Holly's body.

"Oh, that does feel so good...but oh, you've got to stop." Holly pulled away and sat up. "I can't think straight when you do that. We don't have time." She untangled herself from thin faded sheets.

She picked up her T-shirt from the pile of cast-off clothing. It smelled of seawater and sweat and was stiff with salt and sand, as were her jeans and underwear. "No way I'm going to be able to get back into these," she said. "You wouldn't have a T-shirt or something I could borrow, would you?" She flung open Rusty's closet. Within easy reach, several hangers held plaid shirts and blue jeans. Shoved toward the back of the closet were a number of dark suits that despite being jammed together still held the neat drape of expensive tailoring. She pulled out one of the plaid shirts and threw it on. Maybe with shorts underneath? "We've got to do something. What do you mean you've got it all figured out?" She pulled out a dresser drawer and bent over to rummage through it.

"Hold on, Holly. Don't get your panties in a wad. Well, I see you don't actually have panties on at the moment, which I love. But getting back to our predicament, if you go put some coffee on, I'll get decent too and we can make some plans."

"I can do that." Holly pulled on a pair of cut-offs and plucked a belt from an organizer in the closet. Very Daisy Dukes, albeit three sizes too large. Well, it would have to do.

She left the bedroom and crossed the sparsely-furnished living room. Board-and-cinder-block shelves crammed with books reminded her of her college days. Newspapers and magazines covered the coffee table. A TV-and-wheeled-cart combo was classic Walmart. The only nod to luxury was the recliner which by the looks of the worn seat saw quite a bit of use.

"Your nest is pretty humble," she hollered towards the bedroom. Rusty muttered something in reply but before she could ask him to repeat himself, she heard the sound of an electric shaver and an unmistakably-Spanish song pouring out of the bathroom. It definitely sounded like a rude rendition of a Vikki Carr song from Clark's CD.

She stepped into the kitchenette and was startled out of her wits to be greeted with "Hey, little lady." Ohmigod, who had followed them here? She ducked back in the living room and tried to match the scratchy voice to a face. Oh, no. It couldn't be...

She peeked around the door frame. From his perch in a wire cage hung from a tall stand, Doc Roberts's parrot Forceps let out an avian wolf whistle.

What in the world? Holly edged around the bird cage into the kitchenette. A hulking stainless steel espresso machine rivaling anything she had ever seen in a San Francisco bistro dwarfed the small counter. Holly rummaged through Rusty's cabinets and found several chipped ceramic mugs but no coffee. She stood twisting her hair in momentary befuddlement.

"Coffee's in the fridge," Rusty called from the bedroom.

Holly pulled open the tiny refrigerator that looked like it had marched right out of a Salvation Army thrift store. A six pack of MGD beer bottles nestled against the back wall. Next to a can of Vienna sausages and a jar of Cheese Whiz she found a gold foil package of Organic Shade Grown Kona coffee beans. Whole beans. Now what am I supposed to do with these, Holly wondered. Pound them with a rock?

Suddenly she felt herself being pulled away from the ice box and pulled into an embrace. The smell of Old Spice filled her nose and she felt herself respond to Rusty's soft lips and tightening grip.

"Allow me," Rusty whispered in her ear. He poured the beans directly into one of the machine's hoppers, water into another, and hit a switch. The machine's furious whirring released the sharp, sweet smell of freshly-ground beans quickly followed by a strong, steamy aroma that promised a delicious cup of java. Rusty patted the espresso machine. "Could have gotten some serious change for this puppy at First Cash Pawn," he said, "but I just couldn't part with ole Joe here. We'd been through so much together. Sugar?"

"Yes, please," Holly replied, which Rusty took as an invitation to plant another searching kiss on her lips.

"Oh, you mean the granulated kind," he said when they stopped to breathe.

Holly didn't dare ask for cream. "Um, you want to tell me what Forceps is doing here?"

"Oh, yeah. About that. It's not like the Animal Shelter could take him. It didn't seem fair that just because his owner died Forceps would have to be put down. I thought maybe I could find him a new home on eBay or something. Meanwhile I'm trying to clean up his line of patter." Rusty poured two cups of coffee. "Let's sit on the patio and sip our morning brew. I'll fill you in on my plans." Rusty led her by the hand back to the bedroom.

"Wait a minute," Holly yelled stopping in her tracks. "You don't have a patio and you're taking me back to the bedroom. We can't mess around anymore. This is serious. Our lives are in danger."

Rusty laughed and continued pulling her. "I do have a patio, and it's right off the bedroom. Relax. I'll get you back in the sack later when we've got things under control." Rusty pulled a cord and opened the vertical blinds to present a view of a very small patio enclosed by a low fence. He slid open the patio door and the sound of sea gulls squawking filled the air. A snowy egret standing knee-deep in the water suggested that the apartment was located along the flats, maybe the Lagoon. A small round plastic table with two slightly Swiss-cheesed rattan chairs invited them to sit and enjoy their coffee. A brisk wind carried with it the faint aroma of salt water.

Holly planted her cup on the table and twisted a strand of hair. "Feels like a storm is brewing. Folks at the Walmart were stocking up on hurricane supplies. What's going on in the Gulf, do you know?"

"Last I heard, a tropical storm is tracking across the Gulf. Don't worry. It's early in the season for Bonafides to get a storm. It'll probably head for Louisiana." Rusty chuckled. "The weatherman likes to get everyone in a tizzy. What else has he got to report? 'Today it's going to be sunny and warm. Sunnier and warmer than yesterday, not as sunny and warm as tomorrow.'"

Rusty was right. While hurricane season began the first of June she didn't remember her parents ever doing anything about stocking emergencies supplies until closer to Fall. Holly released her hair and reached for the coffee mug. "So what's the plan?"

Rusty grinned. "I have an old friend in the FBI His name is Bill Selig. I got his son out of a jam once and he feels he owes me. Bill's the one that helped me when the drugs were planted in my Lexus. Bill made sure that I was suspended and not disbarred due to an ongoing investigation of the whole case and managed to get my Lexus out of impound. At least I still have that." Rusty paused, sighed.

"And a killer coffee machine."

"That too." Rusty grinned and raised his mug in a toast. "I've been in touch with Bill and he's aware of my suspicions. That's how I infiltrated the crew on the speedboat. Bill set me up for that. The FBI could not step in as the cartel has been too tightly secured. Now that we have the evidence and information we need all we have to do is get to Bill and he'll help us round everyone up."

"What evidence? All we've got is our word against theirs," Holly said.

Rusty grinned. "And a couple of Tejas Bonanza life jackets with some very unusual padding."

Holly had to laugh. "Damn. How do we get to this Bill guy?"

"His office is downtown," Rusty answered. "I called him before I showered. He's expecting us in thirty minutes."

So that was what the muttering had been about, she thought. "Ohmigod, I do have time to shower too, don't I?" She could use at least a rinsing after last night's intimacies.

Rusty laughed. "Honey, you do have time to shower if you want to stay here by yourself. But if you want to go with me, you'd better do whatever you need to as I'm out the door when I finish with this coffee."

"You are not going without me," Holly cried as she flew back into the bathroom to see if there wasn't something she could do about her hair at least.

Minutes later they were in the cab of Rusty's Lexus and heading for the freeway, Holly trying to pull off the Annie Hall look in Rusty's shirt and cut-offs with her hair threaded through the back of one of his ball caps. Country music filled the Lexus instead of the Spanish music that they had played in the PT Cruiser. They harmonized to *A Good Day to Run*. She never noticed the candy-apple red metal-flake Suburban that hung behind them and apparently neither did Rusty until it made its presence known with lights and sirens.

"Wha'?" Rusty said. "We're being pulled over? For what?"

"Pulled over? By that?" Holly said.

"It's a city police van all right," Rusty said, slowing and looking for a safe place to stop. "It's part of a fleet of new vehicles the department got a while back. They made a big deal out of having pulled off this super purchasing coup: vans with special paint jobs that were supposed to be extra resilient in the salt air here. At a smokin' price, too. Only when the vans were delivered they were all this screaming red finish. 'Course, you couldn't get anyone to admit he'd screwed up so they pretended like they planned it that way and kept them."

Holly twisted in her seat. "Oh, no, it's Creaser. Where does he get off? This is official oppression. This is abuse of power. We haven't done anything wrong."

"Except drive down the road with a load of dope," Rusty said.

"In the life jackets. But, but...oh, we are up the veritable creek," Holly moaned and buried her face in her hands.

Ten minutes later, Holly and Rusty were again on their way toward downtown Bonafides, manacled in the back of Creaser's red van.

"Holly, I'm so sorry I've gotten you into this mess," Rusty said under the road noise and Detective Creaser's contented whistling.

"We're not done for yet," Holly replied.

"You mean he hasn't pushed us overboard or run us off the road," Rusty grumbled.

"Guess we're too high profile for that, which means we'll get our day in court. We'll get to tell what we know. And speaking of running people off the road, did you see what I saw?"

"What?"

Holly grinned. "His front bumper. It's all dented. And there's a streak of pistachio green paint smeared on it. I've seen that shade of green before."

Rusty's frown gave way to a grin. "You know, I have, too. On Sam Hill's Jeep."

*****

"So, Holly, is this the latest fashion?" Tres asked as he stepped into Holly's city jail cell. "I've heard of The Boyfriend Jacket, but don't you think The Boyfriend Shirt and The Boyfriend Shorts are carrying the theme a little too far?"

"Very funny," Holly replied.

"Personally, I'd much rather see you in that outfit you had on the day I bought you that necklace at Dmitri's," said Larry Pomposas. He was not smiling.

Holly grimaced. "I didn't have time to change."

"Yes, that's a major disadvantage of getting busted," Larry said. "An arrest doesn't always find one at one's sartorial best. Does it, Burger?"

In the adjoining cell, Rusty simply snarled.

Larry held out a clipboard to which was clipped a small card and handed Holly a pen. "Sign here. Then maybe you can go home and take a shower." He waved his hand in front of his face. "Unless you want to take that shower at my place. In which case I'll put up the bail."

"Thank you but no," Holly replied. She affixed her name to the new bank signature card that Tres had already signed and handed the clipboard to her brother. "So, Tres, you finally get what you wanted. Your hands on Dad's money," she said.

Tres pouted. "A big chunk of it is going for your bail. And his." He scowled at Rusty. "You said I could keep the change."

"Yes, that was the agreement," Holly grumbled. She had placed her one allowed phone call to her brother. Tres, of course, didn't have the ready cash to put up bail for Holly, much less her accomplice. "I would just thank you to get me out of here before you spend it all."

"Don't worry, Sis," Tres said. "You can count on me."

Rusty and Holly groaned in unison.

CHAPTER 32–PUTTING ALL THE CARDS ON THE TABLE

Holly *twisted her hair and returned to Page Number One, Word Number One to read through all 15 legal-size pages of nine-point type one more time. The language of the contract was complicated but she didn't want to overlook anything that would bite her in the butt later just because she was so eager to sign.*

QT Press, publisher of so many "instant books" about people who had gained overnight fame, was as eager as she was to get her story between covers and on the shelves of bookstores everywhere. Across the desk from Holly, acquiring Editor Kurt Tonti twiddled his Montblanc pen. He straightened the pile of manuscripts and galleys at his left elbow. That done, Tonti leaned back in his chair, then leaned forward again. He gave her a strained smile.

"Ms. Berry—Holly—if you have any questions..."

Holly held up an index finger. "I'm fine, Mr. Tonti. Really. I just want to read this one more time." She found it difficult to keep track of all the parties-of-the-first part and heretofores and therewiths. "Um, wait a minute. Do I understand this correctly? I don't actually get to write my own book?"

Tonti sat upright in his high-backed chair. He straightened a tie that didn't need straightening then stretched his gray gabardined forearms across his walnut desk. Tonti clasped his smooth-skinned hands and composed his face into a look of forbearance. "Well, you see, Holly—Ms. Berry—for our

Instant Bestsellers, we have a team of writers. Expert writers, very good at what they do, and they do it quickly. Because of course with our IB books, time is of the essence."

"Oh, no no no," Holly replied, sitting just as straight. "You see, Mr. Tonti, I'm a writer. Writing is what I do and I too am very good at it. If anyone's going to tell how I busted a drug smuggling and gambling ring run by Bonafides's most trusted civil servants and business leaders, it's going to be me."

Editor Tonti came as close to pouting as possible in a professional setting and opened his mouth to respond but was interrupted by the ringing of his desk phone...

The incessant ringing of the bedside telephone rudely pried Holly from the dream. Too drained to speak, she lifted and replaced the phone's receiver without answering. Whoever it was could wait. Like a few years.

The ringing had a different effect on Rusty, however. He bolted upright, launched himself across the bed toward the sound, and with a loud thump landed face down on the Rivera residence's master bedroom floor.

Poor guy must have an equilibrium problem Holly decided as she watched him play tug of war with the bed sheets.

The phone rang again and this time Holly decided to end the torment by answering it. It was her boss. Even though he couldn't see her, she felt odd talking to him in the nude and shrugged into a robe.

"Rivera, there you are. I've been trying to reach you for two days," he said. He sounded chipper, always a bad sign. "Where have you been?"

"I've been, uh, detained," Holly replied.

"I see. I thought you'd like to know that the paper has finally gone to press. Of course, that means we're now working on the next edition. Will I be mailing this one to you as well or do you ever plan to come back?"

"No need to mail it, sir, I'll be back. I just have a few, uh, loose ends to tie up," she said, struggling to tie the robe's belt before Rusty could pull the garment off her shoulders.

"More of your father's legal matters?" her boss asked.

"Exactly," Holly replied. Not to mention her own arrest for drug possession.

"Get it wrapped up and get back here," her boss said, and hung up.

"He's a royal pain in the ass," Rusty said when Holly relayed the substance of the call. "He acts like he owns you."

Holly shrugged. "That's his style. Just my little cross to bear, I guess." She stopped and frowned. "Cross..."

"What's wrong?" Rusty asked.

"Cross...c'mere, Rusty, there's something I want to show you."

Rusty flopped back on the bed and groaned. "Holly, I love ya babe, but I couldn't possibly..."

"Not that," she said. "It's downstairs. Really, I need your help with something."

Rusty sighed, pulled on bright yellow Joe Boxer smiley-face shorts, and followed her.

In her father's study, Holly pointed to the pewter cross under the divan. "Take a good look at this and tell me what you think."

Rusty reached for the object, then pulled his hand back.

"What?" asked Holly.

"Let's leave it right there for the moment," Rusty said. "We don't want to obliterate any prints."

"Huh?"

"We need to get a paper bag."

Holly gave him a questioning look and he waggled his fingers toward the kitchen. As he followed her, he explained. "When I was lawyering, I did civil, not criminal cases. Still, I've seen enough examples of evidence to know bloodstains when I see 'em."

Holly sighed. "I guess I've known all along that's what those brown splotches are. That's what's been bothering me about this cross, why I kept putting off doing something about it. And, uh, don't you think it looks like..."

"The very thing that could have taken a fatal chunk out of your father's skull?"

Holly nodded.

"That's why I think we ought to preserve whatever trace evidence is left on it. Hair, blood, fingerprints. A paper bag is good for that." He frowned. "Have you touched this? Ever?"

Holly twisted a strand of hair and thought. Had she touched that cross? Ever? "I really don't think so. It was just always on the wall, there." She pointed to the empty nail in the wall behind the divan.

Holly got a bag from the pantry and they returned to the office to encase the pewter cross in the sack. "So now we think we know what killed my father. The only thing we don't know is who."

"Whoever did needed three things: means, motive, and opportunity," Rusty replied. "We've got the means..." he pointed to the bag holding the cross. "Who had a motive?"

Holly twisted a strand of hair while she thought. "I guess everyone in the cartel. They were all so eager to get the channel dredged and advance the Tejas Bonanza project and my father stood in the way. So that would be Sidney Qownsill, Noble Barnes, Larry Pomposas, Ted Creaser, Edison Pulitiz—"

"Don't forget Tres. He needed his inheritance and he needed it now."

Holly winced. "Let's not go there. I know Tres is a low-life but I can't believe he'd kill his own father."

"Stranger things have happened. Okay, for now, let's go on. What about opportunity? As far as you know, there weren't any signs of a break-in, right?"

Holly twisted her hair tighter while she tried to recall what had been in the police report. "That's right," she finally decided.

"Which means whoever did it was someone Clark knew well enough to invite into the house. Into this room."

"That's no help. That might have been any of them."

"Damn. You're right. If only there was a way to know who saw him last."

"We can't very well go around asking them. They'd hardly tell us," Holly said.

"Mmmm."

"But wait...wait, wait, wait." Holly quickly high-stepped over the piles of paper and boxes littering the floor and feverishly began clearing the top of her father's desk.

"What?" Rusty asked.

"Under all this stuff, my father's got a calendar pad for a desk blotter. Maybe if he was expecting someone...yes. Rusty, look: probably the last person to see my father alive."

Rusty stood over Holly's shoulder and studied the notation that Clark had made for the day he was killed.

"Shit, how could I have been so blind?" Holly asked. "It was in front of me all along."

"Great. Now we have a suspect. And if that suspect's prints on are the cross we've got a case. Only..." his pleased expression faded.

It was Holly's turn to ask, "What?"

"We can hardly go around fingerprinting everyone any more than we could check their alibi."

"Oh." Holly sighed heavily. Then she brightened. "Whoa. Unless I'm mistaken, I've got a sample of our suspect's prints. Back to the kitchen, Rusty. We need another paper sack."

The print sample safely bagged, Holly said, "Now what? Call the police?"

Rusty snorted. "Creaser's buddies? Surely you jest. No, I have a better idea. C'mon, we've got to—God, I can't believe I'm saying this—get dressed. We're going downtown. And this time, we're going where we want to go. Without a police escort."

*****

Holly squirmed in her chair and tried not to look over her shoulder every thirty seconds, afraid that any minute Sidney Qownsill would emerge from his Shorefront Suites office across the hall. The partition enclosing the cubicle she and Rusty occupied shielded them from view, but that was little comfort.

Across an avocado green steel desk, a thin, balding, pencil-necked man interlaced his fingers behind his head, stretched, then placed his elbows on the desk and leaned forward.

"Burger, that is some tale," said Bill Selig, special agent for the Federal Bureau of Investigation.

"It would be if I were the only one telling it," Rusty replied. "But Holly was there. She'll corroborate."

Holly nodded vigorously. Holly was surprised to learn that the department was housed in a swanky office building. Rusty explained that the tenants so liked the idea of having a law enforcement neighbor that the leasing company gave the feds a break on the rent. "Kind of like free coffee to the cops who stop by the donut shop on the graveyard shift."

"You know, you two very nearly blew a critical federal investigation," Selig said.

Holly and Rusty hung their heads.

"And lost the evidence to boot."

Rusty hung his head lower. Holly said, "At least it's safe in the police evidence locker."

"Sure it is, honey," Rusty and Bill Selig said in unison.

"Still, you may have just given us the very crowbar we need to bust the thing wide open." He tapped the paper sacks Rusty and Holly had laid on his desk, the one containing the blood-stained cross and another holding a soiled drinking glass.

"I can't believe that was still in the dishwasher," Rusty said.

"Sometimes it pays to get behind in the housework," Holly replied.

Selig said. "I'll get these to the lab, have them dusted and checked for trace evidence."

"Creaser's Suburban, too? You'll check that pistachio green paint, see if it matches the paint on Sam Hill's Jeep?"

"That, too. Meanwhile, I'll need something from you two."

"What's that?" Holly asked. "Oh, I know. Our fingerprints."

"Those are already on AFIS, courtesy of your recent booking."

Holly and Rusty looked down at their feet.

"Ms. Rivera, I could also use a sample of your father's DNA, for comparison purposes."

"Oh. But he's already been buried."

"Twice," Rusty said with a grin. Holly elbowed him in the ribs.

"That may not be a problem. Would there still be a hairbrush or comb of his in the home, Ma'am? One that hasn't been cleaned?"

"Yes, there probably is."

"That housekeeping thing again, eh?" Rusty said. Holly elbowed him a little harder.

"Simply bring me the entire brush, just as you find it, in a paper sack like this one. Hopefully, there'll be a hair follicle with the roots still attached. If there's a match, we'll have enough to allege that the cross was used to assault, if not actually kill, your father. That will provide probable cause to investigate further."

"And if the prints match?" Holly asked.

"We have a suspect," Bill Selig replied. He leaned back in his worn vinyl chair. "'Course, a homicide would be a city affair. Not really within our jurisdiction to investigate."

"Not that jurisdictional boundaries ever stopped you before," Rusty said.

Selig frowned. "Burger, you watch too much TV. Seriously, we're more interested in the hanky pank with that gambling ship and the drugs. Still, given your concern about the possible involvement of the local boys in blue, I can probably get my boss to okay our stepping in."

Holly and Rusty thanked the man then left the office, hurriedly to avoid being spotted by Sidney Qownsill.

CHAPTER 33–CALM BEFORE THE STORM

"Dammit, just when we were getting comfortable." Holly said.

"Let it ring. They'll get tired and go away eventually," Rusty replied, but she eased herself off his lap.

"No, whoever it is is persistent and I'm tired of hearing it ring. 'Sides, I've got a pretty good idea who it is and I might as well settle this right now."

He watched her march down the hall, one hand twisting a lock of hair, the other clutching a brandy snifter. With a sigh he slumped deeper into the cushions of the brocade couch in the Rivera family front room. Through the glass pane of the door he could see a figure slouched against the door jamb.

Holly cracked open the front door. "Tres, go away. I don't want to see you right now and I'm not sure I ever want to see you again."

"Aw, Sis."

"That stuff isn't working anymore, you—I can't even think of an appropriate slur. I could understand and try to help you with the gambling and the drugs but what you did to our father was unforgivable. You helped cover up his murder."

Tres pouted. "Holly, I believed them when they said it was an accident and it wouldn't do anyone any good to have an investigation."

221

"No, Tres, what you believed was that it would upset their plans and delay the sale of this place. You were concerned more about getting your hands on the money than your father's death. Cilla Esquivel might not have intended to murder our father..."

"She didn't," Tres said. "Priscilla and Dad got to fighting about selling the house and she got mad and lost her temper and grabbed the first thing she could think of."

The pewter cross that had hung on the wall of Clark's study. The stupid woman had left the murder weapon behind. Had she wondered that if she took it with her, eventually it would be missed? Or maybe she didn't think about it until much after the fact. Holly said that every time Priscilla Esquivel had gotten into the Rivera home the woman had made a beeline for Clark's study. Maybe she planned to wipe the blood and her prints from the cross but Holly never gave her the chance.

Those same fingerprints were found on the tumbler that Cilla had used when she and Holly had shared glasses of iced tea. That glass then sat in the dishwasher with Cilla's prints on it until the day Holly had fished it out and given it to FBI Special Agent Bill Selig.

"Oh, Holly, let him in, for Pete's sake," Rusty called. "You might as well. You're letting all the other hot air in."

Holly turned and regarded him with a scowl. Through the cracked-open door, Tres flashed a timid smile and waved. With a heavy sigh, Holly pulled the door open and let her brother enter. "The fact remains she did kill him," Holly said to her brother's back as she followed him into the front room. "Besides that, what are you doing here? Last I saw you they were hauling you off to jail charged with aiding and abetting, conspiracy or something. How did you get out?"

Tres strode into the front room looking none the worse for his brief incarceration. On the contrary, he looked relaxed and unperturbed in a pale yellow rayon shirt, white cuffed shorts, and leather huaraches without socks. He carried a manila envelope tucked under one arm. "Old Pulitiz bailed me out. Said he felt that's what Dad would have wanted."

"Yes, he's right, Father would have forgiven you once again. He never could face the fact that by excusing your weaknesses he was just enabling you. He rescued you again and again and look at the way you thanked him."

"Sis, I know I screwed up totally. I really am sorry about everything."

Holly didn't appear convinced.

"So, how do you intend to get out of this mess?" she asked. "There won't be any Clark, Larry, or certainly not me to pick you up, dust you off, and tell you that it's okay this time."

Rusty walked over to the liquor cabinet, finished refilling his and Holly's snifters, and turned to Tres. "Want one?"

"Thanks, I sure could use it. I hope you believe me, Sis, I'm not asking you to excuse me. I can't even excuse myself. Getting old Doc to fix the death certificate was wrong. Not telling you the truth and rushing the funeral was wrong. I've faced that and know I'm going to have to pay for what I did. And I will. The bank repo'd my car while I was in jail. Noble Barnes is going to see what he can do but meanwhile I'm cabbing it around town." Tres sank down into the overstuffed armchair and sipped the brandy. "The landlord slapped a padlock on the condo for delinquent payments so I can't even get to my stuff.

"Oh, I can lay it off to the gambling, the drugs, even the sex, but I confess. I knew when Larry approached me on the whole scheme that it was wrong. My lawyer says I might get off with a probated sentence if I testify against Larry and the cartel. Meanwhile I've got to make a show of good faith by going into rehab." He grinned. "Guess I could do without the drugs and gambling but I'm not sure I want any treatment for the sex addiction."

He sipped some more brandy. "Seriously, I do want to try to put things right. I could have used my substitute executor authority to pay everyone off but I didn't." He held out the envelope to Holly. "Here. You get your executrix job back, no interference from me. Just wrap up Dad's estate the way you see best." He gave Holly a beseeching smile. "Can you forgive me?"

Holly sighed. "Oh, I probably will when I get over being mad. Like in a decade or so."

With an uncharacteristically sober expression, Tres nodded. "By the way, what are you going to do about the Rivera land grant?"

Holly looked startled. She looked at Rusty. "In all the excitement, I haven't given that a moment's thought."

Rusty sat back, crossed one leg at the knee, and lifted his brandy snifter in what he hoped was a confident pose. "I have."

"You have?" Holly and Tres said.

Rusty leaned forward. "I think we...uh, you should pursue it, Holly. After all, your opposition's been sidelined. You could get with Gilberto at the Institute and keep running it down without worrying—"

"About being run down myself?" Holly said. She twisted a strand of hair. "I don't know," she said slowly. "There's so much I don't understand. All that legal mumbo jumbo. And so much of that material is in Spanish." She cast her eyes at the ceiling. "I would need help. From someone who could make sense of all those documents, in two languages. I wonder where I could find someone like that. Someone familiar with the law who wouldn't charge a fortune, who would, say, be willing to work on a contingency basis."

Rusty felt warm and giddy and he was pretty certain it wasn't just the brandy. "I might actually know someone like that," he said.

Tres chuckled. He set his brandy glass on the side table and stood. He kissed Holly on the cheek and flashed his trademark winning smile. "So, anyone want to save me the cab fare and give me a ride to Bonafides Recovery Center?"

CHAPTER 34—HAVE THE LAST LAUGH

Rusty sidled up next to Holly, the better to speak without being overheard. For the second time that week, they were in the back seat of a cop car riding behind a law enforcement officer. This time, however, they were not in shackles. They were invited guests.

"Have you ever gone on a ride-along?" Rusty asked.

"Of course I have," she replied. "What investigative reporter hasn't?"

He gave her an indulgent look but did not call to her attention that she wasn't a reporter at all, investigative or otherwise, except in her lofty aspirations.

"Yes, I've been on a ride-along," she said. "The Mission District Police Department held a Citizen's Police Academy. I learned a lot of stuff about search-and-seizure, narcotics investigations, TROs, and yes, I got to go on a ride-along. But nothing like this."

No, nothing like this. Rusty settled back into the rear seat of Special Agent Bill Selig's dark Crown Victoria with Selig at the wheel, accompanied by a second officer. Rusty took a sip of the coffee Selig had picked up for them all from a KwikE-Stop. Behind the Crown Vic additional officers drove a larger Suburban, both vehicles painted more discreetly than the city vehicles' candy-apple red. Rusty contentedly wriggled his shoulders inside the dark nylon field jacket. Big yellow letters over his heart spelled out "FBI." The jacket absolutely was not needed for warmth since early morning temperatures were already above 80, but no way was Rusty not going to wear it.

"Now you two remember the rules," Selig said.

"STAY IN THE CAR," Rusty and Holly replied in unison.

"Stay in the car, right," said Selig. "And out of sight. Doubtless you realize that no one's going to 'fess up to anything if you're present."

"No problem," Holly replied. "After what we've been through, we don't want to get anywhere near any of those people. But I know I'm going to sleep better tonight seeing them in your custody."

Rusty would have preferred to slap the cuffs on the perpetrators personally, especially Larry Pomposas, but he'd settle for second best.

First stop was Sidney Qownsill. The FBI brigade eased to a stop along the curb not quite in front of Qownsill's sprawling red-brick ranch-style house on a grassy tree-lined lot in one of Bonafides's oldest and ritziest neighborhoods. Had he waited a few hours, Selig could have simply marched across the hall from his workplace to Qownsill's Shorefront Suites office. Selig explained that he could accomplish this arrest with a lot less fanfare if he conducted it during the breakfast hour at Qownsill's home. Had it been his choice to make, Rusty would have opted for as much fanfare as could be mustered.

With a second officer at his side, Selig strode up the neatly-bordered concrete walk toward the paneled white front door of Qownsill's house, stooping to pick up the morning paper. Standing out of range of the door's frosted-glass light, Selig extended the rolled-up newspaper and used it to press the bell, then stood back and waited. In his plain dark blue Polo shirt and slacks, Selig looked like he might simply be calling on a buddy to pick him up for a morning round of golf. The loose knit shirt concealed a Kevlar vest. "Not that we're really expecting any trouble, you understand," Selig had said.

Holly and Rusty leaned forward and peered through the darkened glass of Selig's vehicle, breaths held. After what seemed like an eternity, the door opened halfway. Selig held out the rolled newspaper. Over Holly's shoulder, Rusty saw Qownsill framed in the doorway. Bare chested and clad in boxer shorts and his signature cap, the man stood there for a moment. He reached for the newspaper then pulled his hand back. Rusty couldn't hear what Qownsill said but Qownsill's frown spoke loudly. He threw up his hands and backed into the recesses of the house. Selig shrugged his shoulders, signaled to his officer, and followed Qownsill inside.

"Damn," Holly said. "I can't see what's going on."

"Me neither," said Rusty. He reached for the door handle only to find that the back seat of Selig's vehicle wasn't equipped with any. He leaned forward, planning to climb over the front seat's backrest.

"Rusty," Holly said in a warning tone of voice. "Bill said we are to stay in the vehicle."

"I know. I just wanted to, you know, see if..."

"Behave," Holly said. "Sit and enjoy your coffee. I don't think Bill is expecting a gunfight and fisticuffs. I doubt there's going to be much to see."

"Hmmph." Rusty slouched into his seat. "You'd think there'd at least be donuts with this coffee." He had just about gotten to the bottom of the cup when the front door opened. "Ho ho ho, what did you say about not being much to see? You are wrong about that. Look."

Selig and his fellow agent emerged each gripping the arm of a prisoner. Qownsill now wore bedroom scuffs and a short light dressing gown in addition to his cap.

"Ohmigod," Holly breathed as the second detainee came into view. Priscilla Esquivel's beehive of cotton candy hair was a deflated mat. A bright pink satin robe covered her to the tops of her matching high-heeled feathered mules. "Do you think Bill knew this was going to be a two-for-one?"

"I don't know, but I can't say I'm surprised."

The FBI men escorted their prisoners to the waiting Suburban.

Selig slid into position behind the wheel of his vehicle and twisted around to face his passengers. "Normally, I try not to take people into custody in their underwear," he said, "but these two put up such a fuss, so..." He chuckled.

"Something funny?" Rusty said.

Selig started up his vehicle and pulled away from the curb. "We're about to find out." He steered toward the bay and turned onto Shore Drive. Rusty enjoyed the driving tour past Bonafides's premier addresses. Each mansion was bigger than the last, with deep hundred-foot setbacks and curving driveways. Even in the heat of summer, the grass lawns were as green as the finest golf courses. What the owners paid to water them every month would keep him in beer for a year.

Selig slowed as they approached a white-columned two story manor surrounded by a tall black wrought iron fence. "There'll be no sneaking up to the front door of this place," Holly whispered. "How's he even going to get through the gate?"

"Police and first responders usually have an emergency access code," Rusty said and sure enough, Selig simply pulled up to the call box at the gate and punched in some numbers. The gate swung open. Selig pulled up the long wide driveway and parked in the middle, centered in front of the doors to the two-car garage. He and his fellow officer proceeded up the curved concrete walk toward the front door.

As Selig approached the house, one of the garage doors opened. A black Mercedes sedan emerged from the garage and came to a stop, its forward progress impeded by Selig's awkwardly-parked Crown Vic. Rusty saw Noble Barnes spring from the car. Wearing only trousers, he raced barefoot across the grass lawn, Selig's officer in hot pursuit. It wasn't much of a race. The younger man easily caught up to the old banker and led him toward the Suburban.

Bill Selig was nowhere to be seen.

"Rusty, look," Holly cried and pointed toward the house.

At the end of the driveway, the second garage door opened. A silvery BMW convertible emerged, passed the Mercedes, and started down the driveway headed for the street. Rusty thought he recognized Candy Shultklopfen behind the wheel. The convertible's hood was up but it looked like she was as bare-chested as Noble Barnes, perhaps even more so.

"It's Senator Candy," Holly said, "and she's getting away."

"No she's not," Rusty said. He vaulted over the seat back and got behind the wheel. Yes, Selig had left the key in the ignition. Rusty started the car and threw it into reverse. He brought the Crown Vic to a stop parallel with the gate.

"Rusty, we'll get T-boned," Holly yelled and scooted as far left as she could in the back seat.

Behind the wheel of the convertible Candy left the driveway, drove across the grass, and followed by Bill Selig on foot serpentined around the yard but there was no way to get around the Crown Vic blocking access to the street.

Candy brought her car to a stop and pounded on the steering wheel. Pulling his Polo shirt over his head, Selig raced to Candy's vehicle. Rusty could hear him telling the senator that she was under arrest. Through the Crown Vic's rear window he could see her gesticulating and hollering but her reply was muffled by her closed doors and windows. At last she lowered the driver's side window and Bill handed her his shirt. Rusty saw her put it on and only then did she emerge from her vehicle. Bill's shirt covered her top, but not quite her red-thonged bottom. Bill's fellow agent held out an FBI field jacket. With an angry scowl, she snatched it from him and tied it around her waist. As soon as she was covered, the agent cuffed her and delivered her to the Suburban.

Bill returned to the Crown Vic and opened the driver's side door. "Burger. Step out."

Willing the blood not to rise to his cheeks, Rusty exited the car.

Selig waggled his fingers. "I need your jacket."

Selig's Kevlar vest over a sleeveless white T-shirt made for a less-than-professional appearance. "Of course you do." Rusty slipped it off and handed it over. Selig thrust his bare arms through the sleeves and closed the jacket over his bulletproof vest.

Rusty reached for the handle to the rear passenger door.

"Hold on, there, fella," said Selig. "Just what did you think you were doing?"

"Hey, you told us to stay in the car. We stayed in the car. I just didn't want her to get away."

"You wanted her to total my car instead? Crush Ms. Berry in the process?"

"I wouldn't have let that happen. I would have gotten out of the way." Rusty cocked his head to one side. "Meanwhile, it worked, didn't it?"

"Yeah, well so much for your heroics, you're done for the day." Selig harrumphed and yanked open the door to the rear seat. "Get in the car. I'm taking you both back."

"Aww, Bill, I promise I'll behave," Rusty said.

"Yeah, Rusty, no more heroics," Holly said. "Scared me half to death." She sighed, then chuckled. "Noble Barnes and Senator Candy. Talk about all these cartel members being in bed together. Who would have thought that they were literally?"

"Crime makes for strange bedfellows," Selig said, and put the car in gear.

"'Misery acquaints a man with strange bedfellows,'" Rusty said. "That's Shakespeare."

"'Ease and honor are seldom bedfellows,'" said Selig. "That's Proverbs."

"'Politics makes strange bedfellows'." That's Mark Twain. I think," said Holly. "No, wait, Charles Dudley Warner."

"'Politics doesn't make strange bedfellows—marriage does,'" Rusty replied. "That's Groucho Marx."

Selig chuckled. "Wonder who we're going to find paired up next?"

"Who's left?" Holly counted off on her fingers. "Detective Creaser for pushing Doc Roberts overboard and forcing Sam Hill off the road."

"Edison Pulitiz for—"

"Violating basic journalistic tenets," Holly muttered.

"I was going to say 'conspiracy.' Accessory after the fact, at least," said Rusty. "Oh, you don't think we'll find Creaser and Pulitiz together? Ho ho ho," he chortled.

"No, I don't. Nor do I think we'll find Pulitiz at his office." Selig radioed the officers in the Suburban and instructed them to take the detainees to HQ and start processing them. "Then have Team Two meet me at Martita's."

Holly looked a question at Rusty. "Martita's? That's a—"

"Mexican restaurant, right," said Rusty. "And it's just about shift change for the Bonafides PD. They all go to Martita's. So where else would a newspaper man go to get all the juicy stories? Gee, I would think as an investigative journalist, you would know that."

"Don't be a smart ass," Holly said. "Everyone knows you get all the best stories at the Shamrock during happy hour."

"That too," said Selig, "but I don't want to wait that long. Word's going to get out about what's going down and our quarry will scatter like doves during hunting season. With any luck we'll find Pulitiz *and* Creaser. Not *in flagrante*, I hope. That would just be ugly."

If the bright primary-colored murals of a Mexican street scene on the restaurant's stucco façade didn't broadcast "Tex-Mex," the Spanish tiled shed roof over the Martita's entrance and paneled door with wrought iron hardware nailed it. The restaurant was an easy walk from both the Bonafides police station and the offices of the *Daily News*. Nevertheless, Selig and Team Two had to park their vehicles halfway down the street in a lot behind a church as all the street parking was taken up by city police cars—and one Cadillac.

Selig turned off the engine. With his hand on the ignition key, he turned and said, "Dare I leave this?"

Rusty smiled. "I promise, Bill, we'll—"

"Stay in the car," Holly finished.

"And I want to find this car here, right here, in this spot, when I get back." Selig nodded to his officer and they set out on foot for Martita's.

Rusty sank back into his seat. A few minutes passed in silence. He stared at the restaurant's entrance until his eyes hurt. Admitting defeat, he said, "Wanna make out?"

"Rusty!"

"Haven't you always wanted to do it in a police car?"

Holly gave him a long-suffering look. "I can't say that's been high on my list."

"Well, it is mine," he replied, inching a little closer. "At least, it is now."

"With Team Two watching?"

He looked over at the black Suburban. It was hard to see the agents through the dark glass but they probably were keeping at least one eye on Selig's Crown Vic.

"Hmmph," he said and resumed his bored slouch.

Five more hour-long itchy minutes went by.

"I'm hungry, Holly. Are you hungry? Don't you think a couple of *taquitos* would go real good right about now?

"Rusty..."

"Or some chips and salsa?"

"Rusty, stop. You said you'd behave. Now behave."

"Shit, Holly, don't you want to see old Parvo get...hey, what's going on?"

The doors to the other Suburban slammed open. Officers poured out and ran toward Martita's.

Headed for the front seat, Rusty had gotten halfway over the seatback when Holly grabbed his belt and pulled him back. "Where do you think you're going?"

"Holly," Rusty pleaded.

"What part of 'stay in the car' don't you get? What do I have to do to get you to stay put? I know." She threw her arms around him and smashed her lips against his. It took only nanoseconds for the kiss to soften into something seriously irresistible and Rusty was torn between the prospect of having sex in the back of an official vehicle and keeping one eye on the action at Martita's.

Martita's won because he and Holly had no sooner gotten some buttons undone than the restaurant's front door opened. An officer from the Suburban emerged, his arm linked around the elbow of a handcuffed man in a city police uniform. A second FBI officer appeared with another police officer in custody. Selig's officer led a plainclothesman and Selig brought up the rear with Edison Pulitiz in tow. Martita herself, a short, broad woman in a black sheath dress accented with lots of gold jewelry, stood in her restaurant's entrance, flapping her arms and slapping her forehead. Behind her crowded the restaurant's wait staff in chinos and logo'd Polo shirts, cooks in long white stained aprons, and customers in casual clothes and business attire.

Selig and his officers loaded their prisoners into the Suburban. The Team Two officers closed the doors and backed the vehicle out of the parking lot. Selig and his fellow officer returned to the Crown Vic. Selig took his seat behind the wheel, chuckling.

"OK, Selig, give. What the hell was that about?" Rusty asked.

Selig and his officer could barely control their laughter. "We went in, spotted Pulitiz at a round table in the middle of the dining room with a bunch of Bonafides's finest. We go up to the table, I say 'I'm Special Agent Bill Selig with the Federal Bureau of Investigation and I have a warrant for the arrest of—'" Selig sputtered into laughter which got his fellow officer cracking up too.

"What? What?" Rusty and Holly asked in unison.

Selig got himself under control. "Half the table stood up and surrendered." Laughing, Selig and his officer high-fived each other. Selig pulled a handkerchief from his pocket, wiped his eyes, and took a deep breath. "What could we do? We're taking them in too."

Rusty let Selig catch his breath and asked, "And Pulitiz?"

"Either that man has got a set or he is completely self-deluded. He just sat there, all innocent-like. He couldn't believe we really had a warrant for him. Insisted on reading it before he'd agree to get out of the chair." Selig shook his head. "Damn if I didn't think he was gonna edit it."

"Detective Creaser? Was he there?" Holly asked.

"No, dammit. That would have been convenient. We're in touch with BPD dispatch and they know where he should be but he doesn't seem to be there. So we'll be on the lookout for him." Selig took another deep breath. "And one more," said Selig. "Larry Pomposas." His voice was coldly toneless.

"Larry Pomposas," Rusty echoed, trying not to growl. "No telling who we're going to find him with." Holly slid narrowed eyes at him and grimaced.

"And you can't come along for this one, Burger. There can't be even the merest hint of entrapment or impropriety. This has got to go down squeaky clean."

This time Rusty didn't hesitate to growl.

"Nor you, Ms. Berry. I'm afraid you had better sit this one out too."

Rusty stole a glance at Holly. She nodded and her apprehensive expression said she really didn't want to witness that particular arrest. Maybe she was embarrassed about her fling with Larry, Rusty thought. More likely though, she was afraid that Tres would be arrested as well.

Back at Shorefront Suites, Selig pulled into the street-level parking garage and stopped next to Rusty's Lexus. "I suggest the two of you go home and keep a low profile until we get the others under wraps."

"You'll keep us posted?" Rusty said.

Selig nodded.

Rusty and Holly got into Rusty's Lexus. "Home, James?" Holly said.

"Mmmm, not quite yet," Rusty replied. "How about a little celebration lunch?"

"Rusty, Selig said we should—"

"I know what he said, and we will. But first I think we deserve a little treat, don't you?"

"So long as it's not pork rinds and beer at the Marina Bar."

Rusty chuckled. "No. I had something a little more upscale in mind. What would you say to Tico's? It's on the way to the Isla."

"I'd say I haven't been there in ages. You think it's too warm to sit out on the deck? For some reason it feels unusually hot to me."

"Well, at least we've got a healthy breeze. If it's too warm for you, we'll sit inside. We're early enough ahead of the lunch crowd. We can probably get a waterside table." While there seemed to be an unusual amount of people on the road for a weekday morning the traffic was heavier going downtown. This time on a Friday, Rusty would have expected folks to be on their way to The Island for a weekend of fishing or beach-going. Well, not a problem. Less competition for the best table at Tico's. "I could go for some fried grouper or some Gulf shrimp."

"Oh, stop. Now I'm really hungry."

"Just be patient, we'll be there in two shakes," he said although he was taking his time, enjoying the drive around Bonafides Bay.

Not far from where poor Sam Hill had been driven off the road and into the water, Rusty planned to turn off the scenic route and aim for the freeway that would take them across town to the Treasure Island Bridge and the causeway leading to The Island. Ready to change lanes, he checked his rearview mirror.

And saw that they had company.

CHAPTER 35—WHEN YOU'RE HOT, YOU'RE HOT

"Rusty, we don't have to get there that fast," Holly said. "Slow down, you'll get a speeding ticket."

"I'm just trying to get away from this guy."

"A tailgater? You know they say the best way to deal with a tailgater is to decrease your speed. That way if heaven forbid a tailgater does hit you at least you don't rear-end the car ahead."

"Normally that would be good advice but not with this guy," Rusty said.

"What guy?" Holly twisted in her seat to look out the rear window. "Oh. Oh, no."

"Oh, yeah," Rusty said. He took his eyes from the road and checked the rearview mirror again. The driver of the red metal-flake van was talking into a cell phone. And he didn't look happy.

"Rusty, he's flashing his lights. He wants us to pull over. I told you to slow down."

"I'm not over the speed limit. I don't have an expired inspection or registration or broken taillight and there's no warrants out for me. Maybe for him, but not for me. I haven't done anything and I'm not stopping for that asshole." He'd bet anything that cell phone call had just informed Detective Creaser of his confederates' arrests.

Creaser moved into the left lane and came up alongside Rusty. He pointed with his pistol and gestured "pull over, pull over."

"Not a chance," Rusty said through clenched teeth. He hadn't been speeding before but he was now. He wanted to get to the Treasure Island Bridge and onto the causeway leading to The Island as quickly as possible. He wasn't sure why. Maybe because the Isla was his stomping grounds.

And then he found out why he had better get off the freeway. Creaser dropped back in his lane and tapped Rusty's left rear bumper. The momentum threatened to send Rusty's car into a skid.

Rusty's pulse zoomed with panic until with sudden clarity he recalled some casual remarks about evasive driving made by his street-stock-racing former client "Full Throttle" Ipswitch.

Rusty gently steered into the skid and straightened his vehicle, positioning it directly ahead of Creaser's van. The challenge now would be to maintain that position. For several miles they played a nerve-wracking game of chicken, Creaser trying to get alongside Rusty's vehicle and Rusty aiming to stay directly in front of Creaser.

"Because," Full Throttle had said, "the other guy isn't trying to push you. He's trying to clip you, send you into a skid, make you lose control of the vehicle."

Rusty flicked his eyes back and forth between the road and the mirror, taking care not to rear end anyone in front of him and trying to read Creaser's expression, anticipate his moves.

"You're headed for the Treasure Island Bridge," Holly said. "You don't think he'll try to push us off into the water, do you?"

The desperation in her voice made Rusty take his eyes off the reflection in the rearview mirror and give Holly a reassuring smile. "He could try, but the guard rails will protect us."

"You're sure?"

"I'm sure," Rusty said with more conviction than he felt. Over the years he'd certainly seen plenty of damaged guardrails on the bridge, dented by people going too fast or driving drunk. Still he couldn't remember ever hearing of a car breaking through and tumbling into the water. What appeared to be a more likely strategy would be Detective Creaser forcing them to crash into the guard rail or shove them into oncoming traffic in the opposite lane. If Creaser got Rusty into a skid that he couldn't control, the inches-high concrete median barrier wouldn't do much to keep the Lexus on the right side of the road. Rusty felt his scalp and skin tingle at the thought of the innocent drivers who would be injured or killed by an accident that Creaser caused.

They successfully negotiated the bridge and started the four-mile trip across the two-lane undivided causeway over the Intracoastal. The heavy traffic kept Creaser from positioning himself in the opposite lane of the undivided two-lane road to give Rusty's bumper another tap.

Rusty pressed the accelerator. If he could just get them off the causeway and onto the salty flats along the Intracoastal... There were people about: fishing piers, bait stands, and Tico's, the waterfront restaurant that had been their destination. He could go off-road in the SUV if need be.

But as Rusty increased his speed, so did Detective Creaser. He hunched over his steering wheel as if leaning forward would make his van go faster. His red van tapped Rusty's rear bumper. Startled, Rusty felt his vehicle swerve. He struggled to get control and center the car in its lane.

"Rusty, what should I do?" Holly cried. "Call 911?"

"And report what? That we're being chased by a cop? A cop that's probably got some kind of phony warrant out for us?"

"He's a crooked cop."

"They don't know that. Not yet. Bill Selig..."

Selig. He could call Selig. If the man wasn't busy cuffing Pomposas at the moment..."Holly, my cell phone. In my shirt pocket. Call Selig."

Holly dug out the phone and fiddled with the controls and the contact list. "Got him. Dialing. I'll put it on speaker...Oh," she cried as Creaser's van shoved Rusty's car. The cell phone flew out of Holly's hands. "It's gone under the seat. I'll get it." She reached for the seatbelt release.

"No, Holly, keep that belt on." He didn't want Creaser rear-ending them and sending Holly through the windshield. "We're almost to the end of the causeway."

Rusty glanced at the mirror. Creaser's red van was so close that the man's angry face filled the rear view but behind Creaser, red and blue lights flashed. Oh shit, Rusty thought. That was what Creaser was doing on his cell phone. He was calling for backup.

Rusty gripped the steering wheel tightly and struggled to keep the vehicle centered in the lane despite Creaser's increasingly aggressive thrusts. A break in the oncoming traffic let the second official vehicle travel alongside Creaser for just a second before dropping back. Rusty had never been so glad in his life to see flashing lights in his rearview mirror. The bubble gum light was atop a dark Crown Victoria. The cavalry had arrived!

"Rusty, get off the causeway," came Bill Selig's disembodied voice from under Holly's seat. "I'll take care of Creaser."

"Hold on, Holly," Rusty said. "We'll be making a somewhat premature exit. It's going to be bumpy."

The second that Rusty's vehicle cleared the outside guardrail he turned right. Instead of taking the exit road, he steered the vehicle down the grassy escarpment to the frontage road. Not missing a beat, Creaser was hot on his tail. Damn, that van did have a good suspension, Rusty thought. Despite the goofy paint job the city had gotten its money's worth.

Selig's Crown Vic didn't take Rusty and Creaser's shortcut to the frontage road, but it did take the exit ramp at top speed and quickly fell into place right behind Creaser.

"I saw Creaser follow you after you left the parking garage," came Selig's voice over the cell phone. "Figured I'd better keep an eye on him."

Rusty left the frontage road and took his vehicle onto the strand edging the Intracoastal, skirting soft marshy patches.

"Burger, what are you doing? Get to Tico's. I'll take care of Creaser." Selig yelled.

Rusty had been thinking he would do just that, get himself and Holly to Tico's and run inside for help. But what if crazy

Creaser opened fire? The man had already killed two people. Who knew what lengths he would go to? Shoot out the Lexus's tires? Rusty figured that he and Holly were probably safest as a moving target shielded by his vehicle's bulk. He checked his rear view. Creaser kept up with him and Selig was right behind Creaser. Rusty aimed for the Intracoastal Waterway.

"Rusty, what are you doing?" Holly yelled. "This is not an amphibious vehicle. Oh damn, I'm going swimming again."

"Burger," Selig bellowed, "no heroics," but Rusty was too busy executing his plan to respond. Creaser was inches from his bumper. Rusty took his Lexus to the very shoreline. His tires kissed the water and at the last possible second, he shifted into low gear, turned wide to the right, and keeping his wheels pointing straight, set off across the sand. As soon as he had purchase, he turned the vehicle and circled back toward Creaser. Two could play at Creaser's game. Doing donuts in the sand was the stuff of mischievous drunken teenaged beach bums but Rusty closed his circle by clipping Creaser's right rear bumper.

Creaser's speed sent him into an uncontrolled skid that propelled the van to the water's edge. Rusty heard the van's brakes squeal. Big mistake, Rusty thought.

Soft damp sand mounded up against the van's front tires, grounding the vehicle and throwing Creaser forward. The airbag deployed and mushroomed out like a marshmallow over a campfire.

Bill Selig swerved to his left to avoid a collision. The Crown Vic fishtailed on the sand and slowed. Selig turned the car around and returned to where Creaser's van had run aground. Gun at the ready, Selig approached the van.

Rusty saw Selig holster his weapon and went to join him. Already on his cell phone, Selig called for backup and emergency medical service.

"Tow truck, too." Rusty grinned and rocked on his heels.

"Burger, what did I tell you about heroics?"

CHAPTER 36–EVERY CLOUD HAS A SILVER LINING

"...from afar wailing, whistling wind. As it made its way across the prairie, the coming storm bent saplings and flattened the grasses.

Uncle Henry bolted up. 'There's a cyclone coming, Em,' he called to his wife. 'You and Dorothy get to shelter. I'll go look after the stock.' Then he ran out to the sheds.

Aunty Em dropped her work, dashed after him, and stopped when she reached the door. One glance told her that her husband was right. Danger raced toward them. The storm could be upon them at any moment. 'Quick, Dorothy!' she screamed. 'Run for the cellar!'"

"We're off to see the Wizard," Holly thought. She came half awake wondering why in the world she was dreaming of the opening lines of Frank Baum's *The Wonderful Wizard of Oz*. A bright flash of lightning and a rumble of thunder jerked her to full consciousness. Almost as loud as the thunder was rain pelting so hard that it sounded like someone had turned a fire hose on the house.

She shook Rusty, asleep beside her in the Rivera master bedroom. "Storm," she said. "We're having a bad storm. You don't suppose...?" She slipped from the bed. What if the storm that had been brewing in the Gulf for days wasn't headed for Louisiana? I knew I should've checked the weather forecast, she thought.

She shook Rusty again and watched him pull away with a moan, rolling over and over and off the bed.

"Wh-wha happened?" he stammered scrambling to his feet and flopping back onto the bed.

"Good, at least you're awake," Holly answered. "Help me find some candles."

Rusty reached over and pulled her into his arms. "Candles? We don't need candles. It's daylight. Although it does look a little overcast."

"Overcast? Ya think? We just got hit by one serious front. Help me find some candles downstairs in case we lose electricity."

"Cool. Making love in a storm sounds exciting to me."

"Rusty, I'm serious." Holly pulled away. "We should turn on the TV and find out how bad this is."

"I just want to turn you on instead," he said but she leaped up and away. "Okay, I get the message. It's a candlelight and TV moment." He followed her downstairs and into the living room. "How about a drink at least?"

"Mimosas? There's some champagne left over from yesterday. And orange juice in the fridge. Help yourself." Holly grabbed the remote and turned on the television. It was late enough in the morning that *Live* should be on but it wasn't. Instead, in a pre-recorded announcement the mayor of Bonafides spoke animatedly while graphics and text crawls described the different routes citizens could take in the mandatory evacuation that was declared hours ago.

Holly stared at the news bulletin. "Ohmigod, we have to evacuate."

Rusty handed her a mimosa-filled goblet. "Forget that. If the evacuation has already started, the freeway will be a parking lot. The rain's already coming in. Do you want to be stuck out on the road when the wind gets serious?"

Holly shook her head.

"Me neither. I'd rather shelter in place. Let's batten down and tough it out. It's too late to leave the island."

"Oh, I don't know..." She twisted a strand of hair.

"Don't worry, we'll be fine. Hasn't this old house weathered its share of storms over the years?"

It had, that was true. The Rivera house had been built after Celia, one of the most destructive storms to hit the coast, so it hadn't had the ultimate test but it had withstood several Category 3 and higher storms since then.

"It'll be an adventure." Rusty sipped his drink. "Besides, not even a hurricane's going to rain on my parade. I'm still grinning over the round-up yesterday. Bill Selig and his boys did a bang-up job corralling the cartel."

Holly sank into the couch. "That cartel included my brother."

Rusty sat down next to Holly and pulled her into his arms. "I know all this is hard for you. Maybe, just maybe, if Tres has hit bottom, from this point it will be onward and upward all the way. Sometimes a disaster can wake you up to what's really important." He stroked her hair.

Holly wondered if he was talking about his own misfortune. Or maybe he was talking about hers. Her ruminations were interrupted by a sharp ringing. Rusty lifted the receiver of the candlestick phone but the ringing continued.

"My cell," Holly said.

"Oh, no, you don't," Rusty said, and snatched it from her hand.

"Hello," he said. "No, she can't come to the phone and she won't be coming back to work."

Holly felt her heart stop. He was talking to her boss. "Rusty, give me that."

"Not tomorrow, not ever. Goodbye." Rusty clicked the "END" button with finality.

"What have you done?" Holly asked.

"You just quit," Rusty replied.

"I gathered that. Okay, smart guy, now what am I going to do for a job?"

"Start your own damn paper. Here, in Bonafides. It seems to be there's a bit of a journalistic vacuum at the moment."

"You mean because of Pulitiz? There was a journalistic vacuum even before he got arrested. He wouldn't know journalistic integrity if it jumped up and bit him in the butt."

"My point exactly. That paper hasn't been fit to wrap fish. So start your own."

"With what?"

"Your inheritance from Clark. You do have some left, don't you? You didn't spend it all on getting people out of jail."

"Well..."

"And it would mean you could stay here," Rusty said quietly. "To, uh, keep an eye on Tres. And, uh, follow up on the land grant stuff. You do want to do that, don't you?"

Holly was afraid to look Rusty in his beseeching eyes. "I'll have to think about it." Not that she had thought about much else. Run her own newspaper. A longtime dream come true. And research the Rivera land grant. That was a new dream but it was just as tantalizing. And Rusty. Two weeks ago she didn't even know him. Now, she couldn't envision going through a day without a least one warm hug of his strong arms. She imagined that she could get through almost anything if she had the support of his broad shoulders.

A bolt of lightning flashed, followed by a rumble of thunder. Holly peered through the sliding glass door to the back deck at the water of The Gap. If she hadn't been otherwise occupied she might have noticed yesterday how the water level in The Gap dropped dramatically. The brewing storm had pulled the water of the Gulf away from the shore and lowered the tide in the Intracoastal. Storm surge would bring the water back, and with a vengeance.

Depending on the weather and the tides the water's color usually varied from light green to gray to turquoise to sage. The storm had turned it the color of slate with a surface that seemed icy. Little tufts of wind scurried across the water in no particular pattern. If she didn't know that the temperature was in the eighties, she would have assumed it was cold outside. Rusty said he could feel a chill all the way to the bone.

"So, um, would you happen to know if Clark had storm windows for this place?"

"Sure," Holly replied. "There's roll-down shutters for all the windows and in the garage are plywood sheets for the front door."

"Maybe we should get those storm windows in place."

"Sounds like a good idea. I think we have enough food. There's canned stuff in the pantry."

"SPAM?" Rusty asked, a hopeful expression on his face.

Holly laughed in spite of herself. "You and your gourmet sensibilities. No, I don't think there's SPAM but there's probably tuna, chili. The range runs on propane so I can at least make coffee, heat up soup. I'll get some jugs filled with water. Make more ice. You fill the bathtub." They could use the bathtub water to flush the toilets if need be. "I'll get the shutters rolled down and then I'll help with the plywood. As you said, this old place has been through more than one squall so we should be safe."

Squall. Who was she kidding? A hurricane was way more than a "squall." The Galveston hurricane of 1900 had been the worst recorded natural disaster in North American history and Celia in 1970 had destroyed nearly ninety percent of Corpus Christi's downtown.

The sky changed from overcast to gray to ominous black. In the periods of light drizzle between bands of drenching rain, Holly and Rusty pulled all the lawn ornaments and deck furniture into the garage. When the rain was too heavy to work outside, they went inside, moved furniture away from the windows, and covered the costlier pieces with plastic sheets. Holly hustled appliances and electronics up to the second floor to safeguard them against flooding and plugged her cell phone into its charger.

All that was left to do now was to wait and watch the approach of the storm. "Rusty, let's just sit for a bit. We will have to go inside soon enough if this silly thing really gets here. Things have been traveling so fast the last few days. Let's just relax for a minute while we can." Rusty came over, put his arms around her, and pulled her close. She melted into his arms thinking the storm could come or not, she didn't care.

The suddenness of the storm was a surprise. One minute it was coming; the next, it was on them. Sheets of torrential rain marched down the street like moving walls of water. The transformation of the water's icy glassiness to a ripple to a small wave to a swell of waves seemed almost instantaneous. What had been a strengthening breeze became a gust, then a wind with a mind of its own. The palms that had stood tall and straight, their fronds like a crown, creaked and twisted defiantly. The crumpled-paper whisper of their leaves became an incessant rattle. Rain pummeled the house. The wind was a ceaseless howl, impossible to shut out or ignore.

"Let's ride this storm out upstairs," Rusty said with a wink.

Holly doubted that she could relax enough for lovemaking but pulling the covers over her head sounded like a great idea.

In the bedroom, the pounding of the rain on the roof and the banging and thumping of something that came loose was louder than it had been downstairs but in Rusty's arms she felt safe.

"Whew, Holly, that wind sounds ferocious out there," he said. "Seen these before. There's going to be some damage done before this one's over. But I'm glad we're together. I wouldn't want to be riding this out in my apartment. And I'm not just saying that because your house has storm shutters. You were right about the house, I think. Stronger than the storm. They just don't build them like this anymore."

The lights dimmed, brightened, dimmed again, and then went out altogether. The room took on the darkness of midnight. The ceiling fan slowed to a stop. Had the storm not been making such a racket of its own, Holly knew she would notice quiet in the absence of the air conditioner cycling on and off. The sudden stillness of the air made her warm and she thought with dismay that it was only going to get warmer.

As if reading her thoughts, Rusty said, "Hmmm. No A/C. I think we better take off some of these clothes so we don't get overheated." He cupped her chin and turned her head to face him. "Oh, come on. Quit twisting your hair and relax. I'm wanting you right now."

When at last the storm passed, it left faster than it started. The wind went from screaming to whispering almost abruptly. Rain bands became lighter and farther apart until it stopped raining altogether. The stillness was almost as deafening as the storm had been.

When they thought it was safe, Holly and Rusty raised the garage doors and stepped outside to find a landscape that was changed forever. The wind had snapped tree limbs and stripped leaves. Palm fronds blanketed yards. City trash cans had blown down the street and piled up against the side of a house. A white resin lawn chair perched precariously in a tree.

They took down the plywood panel that covered the front door and worked their way around the house cranking up the roll-down window shutters. They came around to the rear of the house to find that a neighbor's dock complete with boat attached half sat on Holly's back yard. Holly climbed the stairs to the deck.

"My God, Rusty," Holly said. "Look at The Gap. It's...gone."

Mother Nature had filled the channel with sand so deep that only She could undo the results.

Rusty laughed. "Forget ever dredging that."

"So much for luxury hotels and gambling casinos." Holly turned to Rusty and said, "Stay right there. Don't go away." She stepped inside and made her way to the kitchen. When she returned she had a chair and a cup of coffee in an old glazed ironstone mug bearing a U.S. Navy insignia. She sat, put her feet up on the railing, and smiled.

The sun broke through the clouds and a gull flew laughing across an apricot sky. Across the sandy ribbon that had been The Gap, the Tejas Bonanza billboard was in ruins, shattered by flying debris. Shards lay scattered at the foot of the supporting uprights. Perched atop of one of wooden beams, a crested cannonbird regarded the passing clouds.

ABOUT THE AUTHOR

JED DONELLIE is an acronym for Jerry Bateman, Don Lowe, Ellie Killian, and Devorah Fox, four book-loving writing friends who in the year 2000 decided to collaborate on a novel.

Jerry W. Bateman grew up in Shawnee, Oklahoma, and graduated from the University of Oklahoma. He served in the United States Army and was stationed in Tokyo, Japan. He went on to have a sales career in Dallas, Texas. The father of two daughters and grandfather to three boys, as a retiree in Corpus Christi, Texas, Jerry was a tireless volunteer. A wise and spiritual man, he always had time to listen and offer a quick word of advice.

Donald H. Lowe was originally from Tulsa, Oklahoma. He served in the Navy as an inventory control petty officer in charge of Shop Stores for Navy Auxiliary Air Station, Cabaniss Field, Corpus Christi. Don was a successful business manager with 25 years'

experience as owner/operator and president of both retail and wholesale businesses. An accomplished artist and writer, Don authored and published various technique booklets and manuals as well as articles for one of the two national ceramic arts magazines. Funny and outgoing, Don was a busy retiree who served numerous community organizations and houses of worship.

Ellie Killian was born in San Francisco, California. She taught reading and writing to elementary students for thirty five years and has written articles for teacher magazines. She has five daughters and 17 grandchildren. Retired from teaching, she lives in Kingsville, Texas, where she is writing stories for children. She is very active in Texas Retired Teachers Association, is on the school board for St. Gertrude's Catholic School, and is a volunteer helper for the Kingsville Food Bank. Email her at ellie-k@sbcglobal.net.

Devorah Fox grew up in New York and lived in Massachusetts and Arizona before moving to Texas. Author of *The Lost King* and *The King's Ransom*, acclaimed literary fantasy novels, she has also written for television, radio, magazines, newspapers, and various blogs. She now lives in Port Aransas, Texas, with her Significant Other and three tabby cats. She writes the "Dee-Scoveries" blog at http://devorahfox.com and columns of the same name for *The Island Moon* newspaper and *TexasNOW* magazine. Email her at devorahfox@aol.com.

EDITOR'S NOTE

Don Lowe passed away on May 14, 2006, Jerry Bateman five years later on January 21, 2011. The story that "Jed Donellie" wrote gathered electronic dust as a collection of files in a subfolder on Devorah Fox's computer but like her departed friends, the book was never far from her memory. The year of Jerry Bateman's death, she decided to dust off *Naked Came the Sharks*, finish it, and get it published so that others could enjoy it as much as she did.

Connect online:

Email: devorahfox@aol.com
Blog: http://devorahfox.com
Facebook: http://facebook.com/DevorahFoxAuthor
Twitter: @devorah_fox
Smashwords:
https://www.smashwords.com/profile/view/mbapub

www.ingramcontent.com/pod-product-compliance
Lightning Source LLC
Chambersburg PA
CBHW060147180626
46813CB00007B/2674